SURVIVE THE COLLAPSE BOOK TWO

D1039457

BRINK
OF CHAOS

T.L. PAYNE

Brink of Chaos
Survive the Collapse Series, Book Two

Cover design by Deranged Doctor Design
Edited by Melanie Underwood
Proofread by Joanna Niederer

Don't forget to sign up for my spam-free newsletter at www.tlpayne.com to be
among the first to know of new releases, giveaways, and special offers.

❀ Created with Vellum

For Jay'vion, whose spirit, energy, and zest for life astound me.

Contents

Preface

Real towns and cities are used in this novel. However, the author has taken occasional liberties for the sake of the story.

While the Unicoi Board of Aldermen, Unicoi Police Department, and Johnson City, Tennessee Commission are real institutions, versions within these pages are purely fictional.

Thank you in advance for understanding an author's creative license.

ONE

Lauren

Lauren Wallace felt a hand on her arm and bolted upright in the bed. "What? What is it? Is it Dad?" Lauren had sat up all night with her father as he gasped for air. It had been touch and go. He'd stopped breathing several times, and a piece of Lauren had died with each episode, knowing he'd take his last breath soon. It was excruciatingly painful to watch someone you love struggle to breathe. Angela had finally convinced Lauren to get a few hours of rest sometime before sunrise.

"No. It's not your dad. He's the same," Angela said.

"What is it, then?" Lauren pulled her mind away from the inevitability of losing her father.

"Benny is here. He needs to speak with you," Angela said.

Lauren glanced toward the window. The sun was barely up.

"I'll be right there."

She pulled on her tactical pants, smoothed her hair back from

1

her face, and stared at her bedroom door with her hand on the knob. She was exhausted and not sure she could handle whatever catastrophe Benny had come to report.

Where the hell are you, Sam?

Her husband, Sam Wallace, had not returned from his trip to Atlanta to locate his murder witness, Tara Hobbs. His fate was still unknown nearly three weeks later. If all had gone to plan, he should have been home by dark that fateful day, but it was obvious nothing had gone to plan. The uncertainty of not knowing what had happened to her husband had Lauren living between hope and hopelessness. She often felt immobilized with confusion as her mind sought relief from the excruciating stress. It was difficult to hold on to hope—especially with all she'd seen since the lights went out. But giving up on her husband felt like a betrayal—like she'd abandoned him. Lauren fought to find a way to shut her mind off when it sought answers that might never come. She had to accept that she may never know what had happened to Sam, and find a way to go on. And now, with her father's failing health and the conditions in Unicoi deteriorating by the minute, Lauren was one catastrophe away from snapping.

Stop! Just stop! He's coming home!

Waffling back and forth was exhausting and Lauren was drained. But she didn't have time to be wary. She had responsibilities. People depended on her to hold things together. She had to keep it all together until Sam got home. She needed him desperately. He'd been her rock whenever she needed him. He'd been there to pull her from the brink of chaos whenever life had come at her like a flood. Lauren missed him with every fiber of her being, and it was getting more difficult to stay hopeful.

Although she desperately wanted to crawl back into bed and avoid reality, Lauren slowly turned the doorknob and stepped into the hallway of her parents' home. She glanced into their bedroom as she passed by. Her mother was in her chair overlooking the backyard while Angela was attempting to cool her father's face with a cardboard fan. Lauren threw her shoulders back and continued down the hall and into the family room to face whatever catastrophic news Benny had brought her.

"How's your dad?" Benny asked as Lauren rounded the sofa.

His police uniform was wrinkled and stained like he'd rolled around on the ground before coming. Why he still wore it was beyond Lauren. Why he hadn't quit and walked away from the impossible job, she didn't know. Maybe it was because he didn't have a family to care for, or perhaps he just couldn't admit defeat —that their efforts were futile.

"What is it, Benny?" She hadn't meant to be so dismissive of his concern about her father. Even though she'd known for months that Bill's health was failing and there was nothing more the doctors could do, she'd never entirely accepted her father's days on earth were coming to an end. She just wasn't ready to talk about it.

"I just received word from my confidential informant inside Corbin's headquarters that someone here is leaking information about our security measures and recovery efforts."

After his escape from Unicoi County jail in Erwin, Tennessee, Nigel Corbin, along with Bobby Russo and others, had gone on a killing rampage, targeting Sam's boss, the district attorney, and anyone who had been involved in putting Nigel behind bars. Afterward, they seized control of the grocery store where the town's residents had fled to escape the carnage. Corbin and his goons now ran the town of Erwin, Tennessee.

Lauren lowered herself onto the sofa and took a deep, cleansing breath, just like Angela had shown her. It wasn't working. She didn't feel any calmer at all. Her heart was still slamming against her rib cage. "Does this informant know what Corbin plans to do in response to this information?"

It had been days since Vince had returned from his trip looking for Sam and reported that Nigel Corbin, a murdering, drug dealing, sex trafficking kingpin, and all-around evil man, had plans to overtake the Town of Unicoi next. This information had everyone in town looking over their shoulders.

Without putting the measure to a vote, Lauren had instructed city crews to begin construction of a border wall of sorts. Inspired by scenes from apocalyptic television series like *The Walking Dead* and *Containment*, Lauren had directed that tractor-trailers left at the truck port, along with those located along the interstate and throughout Unicoi, be pulled into town and placed across the roadways and between houses to form a wall to keep out pedestrian as well as any possible vehicular traffic. Residents near the border wall had been moved to the middle of town and housed inside business premises or other abandoned homes. So far, there'd been no sign of Corbin or his men.

"The informant hasn't been invited to any of the meetings regarding Unicoi. My CI is concerned that their cover may have been blown somehow. Perhaps by whoever is leaking information here in Unicoi."

"Any ideas on who that might be?" Lauren had her suspicions. She and Ralph Cross, alderman for Ward Four, had never seen eye to eye on anything—not until the closing of the town to outsiders came up for a vote. It had been shocking to Lauren that he had supported the measure, considering his ties to businessman Clifford Anderson and others in town who had always opposed Lauren as mayor.

Benny leaned against the wall with his fingers tucked into his Sam Browne duty rig, complete with the handheld radio gifted to the town by her brother-in-law, Vince Wallace. "A few people come to mind," Benny said.

"Ralph?" Lauren asked.

"Ralph or one of his kids."

"His grandson was caught trying to sneak over the wall a few days ago," Lauren said.

"You can't read too much into that. He's a teenage boy, and his girlfriend lives outside city limits."

"Controlling the access points had been difficult enough, but there was no way they could monitor their entire border. The mountainous and heavily wooded terrain both helped and hindered their security efforts, but they'd done their best to use it to their advantage. Lauren hoped the wall would deter Corbin's men and any other mob from attacking with an overwhelming force.

"So, how can we find out who's leaking information?" Lauren asked.

"My CI is going to try to find out, but we should also limit information surrounding security and food storage location to those who need to know."

"Ralph isn't going to go for that."

"So we feed him false information and swear him to secrecy. We've found our spy if that info makes it to Corbin's ears."

"Next would be to find out how he is getting the information from here to Erwin," Lauren said.

"There are too many ways that could be happening. I'm not sure that would be a wise use of our limited manpower. If he's the leak, I think we'd just need to convince the rest of the aldermen that Ralph isn't to be trusted and get him kicked off the council."

"His constituents would freak. I can't see that working at all. They'd be down at city hall raising holy hell."

"Not if we gave them a replacement," Benny said.

Lauren tilted her head to one side and pointed a finger at Benny. "You're sneaky."

"Mayberry would be the perfect choice. He's a veteran. He's been active in the community since the lights went out. He's a straightforward guy—and people trust him."

"I don't know. We don't need to get bogged down with town politics right now. We have too many balls in the air, and there's too much at stake. Lives could be lost—many lives—if we don't solve some of our more critical problems very soon."

"Let's just feed Ralph some fake news and then see where it goes from there," Benny said.

"Okay." Lauren looked back over her shoulder toward her parents' room. "I'll leave that job to you if you don't mind. I'm going to work from home today."

Benny moved closer and placed a hand on her shoulder. "That's fine. I'll let Millie know and I'll be in touch if anything comes up that we can't handle. Otherwise, get some rest and take care of yourself."

"Thanks, Benny. Thank you for all you do for the town, and for me."

"It's my job."

"It's a job that you likely will never be paid for."

"I get to eat."

Lauren sighed. That was what it had come down to now. Two weeks ago, people worked to afford big houses, drive nice cars, and take vacations. Now, if you had food to eat that day, you considered yourself lucky—rich even. But how much longer could their luck hold? Sandwiched between Preston Corbin to their north and his evil son to the south, how long before everything they were working to build would be destroyed?

"Let me know when you hear anything about our spy," Lauren said.

"I'm going to speak to Ralph this morning. We may hear something as early as tomorrow."

Lauren was having difficulty thinking past that day. Worrying about what might happen next was too overwhelming. It was hard enough to keep going as it was. An image of Sam popped into her mind. Was he on the road, putting one foot in front of the other on his way home?

Lord, let today be the day. Please bring Sam home to me.

TWO

Sam

Hammond Veterinarian Services
Franklin, North Carolina
Day 18

"Grab his legs!" Sam Wallace shouted. Becky Shelton remained frozen, staring down at the body on the floor at her feet. "Becky, grab the man's feet. We have to close the door."

Becky didn't move.

Sam yanked on the dead man's arms, pulling him backward and across the threshold of the veterinary exam room attached to Doctor Hammond's stable. Sam stumbled, struggling as he put weight on his injured leg. Becky raced over and picked up the man's legs, helping Sam carry him out into the aisle between the horse stalls.

"I had to do it," Becky said, allowing the man's feet to drop to the ground.

"I know. You did the right thing," Sam said, grabbing her arm.

She looked back over her shoulder as Sam pulled her toward the door. "He was going to kill me," she said.

Images of Tara's lifeless body flashed through Sam's mind.

"Let's get inside and bar the door," Sam said.

The townspeople had surrounded the stable—some with clubs, others with bats or hammers—all demanding the veterinarian send out Andrew Titus, the injured boy that the doctor was attempting to save.

The town of Franklin, North Carolina, had been home to four thousand full-time residents before the EMP. As a tourist town, it was in peak season, and the population had nearly doubled. Not all of Franklin's visitors were friendly. As Sam had learned, some were takers, leading to clashes between the locals and the "outsiders," as they referred to them. The residents of Franklin had managed to oust some of the tourists who had formed groups and started stealing, raping, and even killing residents in some instances.

"Grab that two by four," Sam said, holding the dead man's hammer in his hand.

Becky picked up a board from the stack of lumber assembled by the door to the exam room that had become Sam's home away from home for the last twelve days as he recovered from his leg wound. "Is this going to work?" she asked, handing him the board.

Sam didn't answer her. He couldn't be sure how many people were out there. As far as he could tell, none of them were armed with rifles or pistols. If they could secure the doors and windows to the room, he could hold them off with Becky's hunting rifle until help arrived.

"Hold that end," Sam said as he used the hammer to drive a nail through the board and into the door jamb.

The shouting outside continued as Sam and Becky barred the door with boards and moved on to cover the window with plywood.

"How's he doing, Doc?" Sam asked.

"I could use a hand. I'm trying to clamp off an artery, and I need someone to hold the retractor."

"Go, Becky. I've got this," Sam said, hoisting up the square piece of plywood and holding it against the window.

"There's a box of gloves on the counter. Put those on," Doc told Becky.

Something crashed against the window. The glass broke but thankfully, the four nails holding the plywood held. Sam removed the nail he'd been holding between his teeth and quickly hammered it through the sheet of engineered wood and into the casing.

"Send him out and we'll go away," a gruff male voice shouted.

"Maybe we should—" Mrs. Hammond started to say.

"No!" Becky yelled. "No. They won't go away even if we hand Andrew over to them. If we open that door, they'll kill us all."

"It's going to be okay, dear. Andrew's family and the rest of the neighbors will be here soon. Just sit over there in the chair and let me work," Doc Hammond said.

With the door and window barricaded against the mob outside, Sam turned his attention to his weapons and ammo. Becky's .30-30 Winchester held six rounds and her pack had an additional twenty-round box. He felt confident with that. After shooting the first few people through the door, the others would likely run away, especially if the leader was the first one taken down. Could he get that lucky? His luck hadn't been great so far. He had to be prepared to fire at and hit at least five, maybe six. That would leave him with twenty rounds if he had to take the fighting to them later.

Something hard rammed the door, and Sam spun to face it. "Doc!"

"I need a minute more," Doc said.

"Mrs. Hammond, I'm going to need you then."

"I can't," she whined.

"Nancy!" Doc yelled. "Pick up the damn shotgun."

Mrs. Hammond rose from her chair, slowly crossed the room, and retrieved the shotgun from Sam's cot in the far corner of the room.

"I need you to stand in the middle of the room and point the barrel toward that door. As soon as you see one of those sons-of-bitches, you fire," Sam said.

"What if it's—"

"It won't be. Your friends and neighbors aren't going to be the ones to bust through that door. It will be rapists and killers, Mrs. Hammond."

Her mouth dropped open, and her eyes grew wide. "I'm not sure if I can pull the trigger."

"You know how. Remember, we used to shoot years ago. You were a good shot then. You can do this, Nancy," Doc Hammond said.

Sam knelt beside Mrs. Hammond, supported the barrel of his rifle on the back of a metal folding chair, and aimed it at the door. At his feet was the box of ammo. He would need Mrs. Hammond to shoot when he needed to reload. The report of a shotgun would likely be enough to have them hesitate. He was banking on only having to fire a few rounds to cause the rest to flee. Sam didn't think the mob was willing to die to exact their revenge, but the leader—the father of the young man that Hammond's neighbor, Andrew Titus, had killed might—be angry enough to keep coming.

The wood splintered and a hole appeared in the center of the door. A hand reached through and Mrs. Hammond freaked. Her shotgun boomed, blowing a larger hole in the wood as the empty shell fell to the floor. The hand disappeared, and something large and metal was thrust through the hole. In seconds, the boards gave way, and the door was flung open. Mrs. Hammond was bent over, trying her best to reload as a large man stepped into the opening. Sam aimed at the center of the man's chest, exhaled, and squeezed the trigger. The big man fell following the thundering roar, and another man appeared. Sam worked the rifle's lever and fired a second round, causing the second man to fall onto the first. As a third man appeared, Mrs. Hammond fired her shotgun. The man dove to his right and landed outside the door. Sam hopped over to the door and put two into the third man, then pivoted to his left ready to deal with anyone who was still standing—but saw no one. However, when he moved to the open barn door, he caught a glimpse of six men running away across the Hammonds' west pasture.

Sam stepped out and scanned from left to right but saw no other perps. Just as he turned to go back to ensure the three inside the barn were dead, Andrew's family came running across the lawn toward the barn.

"Is my son alive?" a middle-aged man yelled.

"I believe so. Doc is working on him inside," Sam replied.

Andrew's family members moved him inside the Hammonds' house, where Doc Hammond had set up a surgical suite of sorts. They were extremely low on antibiotics and lacked blood and ventilators, but Doc had the training to stop the bleeding. Unfortunately, as a large-animal veterinarian, he did not have sufficient equipment or supplies to operate on humans effectively; the rest would be up to God.

Mrs. Titus and her daughter visited Andrew after the doctor had done all he could. They brought herbs and wild medicinal plants that had served the Appalachian people for generations.

"My Cherokee grandma used this all the time," Mrs. Titus said, applying a herbal salve to Andrew's chest wound. Her daughter sang hymns and prayed as her mother applied the folk medicine. Soon, more than ten family members surrounded the bed, and gospel music filled the home.

Sam and Becky left the Titus family to tend to Andrew's physical and spiritual needs and returned to the barn to take care of the bodies piled up there. There would be four fresh graves in the Hammonds' growing back-forty cemetery. Sam said a silent prayer that they would be the last. He was so tired of death.

Becky tied a rope to one of the men's legs and pulled him to the cemetery with Doc Hammond's bay mare, Jingles. As Sam tied a second rope to one of the remaining dead men, he couldn't help but think about Lauren, Charlie, and the rest of his family back in Unicoi. Franklin wasn't much different than his hometown. There would be troublemakers for Lauren and the others to contend with sooner or later.

Sam found some solace in knowing that he and Vince had prepared for that scenario. The compound was fairly secure, and the occupants were well trained. But he also knew that in a town of three thousand residents, it wouldn't be long before they'd be knocking at the gate, wanting to share in the group's resources. He hoped Lauren had found the strength to turn them away. He had no doubt she would die to protect Charlie and her parents and cursed his injured leg. The wound was healing too slowly for his liking. He needed to get on the road to Unicoi. As much as he wanted to help the people of Franklin, Sam needed to find a way home to his family. If the Baofeng handheld ham radio hadn't gotten smashed when the Russos crashed into Sam's vehicle, he might have had a way to get a message to his brother and let them know he was alive.

"Becky, before the lights went out, did you know anyone who was an amateur radio operator?" It was a long shot, Sam knew. Even if she knew of someone, the likelihood that the person had had the forethought to store spare ham radio equipment in a Faraday container and have a way to power it up after the EMP would be extremely unlikely. He couldn't be sure that the base station he and Vince had set up would still work anyway. It should, though, according to everything Sam had read. They'd stored the spare equipment in a Faraday box and had enough solar panels and batteries to power it.

"There was this paramedic that I dated for like two weeks. He was an amateur radio operator. He had radio equipment at his house and a huge ass antenna in his yard. He often used these little walkie-talkie-type radios when he assisted on search and rescue missions, too."

Sam's heart rate sped up.

What if?

"Do you think you could take me to his house?"

THREE

Benny

Ralph Cross's Residence
Unicoi, Tennessee
Day 18

As Benny traversed the narrow, one-lane road with its hairpin turns and sheer drop-offs up to Alderman Ralph Cross's home nestled on a hilltop overlooking the Town of Unicoi, he thought of his great-grandparents' place in the mountains. It was so remote and the terrain so difficult that they were often cut off from the outside world for weeks during the rainy season.

Ever since the event, Benny had considered taking a trip up the mountain to check out the old log cabin. Although Vince Wallace had kindly offered him a place at his compound, Benny wanted another place to hole up in if he had to bug out quickly.

Instead of exiting and walking toward the door, Benny honked the horn to announce his arrival. He didn't want to risk being mistaken for a trespasser and shot by one of Ralph's kids. He exited quickly and moved behind the truck with his pistol drawn. The front door to the ranch-style brick home opened, and Ralph's

14

oldest son appeared. Clay Cross waved and stepped out onto the porch.

"Hey, Benny. What can we do for you?" Clay asked.

"I need to speak with Ralph about town business," Benny said, holstering his sidearm.

Clay gestured for him to come up to the house. "Dad's out back in the pool. Can I get you some sweet tea or anything? We don't have ice, but it's been chilling in the spring, so it's pretty cold."

"I'd love a glass of sweet tea." Benny would never turn down his favorite beverage.

Clay led Benny through the house and into the backyard where the family had gathered around an in-ground swimming pool. Ralph climbed the steps to exit the water, and Benny looked away.

I'll never be able to unsee that.

"What's going on, Benny?" Ralph asked, plucking a towel from the back of a lounge chair and drying off before attempting to wrap it around his rotund belly.

"Can I speak with you in private?" Benny motioned to a seating area near a rose garden at the back of the lawn.

Ralph picked up a glass of tea and motioned for Benny to go first down the pea gravel path.

After lowering himself onto an Adirondack chair, Benny took a long pull of sweet tea. It was ice cold. He closed his eyes and took another. Everything that had occurred in the last eighteen days faded for a moment. It was like he was transported back to a time when there were hot showers and cold beer, pepperoni pizza was a phone call away, and you could spend hours of your life scrolling through social media.

"What news did you bring me?" Ralph asked, bringing Benny back to the present.

Benny took another sip and set the glass down on a side table. "I just came from speaking with the mayor." That much was true. "Our hunting party came home last night with news about finding a huge cache of food and weapons at a cabin up on the mountain."

"And?"

"There are some military-type weapons there. Grenades and rocket launcher-type shit. Enough ammo to fight a small war."

"Any idea where it came from or who put it there?"

"There was a militia group in the area a few years back, but they got busted up by the FBI." That was also true.

"And you want the board to do what about it exactly?"

"I would like permission to seize everything and bring it all back to Unicoi and store it at Ike's hardware store until we can get a more secure place built. I'd like to keep it secret, though. We wouldn't want any crazies knowing where something like that was stored."

"You don't want to tell Maryann and Gretchen then. They couldn't keep a secret if their lives depended upon it. The whole town would know by lunchtime."

"The mayor wanted at least one of you to sign off on it," Benny said.

"She did, huh? Well, I approve. Make sure you keep that secure and post guards on it. I don't want the Henley boys or some other yahoos getting ahold of that stuff and making a ruckus in town."

Benny stood and picked up his glass of tea. "Great. I'll arrange to have it brought in tonight." He downed the rest of his drink and turned to go. "Cody said there was a small fortune in gold up there too, but that shit's worthless at the moment. I was thinking of just leaving it for now."

Ralph's eyes widened for a split second, and then his expression returned to normal. Benny had piqued his interest. "You never know. We might be able to convince some fool it still has value and get something in trade," Ralph said.

"You think?"

Ralph nodded.

"All right then, I'll have the boys bring that to town, too. We'll take it to the old Bank of Unicoi and lock it in the vault."

Ralph nodded. "Okay. Keep me informed."

Benny was surprised that Ralph didn't insist they bring it to Corbin's bank. Maybe that would be too obvious. The Bank of Unicoi, which had closed thirty years before and still had its original safe from 1905, had been converted into a cute little ice cream shop.

Benny had set the trap, but in order to make it convincing, that evening, he would need to send Mayberry up into the mountains with a couple of guys with instructions to get a load of wood and cover it with a tarp. In the dark, Ralph or anyone he sent to spy on them would believe it was the gold and weapons. Benny would soon have his answer about whether Ralph was their mole.

Back at the police station, Benny was going over the security force duty roster to determine who he could assign to keep tabs on Ralph and his kids when Officer Brian Wilson hurried into his office.

"We have a problem out at Ike's warehouse."

"What is it?" Benny asked.

Officer Wilson's uniform shirt was drenched in sweat as if he'd run the mile and a half back to the station.

"The mayor asked me to scout additional locations to store food and supplies, so I checked out Ike's old warehouse. I found a group of people living in there."

"Locals?"

"No. It's some of the people we cleared out of the truck port and the Unicoi Inn before we burned it down."

"We escorted them to the city limits. I watched them walk down the interstate."

"They must have doubled back somehow because I recognize their leader. He's that mouthy fella with the fancy clothes—the one who was complaining about leaving his Beemer unattended at the travel center."

"What the hell have they been doing for the last week?"

"Stealing, from the looks of it."

Benny spat out a string of curse words and stood, pushing back his chair.

"We have to get rid of them. How many are there?"

"I saw at least twelve, but there could be more. I didn't want to alert them to my presence before I had backup."

"Get a team together, but wait until they're sleeping to go in."

"Roger that," Wilson said. He keyed the Baofeng UV-5R handheld ham radio that Vince had so generously donated to the department and gave his call sign like proper radio protocol still mattered. Alan Mayberry's voice came through the radio. "Meet me at the station. We have a mission to plan," Wilson said into the radio.

"On my way," Mayberry replied.

Benny thought of alerting Vince, but his radio transmission couldn't make it over the top of the mountain.

An hour later, Benny was just getting ready to task Joey Hoffenberg with following Ralph when Randy Turner's boy, Colin, came barreling into the police station.

"Come quick," Colin said.

"What's with all the shouting?" Benny asked, exiting his office.

"I tried to stop him, Chief," Desk Sergeant Belinda Salter said, waving her hands in the air. "He just wouldn't listen." The grayhaired woman returned to her seat behind the counter.

The door that would normally be closed and locked in the past had been propped open for ventilation.

"What do you need, Colin?" Benny asked. The preteen boy was dirty and soaked in sweat.

"You have to come quick. He's going to shoot my daddy."

"Where? Are they at your house?" Benny said, rounding the counter.

"Yes. Please hurry." Colin took off before Benny could get more information from him, but he had an idea who was involved. He'd been called out to the Turner residence numerous times over the years.

Sliding behind the steering wheel of the pickup, Benny raced through town and pulled to a stop two doors down from the Turners' house. He reached back, removed the shotgun from the rack mounted to the rear window, and exited the vehicle.

"Hurry!" Mrs. Turner screamed, waving her arms frantically. "He's going to kill him. He's going to kill him."

Benny ran around the side of the Turner house. A shot rang out, and Benny stopped dead in his tracks, assessing where the shot had come from. He ran to the back corner and peered into the Turners' backyard. Twenty feet away, Randy Turner lay on the ground between two rows of corn. Ruben Reardon stood over him with a pistol in his hands. Mrs. Turner ran over to her husband in a panic, dropped to the ground, and threw her body across his, shielding him from any more possible gunfire.

"Drop the weapon, Reardon," Benny ordered, stepping into the backyard and raising the shotgun. "Drop the weapon, or I will shoot you."

Reardon's gaze shifted toward Benny. His eyes were wild. Benny had never seen him look so crazed. "Just drop the..." Reardon suddenly turned toward Benny. Benny's shotgun boomed, and Reardon dropped beside Randy, his arm landing on Mrs. Turner's back. The pistol landed near her right foot. Mrs. Turner jumped back onto her knees, screaming and pounding on Reardon's chest.

"You killed him! You bastard. You killed him."

Benny rushed over and secured the pistol before checking Randy for a pulse. Mrs. Turner was right. He was dead. A round had struck him right between the eyes. Benny stepped around Mrs.

Turner and checked Reardon for a pulse. He, too, was dead. He took Mrs. Reardon by both arms and lifted her to her feet. She lunged toward him, wrapped her arms around him, and sobbed into his chest.

Colin ran over and stopped at his father's feet. He stared at him for a moment, then glanced at Reardon.

"He killed my dad?" Colin asked.

"I'm afraid so."

"Did you do that?" he asked, pointing to Reardon.

"Yes," Benny replied.

The boy took his mother's arm and led her away without another word. Benny pivoted, scanning to see whether any of Reardon's family had heard the commotion and decided to join the fight. He saw no one. Benny walked over and inspected a line of newly installed fence posts. "All this over a few feet of earth," he said out loud to himself.

"You can feed a family for a week with a few feet of earth."

Benny spun on his heel with his shotgun raised, searching for the owner of the voice. Marie Roberts stepped out of the cornfield and approached the bodies. She stared down at them for a moment and then turned her gaze to Benny. Her long black hair was pulled into a ponytail that had been threaded through the opening on the back of her ball cap. She wore tight running shorts, a tank top, and thong sandals. On her hands, she wore leather gloves.

"I guess that's true these days," Benny said.

"They've been fighting back and forth for days. I suspected it was going to come to this. It started when Reardon accused Randy of trampling his green beans."

"I'm surprised I haven't had to deal with a lot more of this type of thing," Benny said, moving toward the house.

"It's not because it isn't happening. Folks are trying to deal with this shit themselves. Everyone knows you guys have your hands full keeping the town safe from outsiders."

"That's true. I don't have time to run out here for property line disputes anymore, but when they get to this point, someone needs to step in before bullets start flying," he said, pointing back toward the bodies.

"Tensions are running high. Pastor Billings has talked about loving your neighbor through this mess. It just fell on deaf ears with these two," Marie said.

Marie followed Benny back to his truck. "Have you heard from your sister today?"

"Not today. Not yet. She probably won't try to contact me unless she has something big to report. She's getting nervous."

"Ronnie's one tough chick. I wouldn't blame her if she wanted out. We could put her out at Vince's and keep her safe."

"I told her that. She's scared and doesn't know who to trust. If we know who in town was leaking information to Corbin, she might feel safer about leaving Erwin and coming here."

Benny climbed into the pickup truck and closed the door. "I might have that answer soon. Let me know the minute she contacts you. Okay?"

Marie leaned on the door and poked her head inside. Their lips met, and Benny forgot all about the shooting incident and Corbin's spy for a moment. He forgot that the world had gone to shit and that he and Marie might never get married and have kids now. All he thought about was how good she smelled and how soft her skin was to his touch.

After saying goodbye to Marie, Benny stopped at the church to talk with Pastor Billings. Twice in one day, the minister's name had been brought up. Benny took that as a sign.

He entered the church through an open door. Gone were the pews; cots had been put in their place. Women, and girls as young as thirteen, filled the room. Some played card games while others stretched out reading paperback novels.

"Chief Jameson."

Benny turned to face the pastor. "Pastor, who are all these people?"

Billings scanned the room. "They're refugees."

"Are they Unicoi residents?"

"Yes. Most have been in Unicoi for months. Some of them a year or more."

"I don't know any of them." Benny took two steps to his right and spotted a redhead that he did recognize. Sharon DuBois, Billy Mahon's top girl. "What's she doing here."

"You burned down their home," Billings said.

"Are all of these girls from the motel?"

"Most of them."

Lauren was not going to like this one bit.

FOUR

Charlie

Wallace Survival Compound
Unicoi, Tennessee
Day 18

From the road, the gate at the entrance to the compound was nondescript—just a twelve-foot wide cattle panel hinged from one tree along the ditch and chained closed to the next tree. A sign hanging on it read, "Closed." A gravel drive arced from the gate toward the woods and proceeded toward the back of the property, where visitors were greeted by a giant dirt-filled coyote-brown Hesco barrier wall and a second, more substantial gate. This second gate and barrier wall had been installed after the EMP. It was twelve-foot high and solid so trespassers couldn't see past it— and always guarded on the inside by an armed member of the group. A peephole allowed the guard to see anyone approaching.

Charlie leaned out the window and waved at Lindsay, Uncle Vince's longtime girlfriend, as she emerged from behind the gate, pushing it open for Vince and Charlie to enter.

"Hey, Charlie boy," Lindsay said. "You come to help guard this place with me?"

Charlie shrugged. "Lauren sent me to stay until my dad gets home."

Lindsay smiled. "Cool. Casey will be glad to see you, I bet."

Charlie's face flushed. Casey was the only girl there is age. He wasn't sure she would care whether he was there or not. He didn't know Casey very well. They'd met on the road home from Knoxville on the day of the event. She'd gone to the compound as soon as they arrived in Unicoi. Charlie hadn't seen her since.

Vince pulled the Wagoneer through the gate, and Lindsay closed it behind them. They continued toward the back and stopped at what had once been the office and store for the shooting range. Charlie climbed out as Vince went around and grabbed his bag from the back. "You can stay in my room. You don't snore, do you?" Vince said, smiling.

"No. Well—not that I know of."

"Good deal. Let's get you settled and then I'll run you through our routine and get you up to speed with all of our safety protocols. After that, we'll see Dave and get your work assignment."

Charlie stopped on the porch. "I don't think I'll be here that long."

Lauren had said she was sending him there until his dad got home. It was supposed to be to keep him safe, but Charlie thought it was because of what he'd done. He'd shot that man. He hadn't had a choice. The man would have killed Lauren if he hadn't stopped him. Lauren acted differently toward Charlie after that. At first, she was caring and concerned about how he was coping with it, but the next day, she was quiet and avoided him.

His dad wouldn't have sent him away. His dad would have wanted him to stay at the Taylors' and help watch out for Lauren and her parents.

"I know. Your dad will be home anytime now, but when he gets back he'll convince Lauren to move Bill and Edna out here, too.

That was your dad's plan all along. He just hadn't convinced Lauren yet."

"I don't think she'll leave the town. She feels responsible for everybody," Charlie said.

"We'll leave that task up to your dad."

Uncle Vince led him past the wall of sandbags stacked in front of the window. They went down a side hall to a back room. Vince flicked on a lamp and tossed Charlie's bag on one of the two twin beds situated along opposite walls with a chest between them.

"How is it you have lights?" Charlie asked.

"Solar." He peeled back a curtain and pointed to a row of solar panels on stands behind the store.

"Does it power anything besides lights?"

"We use it to charge batteries, like the ones for the machine that makes oxygen for Bill's breathing machine. Also for the batteries used in our scopes, radios, and flashlights."

"We'll store your clothes in this foot locker for now. Once your dad and Lauren move out here, you'll have your own room in one of the bungalows with them."

"You mentioned radios. Lauren said you have one that lets you talk to people far away."

"I do. It's called a ham radio. I've talked to people as far away as Norway."

"Does my dad know about it?"

"He helped me pick it out and set it up."

Charlie wished their phones still worked. He could call his dad and find out where he was and how soon he'd be home. He could call his mom too; she got all freaked out if he didn't call her every day when he came down to his dad's for visits.

As he placed his clothes inside the locker, he asked, "How long does it take to drive to Toledo from here?"

"Before all this, I would say eight or nine hours. Now, with the roads like they are and all, I'd say maybe a couple of days. You thinking about your mom and little sister?"

Charlie nodded.

"I know you miss them."

"I wish I could call and let mom know I'm okay and everything."

"I can put a message out on the radio. I know she doesn't have a ham radio, but there's a chance someone near her house might. It wouldn't hurt to try."

"Thanks, Uncle Vince."

He closed the lid on the locker, turned, and sat on the bed. "Do you think I could talk to her if someone can get a message to her?"

"Of course, if she can get to the radio. It's possible."

Charlie smiled.

"How long do you think it'll be before things get fixed and I can go home?" He loved his dad and stepmother, Lauren, but he missed home. He wanted to sleep in his own bed in his own room. He wanted to hang out with his friends and swim in the pool in his backyard.

"I'm afraid I don't know the answer to that, Charlie. No one does." Uncle Vince rubbed Charlie's shoulder. "Let's go give you the ten-cent tour."

Outside, they walked past more sandbags. Holes had been dug in the ground, and sandbags were stacked around the top on the ground. Cody and a couple of other men approached from a large metal building near what had once been the shooting range's classroom. Rows and rows of different vegetables were growing next to the structure.

"Hey, Charlie. Good to see you again," Cody said. He was dressed in hunter's clothes and carried two rifles, one in the front and one attached to a large pack on his back.

"Hi, Cody. Where you headed?"

"Hunting."

"Where at?"

Cody nodded his head to the side. "Out Highway 107 toward Limestone Cove. You wanna come?"

Charlie frowned. He would, but he knew Lauren would freak on him. "Nah, I'm not allowed to leave the range."

"Maybe next time," Cody said as he continued on past Charlie.

Charlie would have liked to have gone hunting with Cody. He would've liked to do anything that felt normal. He and his dad used to hunt before his mom moved him to Ohio. "Good luck," Charlie called after him.

"I'll see you in a day or two," Cody called back.

Charlie hoped to be back in town by then, whether his dad was home or not. Memaw and Papaw Taylor needed him, even if Lauren didn't.

FIVE

Lauren

Wallace Farm
Unicoi, Tennessee
Day 19

"How could you do this to me, Dodge?" Lauren asked as she tugged on a ram with his head stuck through a broken wooden slat in the gate. She wrapped her arms around the one hundred-pound Shetland sheep's neck and yanked and twisted his head, trying to free his horns from the narrow space. He bucked, jumped, and kicked, slicing her shin with a sharp hoof. Wincing in pain, Lauren released her grip on him and straightened. Wiping tears from her eyes with her sleeve, she moved to the opposite side of the animal to get a better grip on its horns.

"I don't have time for this. I have too much to do to keep saving your butt." Strands of electrified wire and a strong fence usually kept the sheep, goats, and donkeys in their pasture. But the solar fence charger hadn't survived.

Lauren was exhausted, not only from biking nearly two miles from her parents' house to the farm every day, and now wrestling

28

to free the ram, but also from everything she'd been through since the electromagnetic pulse had ended life as she knew it. It had been two of the hardest weeks in her thirty-six years of life. As strong as she was, Lauren was nearing her breaking point, but there was nothing she could do about it. So many people depended on her—she couldn't slow down now. She had to keep pushing herself to get everything done so she and her loved ones would survive one more day.

She was at the point where she was mentally breaking jobs down into hours and sometimes minutes just to focus on the job at hand instead of the mountain of tasks in front of her. That was how she managed her emotions. It was how she could bear the grief of missing her husband, Sam, and the unbearable ache of not knowing what had happened to him. He'd gone to Atlanta to find Tara Hobbs, a witness in Nigel Corbin's murder trial, and had yet to return home to Unicoi, Tennessee. One moment at a time. You can get through the next five minutes. That was how Lauren managed to cope with the piercing pain in her chest and the hollow pit in her stomach.

You can do this.

Lauren drew in a deep breath, stuck her hands through the gate's slats, and wrapped her fingers around the ram's horns.

I just need to get Dodge's head unstuck, water the garden, gather the eggs, and then rush back and check on Mom and Dad before I prepare for the town hall meeting. That's doable. I've done this a million times. Nothing new.

Nothing new? Well, except that she was doing it all without the aid of modern technology, and her husband wasn't there to help her.

"You need some help?"

Lauren glanced over her shoulder as her stepson, Charlie, approached from the old wooden barn. She released her grip on the ram's horns and turned to face him, heat flushing her cheeks. Lauren gritted her teeth. "Why aren't you at the compound?"

"I... um..." Charlie stammered and backed away, unaccustomed to Lauren's anger being directed at him.

"You know it isn't safe outside that wall."

Where the hell is Vince? He was supposed to be keeping his nephew safe. He had promised not to let him out of his sight.

"Vince, Lindsay, and Maggie are in the garden. They told me to come help you."

Lauren swept her gaze toward the one-acre garden at the back of the farmhouse-style home that she and Sam had built on his family's property soon after they married. She loved this slice of heaven, especially her view of Buffalo Mountain from the wraparound porch where she used to have her morning coffee and an evening glass of wine before she'd moved into her parents' home in town to care for them.

Sam's family had owned the two-hundred-acre property nestled on top of a hill and down along the winding entrance road for nearly a century. Sam's brother, Vince, lived down the hill, across from the gun range he and Sam owned. The gun range had been turned into the Wallace survival compound. It was where Charlie should have been—safely behind its gate.

Although keeping up with the chores and maintaining the garden with all that was going on in town had been nearly impossible by herself, she hadn't asked for help. Vince had his own responsibilities leading the group who'd gathered at the compound. Everyone was struggling to do what this new world required. They didn't have time to take on more work as well.

It had been days since Vince had come back from his last search for Sam. Neither of them wanted to give up hope that Sam would make it home, but continuing to search every day wasn't feasible—not with so much to do back home.

After the news that Nigel Corbin had been released from jail and had established a base in Erwin, only five miles south of Unicoi, Lauren had sent Charlie to stay with his uncle. There he would be surrounded by a twelve foot wall and two steel gates, and guarded by fifteen well-trained and well-armed people who'd been hand-picked by Sam and Vince to defend the survival compound they'd established prior to the shit hitting the fan.

Lauren turned her attention back to Charlie. "Where's your pistol?"

He lifted his shirt revealing his holstered Glock 17.

"Extra mags?"

"In my pocket." He reached into the back pocket of his jeans and produced a seventeen-round magazine for the pistol. "I've got my Benchmade folding knife in my front pocket. You want to see it too?" There was hurt in his voice.

He didn't deserve this level of scrutiny. Lauren shook her head and turned away. "I'm sorry. It's just that—"

"I know," Charlie said, interrupting her apology. "How can I help?"

"You want to get on the opposite side of the gate and push his head while I pull from this side?"

Charlie climbed over the gate and hopped down beside Dodge's head. He reached out a hand to pet the ram's nose and then stopped.

"Never rub a ram's head. They aren't pets. It can make them aggressive," Lauren reminded him.

"He's never rammed me."

"Never—ever—trust a ram. Never turn your back to one. Understand?"

"Yes," Charlie said.

"Grab his horns and try to turn his head to one side," Lauren said.

Dodge balked and threw his head back as Charlie took hold of him, but after several minutes of twisting and tugging, Dodge was free and ran off to join his ewes.

"Thanks, Charlie."

Lauren picked up the empty feed bucket and shut the gate behind her.

"You want to help me gather the eggs?"

After Charlie placed the carton of eggs into the basket on Lauren's bicycle, he and Lauren joined Vince and the others in the garden.

Lindsay stood guard as Vince and her sister, Maggie, cleared weeds between two rows of Appalachian heirloom green beans with garden hoes.

"You look like shit," Lindsay said as Lauren approached the gate.

Lauren glanced down at her dirt-stained shirt and tactical pants. "I had to wrestle my ram again." Lauren wiped yellow lanolin from Dodge's fleece onto her pant legs and leaned on the chain-link fence that surrounded the garden.

"I'm not referring to your dirt and grime. You look like you haven't slept in weeks."

That was because she hadn't—not much. When she tried, nightmares woke her. Images of the people she'd killed on her way home from Knoxville, along with her imagination brewing up dangerous encounters that Sam likely had to face in Atlanta, kept her staring at the ceiling most nights.

Lauren gestured to Vince and Maggie. "I appreciate you guys coming to help."

"We were out of eggs," Vince said, stopping to lean on his hoe. He wiped the sweat from his brow. "It takes a lot of food to feed that crew."

"I know what you mean. We're rationing pretty tight in town, but I'm trying to keep our work crews as well-fed as possible."

"How's your inventory?" Vince asked.

"We have a couple more days of food."

"Days?" Lindsay asked.

"We suspended our search of the full tractor-trailers to begin constructing the wall around town using the empty ones."

Once word came that Nigel Corbin intended to extend his kingdom to Unicoi, a defensible perimeter became the town's only option. He had more people and more weapons. If Unicoi was going to keep the food and supplies they'd gathered, they needed a way to keep marauders out of town, including the Corbins and their crews.

"It's going to be weeks before the gardens will be producing enough to feed them," Vince said.

"I know. If we could just hold on somehow; we have a lot planted already. Once the wall is finished, we can turn our attention to planting more food. Both Stephens' Farm Market and the Johnson & Carter Farms have donated their acreage, seeds, and fertilizer to the town."

With flat land being rather scarce in the area, having the two commercial farms donate their land to feed the residents of Unicoi had been a godsend. Both were family-owned and operated. The families had lived in the area for generations. Their commitment to the community had begun long before the lights went out, and Lauren wasn't sure how the town would survive without them.

"It won't be enough. You know that, right?"

In her heart, Lauren knew they were way behind on securing enough food to feed all three thousand residents of Unicoi. They would need at least six thousand acres to grow enough food, and maybe even twice that to cover livestock for meat. They'd already begun cultivating hay fields to raise crops. Every family had been required to turn their lawn into garden plots to feed themselves, but even with what the town could provide, it wouldn't be enough to see them through an Appalachian winter.

Lauren hadn't even begun to contemplate how the town would manage winter without electricity. Most of the residents didn't have a way to heat their homes. Everything would be more difficult in the cold, damp winter. Shaking her head in frustration, Lauren pushed the thought aside. She had to address the immediate needs of the community first.

"I have to do what I can. So many people are pulling together to make this work. We just have to find a way to feed everyone until the crops come in."

"And then what? They eat this summer and then have nothing until next summer's harvest?" Vince asked.

"Cody and his hunting party—"

Vince cut her off. "Not enough." He walked over and placed a gloved hand on her arm. "Five guys cannot hunt enough game to feed three thousand people."

Lauren pulled her arm away and glared at her brother-in-law. "I can't just abandon the town, Vince. What am I supposed to do?"

What was she supposed to do? She didn't have a clue. It seemed that no matter what she did, it wasn't enough to save the town. No matter what she did, it wasn't good enough. There wasn't a way for her to bring Sam home, and there was nothing she could do to improve her father's heart condition. But she couldn't quit. It just wasn't in her to give up—not on the town, not on Sam, and not on her father—no matter how bleak things looked.

Vince looked away. "I don't know," he whispered.

"I admire you for working so hard for the town, Lauren," Maggie said. Lauren ignored her. She didn't want to be rude to Lindsay's little sister, but she couldn't ignore the fact that Maggie was married to one of the hitmen hired by the Corbins to take out Tara Hobbs—and Sam, if he got in their way. In the back of Lauren's mind, a part of her blamed Maggie for Sam not making it home. It wasn't logical, but it was what it was. Lauren knew Maggie hadn't been a part of the Corbins' criminal deeds, but Maggie was here and she was a convenient target for Lauren's stressed-out mind.

"All we're trying to say is, at some point you're going to have to step back and take care of yourself and your own family," Lindsay said.

Lauren turned on her. "What? Are you accusing me of not taking care of my family?" The words came out like automatic weapon fire. She'd been taking care of her parents for three years. Her whole life revolved around doing what was best for them. She was doing her utmost to take care of their needs and save the town. Her father understood. He'd served as mayor for nearly a decade when Lauren was a kid. He knew the burden. She recalled the time he spent caring for the town's needs. Lauren knew she had spread herself thin, but what choice did she have? Until Sam returned, she had to do it all. Thankfully, she still had her parents' nurse to rely on. Without her, she couldn't continue to be mayor of Unicoi.

Lindsay threw her arms around Lauren's shoulders and tried to pull her close, but Lauren pushed her away. "I'm not saying that at all. We…" Lindsay pointed to Vince and then to herself. "We aren't saying that. You are doing a phenomenal job, isn't that right, Charlie?"

"Very much," Charlie said.

Lauren nearly lost it. She choked back tears, swallowed hard, and turned her back on them. "I'm sorry, guys. I'm just tired. I do appreciate the four of you coming to help. I need to get back to town. I have a meeting this afternoon." Stones crunched under Lauren's boots as she stepped around Charlie and headed up the path to the house.

"We love you, Lauren Michelle," Lindsay called to her back.

"I love you guys, too. So much!"

SIX

Sam
___

Downtown
Franklin, North Carolina
Day 19

The town of Franklin, North Carolina, had once been an idyllic, picturesque small town. Nestled in the Nantahala National Forest at the foothills of the Smoky Mountains, Franklin attracted outdoor enthusiasts of all kinds, causing the town's population to swell to more than four thousand residents in summer.

The once quaint downtown now lay in ruin with shops, restaurants, and businesses burned. The brick facade shells of most of the buildings were all that was left standing, gutted by the fire.

"They say a candle started the fire," Becky said.

"And without running fire trucks, there was no water to put them out," Sam said.

"Exactly. Of course, they'd been looted a week before that."

The Lazy Hiker's roll-up door had been smashed and all its food and brew looted, but it hadn't been burned. Inside, Becky ran a finger over a name scribbled on the wall.

"I imagine you met your share of hikers coming through town," Sam said.

"Every year." She lingered, staring at the name.

"I'm going to see if there's anything useful left in the back," Sam said, leaving her to her memories as he limped toward the storage room.

The back room was empty. Even the paper products had been taken. Sam returned to the front and found Becky outside with her pony and its wagon. She wiped a tear from her eyes as Sam limped toward her.

"You want to talk about him?"

"Nothing to talk about really. He came into town just before the lights went out, stayed a couple of days, then he got back on the trail heading north." She grabbed the pony's reins and gestured for Sam to climb back into the flatbed wagon.

"How much farther?" Sam asked.

"Randall Gershwin lives three miles outside of town up on a ridge off Patton Road."

Becky was quiet as she walked, leading Brownie and Sam southwest through town. As they went along, the damage appeared to be less and less, with some businesses still intact but unoccupied. They saw no one out and about until they crossed over Highway 64 and turned south into a more rural setting.

A man and woman tending a garden beside the road stopped and waved as Becky halted the pony and its cart and took a step toward them. The man reached down and grabbed his rifle. Sam brandished his pistol but didn't point it at the man. Becky took a step back with her hands out, her shotgun slung on her shoulder. "Whoa! I just wanted to ask if you've seen Randall Gershwin lately." Sam hopped down and hobbled over in front of Becky, holding his pistol at his side.

"He's dead. He had a bad ticker. It's hardest on those dependent on meds," the man said.

"Is any of his family still there?" Sam asked.

"No, Elisa's kids came and got her right after Randall passed. They live up in Bluff City somewhere."

"We came to see if Randall's radio still worked. Do you know anything about that?"

"As far as I know, it was fried with everything else," the elderly man said.

"Thanks for your help," Becky said.

"You folks heading through town?" the man asked.

"We are," Becky said.

Sam wanted to stop her, but she'd spoken before he could catch her attention.

"You're staying with Doc Hammond?"

Sam grabbed Becky's arm. "We got to be going. Thanks again for your help," Sam said, pulling Becky back toward the cart.

"I'd take Wilkie Street toward Harrison and avoid town if I were you. Ain't safe no more. The whole damn town is now run by those outsiders holed up in the motel up there," the man said.

"All the locals left town and headed into the rural areas to get away from them. I always said the tourists would someday overrun the place, and it would never be the same. This wasn't what I envisioned though," the woman said.

"Thank you. I think we'll take your advice," Sam said.

He hopped back into the cart, and Becky tugged on Brownie's reins. She was walking faster now. After rounding a curve out of sight of the couple, Sam asked, "Is there another way to Randall's place? I'd really like to take a look at his radio and see for myself since we came all this way."

"Not unless you want to climb the ridge, and I don't think your leg will like that very much."

"Everyone around here would want to know if his radio is working. We could have information about the outside world. People would want to know if help was coming from Raleigh or the federal government. I wouldn't tell anyone if I had a working radio. I wouldn't want it stolen."

"We could try, but I think you're risking greater injury, and I'm not sure it's worth it. I mean…" She stopped in the middle of the road and walked back to the cart with reins in her hands looking at him.

Sam didn't want to give up on finding a working ham radio. They'd come so far, but Becky was right. He was in no shape to climb mountains. "All right. Let's head back."

On their way back, as they approached a blind curve, Sam heard voices. "Becky, stop the cart," he said in a fierce whisper.

"Whoa," Becky told Brownie. When Becky stopped, Brownie did as well, and Sam could hear the people more clearly. Sam climbed down from the cart and moved up beside Becky. Brownie nibbled on his hat as Sam put one finger to his lips, gesturing for Becky to remain silent.

Someone was arguing ahead, but Sam still couldn't make out their words. "Two men and one woman," Becky whispered. Her hearing must have been better than Sam's because he couldn't make out the second male voice. The female voice was clear. She was shouting, "Stop! Stop it!"

"What do we do?" Becky asked.

Sam looked behind them and then left and right. To the left was a cliff, and to the right, an open field. Beyond the field was a creek. "We may be able to cross there and follow the stream north until we bypass them," Sam said.

"She sounds like she needs help."

"We can't help. I'm not in any position to fight. And you only have two shotgun shells left. We have to avoid trouble."

Becky shook her head.

He knew exactly how she felt. It went against every instinct in Sam's body not to run to the woman's aid, but he could barely walk. There would be no way he could physically fight and win with an unknown number of assailants, most likely armed with some sort of weapons. He wouldn't put Becky in that situation. It was too big a risk. "Becky, we can't help her."

He pointed to the field. Becky closed her eyes and cursed under her breath.

"I'm not sure the cart will make it up the creek, Sam."

"Can we cross over? That cornfield on the other side seems flatter."

"It might get stuck," Becky said.

"Let's try."

Sam walked alongside Becky as she led Brownie across the field and down into the shallow water. The splashing sound the pony made as they crossed the creek echoed through the valley. Sam walked backward, keeping an eye on the road. Trees lined the bank of the creek and blocked their view of the homes on the opposite side from where the raised voices had emanated.

"You have any idea where this stream goes from here?"

"No idea."

"Once we get clear of these houses, let's look for a place to cross back over and return to the road." Sam's leg was throbbing, and he was nearly dragging it behind him. He held onto the side of the cart to steady himself. By the time they cleared the homes, Sam was barely able to walk. The pain was intense, but they couldn't afford to get the cart stuck in the muddy field.

"What are you doing?" a gruff male voice shouted.

Sam spun and nearly fell as his leg gave way. He pulled himself around, holding the wagon for support. He leaned against it and unholstered his pistol, holding it at his side out of view of the approaching farmer. "Look at the mess you're making of my corn."

"I'm sorry," Becky said.

"You're sorry. That was food for my children, and you're sorry?"

"Stop beating him! You're going to kill him!" Sam could hear the woman clearly now. So could the farmer. His shotgun came up, and he stepped toward the edge of the field, peering through the trees.

"Linda? What's going on over there, Linda?"

A shot rang out, and Sam dove for Becky, pulling her down to the ground. Brownie bucked and yanked his reins free from her grasp, then bolted across the cornfield away from them, taking Becky's pack and their only water supply with him. Another shot rang out, and the woman screamed. The farmer was crossing the stream calling the woman's name when a third shot rang out and struck him. He went down on one knee and returned fire.

"We have to get out of here, Becky, but I can't get up." Sam's leg was too weak. If he had any chance of getting up off the ground, he needed her help.

"They shot him."

"Becky, if you don't help me up, they're going to shoot us, too." She slowly turned to look at him, shock evident on her face. Sam took her arm. "Help me, Becky."

She got to her feet and tugged with all her might. It took all Sam's strength to assist her. Once he was upright, he aimed his pistol toward the houses with his right hand and held onto Becky's right arm with his other hand. He hopped to the tree line, and they rested behind a tree for a moment so he could assess where they could go to cross and get to safety.

From that position, the side of one of the homes came into view. A man lay on the ground outside a detached garage. Draped over him was the woman. Standing over them both was a huge man with broad shoulders holding a scoped AR-15. They were well within the rifle's effective range. If they stood and attracted his attention, he could kill them both before they had time to run away.

"I think our best option is to stay small and remain quiet until he leaves or goes inside."

"He killed them?" Becky asked.

"It looks like it. If not, there's nothing we can do for them."

"Doc could."

"We don't know if there are others we can't see. There could be more perps inside. We can't help them," Sam repeated. "I'm sorry."

Tears streamed down Becky's cheeks. "I feel so helpless and weak. I hate feeling this way."

Sam understood how she felt. He wasn't exactly strong and in control at the moment. He wasn't used to feeling that way—not since he'd been shot in the line of duty. He'd been assigned to a desk while he recovered, and although he couldn't be out there catching the bad guys, at least he'd been able to do something to help put them behind bars. Now, all he could do was watch as people stole, maimed, and killed each other.

As the assailant moved toward the garage, Sam started to rise, holding onto a tree trunk to steady himself. The man turned swiftly. Sam hadn't been aware that he'd made a noise. He froze. Behind him, he heard the squeak of the wagon as Brownie trotted across the field.

The man stared off in that direction for a moment and then walked into the garage through the open door.

Sam reached down for Becky's hand. "Let's go. Stay low and remain quiet. We'll follow the tree line and the creek until we're out of sight."

Becky stood, and Sam took her arm. They hurried, having to step over deadfall and around briar bushes until they reached the end of the field and the road came into view.

"Let's cross here. It'll be easier to travel on the road. I can't keep lifting my leg over logs and rocks," Sam said.

As they crossed the cold stream, Sam's dry mouth longed for a drink. The cool water felt good on his feet, but they couldn't afford to linger.

On the opposite side, Becky held out her hand and pulled Sam up the muddy bank. Sam fell face forward into the mud, striking his chin on a tree root. As she tugged, Becky's foot slipped, and she slid to the ground.

"Are you okay?" Sam asked.

"I'm okay. I just don't have any more energy in me. I don't know how we're going to get back to Doc's now that Brownie ran off."

"We're going to look for some other form of transportation, but in the meantime, we need to keep moving," Sam said. He wasn't sure what other forms of transportation they could find, but anything that would get him off his leg would work.

He and Becky rested on the bank under the shade of the trees listening for the squeak of the wagon. If they could catch up with the pony and cut him off, that would be their best option.

"Wait here. I'm going to climb up that hill there and see if I can spot him," Becky said.

"Be careful. Keep your head on a swivel and ears alert for anyone approaching you," Sam said.

"I know to do that. I'm a hunter, remember?" Becky said, shouldering her shotgun.

SEVEN

Verónica "Ronnie" Morales

Shop 'n Save
Erwin, Tennessee
Day 19

Everyone fell silent as Nigel Corbin strode into the cavernous former grocery store. His deputies visibly tensed when Nigel fixed his gaze on them, as did Ed Billings, Erwin's former mayor. Former because Nigel had appointed himself the town's leader after ordering the Z-Nation boys to kill any government official who dared to oppose him. Alberto Vazquez Mereno ran the Z-Nation like a business. Before the lights went out, Mereno had owned several local businesses and often dined with commissioners and other prominent citizens, none of whom knew of his ties to Corbin and his illegal enterprises.

As the handsome, muscular, middle-aged man in charge, Nigel had his pick of the women who now called the Super Saver home. Verónica "Ronnie" Morales prayed he would choose anyone but her. When his gaze fell on her, she stiffened for a split second before softening her shoulders, tilting her head back, and throwing her long black hair over her right shoulder, pretending to be interested. Inside, her stomach churned.

Ronnie lowered her head and looked at the floor as if showing respect to the king. Nigel ate that shit up. Ronnie didn't want to do anything that would put her on the bad side of the Corbins. She didn't want them to have any reason to look into her activities and learn that even before the shit hit the fan, Ronnie had been working with the cops and informing them of what she knew about the Corbins' illegal activity.

Ronnie wasn't a close confidant. She wasn't part of Nigel's inner circle, but she knew how to loosen up someone who was. Nigel was adamant that those under him refrain from drugs, even though he used them to control others. If he knew that Bobby Russo was snorting coke, Ronnie might lose her access to inside information.

"We called this meeting today to address a serious issue," said Lee Brodrick, Corbin's chief of security. Brodrick squared his broad shoulders and clasped his hands together in front of him, letting his arms rest on his tactical belt. Mereno and his top lieutenant, Dexter Murray, stood behind him.

"It seems some of our neighbors have decided not to play nice. When our county officials attempted to go into Unicoi to address the town council about working with Erwin and Johnson City for the good of the people, Unicoi turned them away." He paused and scanned the crowd. He continued, raising his voice above the murmurs of the group. "They've stolen food and other resources from businesses, taken private property, and walled themselves in to keep those resources for themselves and from the people who need them."

The crowd grew louder, with some shouting to tear down the wall. This wasn't Corbin's first attempt to gin up support for attacking Unicoi. He'd been trying to justify a raid for days. But with their stomachs full and alcoholic beverages still flowing, there had been little appetite for war. Corbin had remedied that by reducing rations and limiting alcohol, claiming everyone needed to be ready to fight because it wouldn't be long before Unicoi came for them.

It appeared that Corbin would soon have the support for the war he wanted. Ronnie's days here were numbered, and she'd soon need to make her move to escape.

"Bronson over there has set up a registration table. Everyone over the age of fourteen must register. Training will begin immediately."

"Training?" a young woman from the crowd shouted. "For what?"

"To defend our community," Brodrick said.

"Defend it from whom?" another woman asked.

"From our aggressive neighbors to the north—Unicoi."

Ronnie searched the faces in the crowd. She saw reluctance. They might require a little more persuasion to be convinced to take up arms.

"I got kids and grandkids in Unicoi. They're not—"

"I have family there too. My brother and his wife. They're good people. They're struggling just like us."

Brodrick glared at them. Ronnie kept her eyes on Nigel. His jaw tightened. He was growing impatient. He didn't suffer any dissent among his subjects. If Brodrick didn't devise a way to control these people and get them to do what Nigel wanted, they'd all find themselves doing hard labor—or digging their own graves.

Ronnie took a step back, and then another, blending into the group and moving toward the door. She needed to get word to Unicoi. She wanted to let Benny Jameson know the hammer was about to come down. There would first be a cleaning of house. Examples would be made of the people who spoke out against attacking Unicoi, and then anyone who failed to comply would find themselves and their families at the end of a rope.

"Can you believe this?" a woman in her mid-fifties asked her. Ronnie turned to face the woman. "They're nothing more than thugs and warmongers," the woman said. "They killed the mayor and most of the town council and set themselves up here as kings." Ronnie put her finger to her mouth, trying to stop the woman from continuing and getting herself in trouble, but the woman was on a roll. "They've taken everything from the town, and they won't stop until there's nothing left in Unicoi either."

Ronnie touched her arm and leaned in close. "You can't talk like that. You'll get yourself killed. Corbin and his henchmen don't allow it. If you can, I'd take your family and get as far from here as possible."

"I've been here all my life. I'm not going to let some douchebag like Corbin run me out of town." Her voice was loud enough that if the murmuring of the gathering hadn't drowned out her words, she might have found herself at the wrong end of Brodrick's gun.

Without another word, Ronnie turned and sliced through the crowd, putting distance between herself and the stupid woman. When she reached the door, she pointed to the porta-potties at the back of the parking lot. "I gotta go," she mouthed.

The handsome guard at the door smiled. "You need some help, Ronnie?" Jose asked.

Ronnie dropped her chin and flipped her hair over her shoulder. "Maybe later." She pushed through the double doors and stepped onto the walkway. Jose followed her outside. "How much later?"

She smiled. Ronnie put a hand on her curvy hip, arched her back slightly, and bit her bottom lip. "Tonight? Around midnight?"

Jose bobbed his head and pumped his fist in the air. "Yes! My place or yours?"

"Yours."

Jose lived in a trailer park just north of the Tractor Supply store and one mile from the church where her cousin was pastor. Benny would really owe her after this one. She would leave a message with her cousin that she needed to meet Benny face to face. She needed to know whether choosing to align herself with Unicoi was still worth the risk. She wanted to hear him say that she'd be accepted in town after all she'd done to help them.

I get off at seven o'clock," Jose said as Ronnie sprinted off toward the porta-potties.

"I'll be there at midnight," she called back.

EIGHT

Benny

On the way to the northern checkpoint, Benny was flagged down by Joey Hoffenberg. Benny turned his truck around and pulled to a stop in the road next to him. Joey dismounted from his bicycle and climbed into the passenger seat of Benny's truck.

"I watched Ralph and his family as you asked, but he's not your spy," Joey said.

"Are you sure Ralph never left his house yesterday?" Benny asked.

"He never left his pool. I think he's afraid if he did, his ass would melt in this heat."

Benny wiped the sweat from his brow. Unicoi usually had pretty mild weather. But without air conditioning, their mild weather seemed like an unusually hot and muggy summer.

"What about his kids? Did Clay Cross leave? Did they have any visitors?'

"No. No one left, and no one came to visit."

Benny shook his head. Ronnie hadn't reported in yet, so it was still possible that Ralph was waiting for someone to pass the information along. "Go back and continue watching them. Let me know if anyone leaves or they get a visit from anyone."

"Okay, Chief."

As Joey pedaled back toward Ralph's house, Benny continued toward the checkpoint to talk with Alan Mayberry about the group holed up in the warehouse. Wilson had returned with a concern about the safety of women and children there if they went in to clear out the place as they'd originally planned. They would need a larger show of force to head off any potential flying bullets and keep the women and children safe.

Benny took a detour for a few blocks and drove by the church. He still hadn't informed Lauren of the issue. She had enough on her plate with her father's health taking a turn for the worse. He hoped to find a solution before having to tell her about Sharon and the other girls from the motel—that was a sticky situation.

In many ways, Benny felt compassion for the young women— some of whom were only teens. They had been victims of Billy Mahon and the Corbins. Most had been unwilling participants in the sex trade. Benny wasn't sure how the town would respond to their presence, but if he could convince Billings to make sure they all signed up for work assignments and were contributing to the support of the town, he could justify allowing them to remain in Unicoi.

Pastor Billings was out in front of the church, leaning on a rake, talking to a young man. As Benny pulled the pickup to a stop at the curb, Billings and the young man turned their attention to Benny.

"Can I get a word with you, Pastor?" Benny leaned across the seat and opened the passenger-side door. Billings slid into the seat but left the door open.

"Pastor, we need to talk about the girls from the motel."

"You cannot judge them for their past. They're all God's children and deserving of forgiveness."

"There's nothing to forgive, Pastor. I assure you I'm not judging them. I just wanted to ask you to encourage them to go to the distribution center and sign up for a work assignment. I think that would go a long way to help the town's people accept that they've been allowed to remain in Unicoi."

"They're working. They're pulling weeds and watering, and—"

"In addition to what they're doing for the church, having them do something that contributes to the town would help. Everyone will soon be required to work, Pastor. It would be good if they signed up before it was mandatory—sort of a goodwill gesture."

"I'll speak to them," Billings said, climbing out of the truck. "By the way, how is Bill Taylor? I heard he was having difficulties with his health."

"That's what I hear," Benny said. He didn't feel it was his place to give out news about the mayor's father.

Benny also stopped by Marie Roberts' house on his way out to the checkpoint. Marie's neighbors, Mrs. Turner and her son, Colin, were out in front of their house working their front garden. They looked up as Benny approached. Mrs. Turner looked away. Benny gave Colin a curt nod and proceeded on to Marie's house.

She, too, was working in her front garden. Marie came from a farming family and her vegetables looked amazing. Her parents had come to Unicoi as migrants to work the commercial farms. Now, they owned a farm of their own and, before the event, sold produce to both Stephens' Farm Market and the Johnson & Carter Farms. They knew a thing or two about growing food.

"Hey there, sexy," Marie said, dropping the garden tool and walking toward the truck.

"Your garden looks amazing."

"Thanks." She cupped her hand around her mouth and whispered, "It's the rabbit poop."

"Where'd you get rabbit poop?"

"In my basement. I trapped some cotton tails. Don't tell Park Ranger Sullivan."

"That's illegal," Benny said, smiling. "I could arrest you, you know."

She threw her head back, exposing her long neck, and stuck out both hands, clasping them together. "Arrest me, officer," she said in a sultry voice that made Benny's toes curl in his boots. Her dark brown eyes lured him in for a kiss. When their lips parted, Marie whispered, "Ronnie sent word. She said Corbin got some news from Unicoi, but she hasn't been able to find out what exactly he learned. Whatever it was, it made him mad as hell. The attack has been delayed for now."

"She still doesn't know who's bringing him the information?"

"No. I'm afraid for her, Benny. She may never make it out if she tries to get closer to Corbin's inner circle."

"I know. I'm sorry. When you speak with her, tell her she can get out any time she feels it's too dangerous. We'll find another way to get information."

"Thank you, Benny. You're the best. I don't know why my mother dislikes you."

"I don't either."

"You could convert."

"I don't think my converting to Catholicism will be enough for your mother to approve of us getting married. She just doesn't think I'm good enough for her daughter."

"Things have changed. My prospects have changed."

"Does that mean I have less competition?"

She smiled. "You have no competition."

"That's what I want to hear," Benny said.

Her expression flattened. "Do you think things will ever return to normal?"

He stroked her hand. "I'm afraid not. I can't see how things will ever be the same, even if they were somehow able to get the lights back up and running. People are forever changed by this experience."

Marie waved and returned to her garden as Benny drove away. He thought about just how much things had changed. Almost every aspect of his daily routine had been altered. It took hours to do what had taken minutes before the event. The death and destruction that everyone had witnessed since the lights went out nearly three weeks ago had left indelible scars that would stay with them long after life returned to anything resembling normal.

NINE

Sam

Cartoogechaye Creek
Franklin, Tennessee
Day 19

While Sam waited for Becky to return from her search for Brownie and the pony cart, he removed a med kit from the new pack that Becky had found for him in town. The backpack had likely been abandoned by a section hiker as it was loaded down with too much gear, and none of it was the ultralight stuff that a thru-hiker would carry. He'd gone through it and ditched more than half the equipment. Sam had stashed the extra items under his cot because everything was useful these days and irreplaceable in most cases.

Sam had kept only the LifeStraw personal water filter, the water purification tablets, and the collapsible water bags in the pack to keep it as light as possible.

Sliding sideways and scooting on his butt, Sam made his way to the edge of the stream, primed the LifeStraw by inserting the base about an inch below the water, and then let it sit for about thirty seconds to soak the inner membrane. Once the straw was primed, Sam lowered his face toward the water and sucked on the mouthpiece about four or five times. A second later, he was drinking filtered ice cold water.

Once his thirst was quenched, Sam submerged the Whirl-Pak collapsible water bags below the water and filled all three. The bags gave him three liters of water but added over six pounds to the pack. Water was usually the heaviest item he carried, besides weapons and spare ammunition. He'd ditch other things if he had to, but water, weapons, and ammo were absolute essentials.

He still had the same everyday carry (EDC) items in his cargo pockets that he had carried before the shit hit the fan. Among other things, those always included a means to purify and carry water, three ways to make fire, and a few first aid items.

With water taken care of for the moment, Sam returned to refining his pack and making a list of items he lacked and where he might go to obtain them. He needed some way to catch fish, snare rabbits, and kill squirrels as these were the most plentiful and best source of quick food in the area. Becky was an excellent hunter, and she would have snare wire. He usually hunted squirrels using his scoped Henry .22 rifle, but what he really needed in this situation was a long bow. It was a quiet way to hunt without attracting unwanted attention or scaring away other game. He wrote longbow on his notepad. He'd ask Becky if she knew where he might locate one.

After an hour, Sam had filled three pages of the small notepad with items he needed to obtain for his trip home. Ammunition was at the top of the list, but he doubted he'd be lucky enough to stumble upon a cache of weapons and ammo. What he wouldn't do is take it from someone else. That would be akin to taking food from their mouths or sentencing them to death by leaving them defenseless.

The most troubling item on Sam's list was transportation. He'd listed every means of travel he could think of, including a skateboard.

You're grasping at straws now, Wallace.

Sam chuckled at the image of him rolling into Unicoi on a skateboard. Benny and Vince would never let him live that down.

At the crunch of breaking branches, Sam drew his pistol, aiming it toward a stand of trees to his right in the direction the sound had come from. A horse's nose was the first thing to come into view. Becky sat high on its back. She led a second horse behind her.

Sam smiled.

"What are you smiling about?" she asked as she hopped down from the horse.

"Nothing. Where did you get those?" he asked, pointing to the horses.

She stroked the black mare, then led it and the quarter horse to a tree, and tied the reins to a limb. They began munching grass, waving their long tails in the breeze.

"I traded for them. Mandy Platt barrel races—at least she did before, well, you know. People have been stealing them. She even had a gun pointed at her while she was riding to visit her momma and some asshat took her favorite mare, Jelly Bean. She said she might as well get something for them rather than have them just outright stolen."

"What did you trade her?"

Becky's mouth curved into a smile and her face turned a shade of scarlet. "Condoms."

"Condoms?" Birth control wasn't something that Sam would have thought would be a high-value barter item in the apocalypse, but it made sense. Intercourse was still going to occur, and pregnancy under the current circumstances would pose many additional problems. The lack of medical staff, scarcity of baby items, and many other considerations would factor into the decision to avoid pregnancy.

Sam was surprised that Lauren and Lindsay hadn't mentioned it while their group was preparing supplies and stockpiling barter items. But after Vince had questioned stocking feminine hygiene items, maybe they felt uncomfortable bringing it up. Besides, Lindsay wanted a baby in the worst way. Sam didn't think she'd let a little thing like the apocalypse prevent her from becoming a mother. Lauren, on the other hand—Sam was sure she had several years' worth of birth control pills upstairs at her parents' house, along with the medication she'd stashed for her father's heart condition. She wouldn't want to bring a child into this mess.

"That's pretty sound logic, I'd say," Sam said. He thought of asking Becky about why she was carrying the condoms in her pack but decided not to go there—none of his business. From her flushed face, he could tell she was embarrassed about it.

"I know it will be difficult for you to climb up on a horse, especially bareback. But Mandy wouldn't part with any tack. She has a sentimental attachment to all of it from her racing days."

Sam looked around for something he could stand on that would make it easier to mount the horse.

"What about that boulder there? You think you could climb up on it and throw your leg over. Once you lay your torso across her back and throw your good leg over, I could help push you upright."

Sam studied the boulder. The mare looked to be about fifteen hands. The height of the boulder was about right.

Sam groaned as Becky pushed on his hip and shoulder, trying to shove him upright. If anyone had been watching the scene, he was sure they'd be rolling on the ground laughing. Sam would have too if it hadn't been so freaking painful.

Becky was petite, but she had to be all muscle under her loose-fitting, long-sleeve, button-up shirt and baggie cargo pants. It was a good thing she was strong because Sam would have never made it up onto that horse without her.

The horse reared its head in protest a few times before taking off in a gallop and following Becky's horse toward the blacktop road. Sam bounced on the horse's back uncomfortably as they raced along. He was using muscles he hadn't used in years and was having difficulty balancing due to his inability to grip the side of the horse with his injured left thigh. Having his leg dangling was incredibly painful and he wondered how he'd do with a saddle. When he'd first seen the horses, he'd thought they might be his ticket home, but now, actually riding one, he wasn't sure he could endure that much pain.

"What about Brownie and the cart?" Sam asked.

"I looked everywhere for him. When I got to Mandy's and saw her horses, I abandoned looking for him to get back here and get you home. But I intend to come back tomorrow and try to find him."

It's a long way to go, Becky. You don't have to—"

"I owe it to him. He's been good to me. Besides, I've wanted to try hunting down this way. I was hoping to bag some turkeys."

Sam and Becky rode into town without talking much. Sam was concentrating on staying on the horse and watching for people. He wasn't sure what had Becky so quiet. She didn't seem the type to open up about her problems. Should he ask?

"It's a dangerous world we're living in now, isn't it?" she said as they neared the outskirts of Franklin.

"Getting more so every day," Sam said. "People are more desperate now. They know help isn't coming and they worry about how long they can hold out. Many are slowly starving to death. Can you imagine watching your child wither away like that?"

"No. I worry about my mom and family sometimes, but they're tough mountain folk. I come from a large family, and they all still live close to each other. Life won't be much different for them. They've always been wary of strangers, and the remoteness of their homes makes it unlikely they'll see many trespassers."

"Have you thought about trying to make it home to your family?" Sam asked.

"I've thought about it, sure."

"And? What do you think?" Sam asked. It would be better to have a travel buddy. If Becky did decide to go with him, Sam could leave sooner than if he had to go it alone. Their survival chances would improve if they traveled together. After realizing how weak he was from just moving the short distance from the rock to the stream earlier, Sam doubted his ability to make it one hundred and twenty miles to Unicoi, but taking a horse was probably going to be his best bet for making it home.

Maybe in a few more days.

He would work on building his core strength and try to find a saddle. That should make riding somewhat easier, but he needed fuel for that. Protein, carbs, and fat. It was the most foreign thing to Sam to be almost totally dependent on others for everything, but he was stuck. Sam couldn't ask Becky to provide him with more game than she was already giving him.

In addition to feeding Sam and the Hammonds, Becky was providing meat for two of Sam's fellow A.T. hikers, Moondust and Tumbleweed, whom she'd rescued from a potentially violent encounter with some locals. They'd been staying with her for several weeks. Recently, she'd managed to convince Mrs. Hammond that they'd be useful cutting firewood, helping with the laundry, and cooking. But they'd remained a burden on Becky as more mouths to feed.

"I need to teach Moondust and Tumbleweed how to handle a weapon. They need target practice, but we can't spare the ammo," Sam said. If they were going to stick around, they had to learn to be more self-sufficient and contribute more.

"Moondust has shown interest in learning to trap and set snares. I think I'll ask her to come with me in the morning," Becky said.

"That's a great idea." Sam firmly believed in the old adage that said if you gave a man a fish, he could eat for a day. Teach a man to fish—or in this case, snare and set traps—he could eat for a lifetime.

"While you were looking for Brownie, I inventoried my new pack—thank you again for giving it to me—and I made a list of things I'll need to make it home. When we get back to Doc's, do you think you could review it with me and see if you know where I might find any of the items?"

She looked back over her shoulder. "Sure. I'll also keep my eye out when I go out tomorrow."

"I don't want you to put yourself at risk, Becky. If you would just suggest where I can look for them."

"I don't mind looking. If I think I can get them without trouble, I will. I won't do anything stupid," Becky said, her tone sharp. Her North Carolina accent was thickest when she was perturbed. Sam hadn't seen her angry yet.

"I know you won't do anything stupid. You wouldn't have made it this far if you weren't a very bright and capable woman."

"Thanks," Becky said flatly.

"I mean it."

"I know. I've had to scrape by all my life. I don't know anything different. When I was married to Darrell was the only time I ever had two nickels to rub together." She stopped the horse.

Sam pulled on the reins, but his horse kept moving. "Whoa, boy!" he said as the horse stepped up beside Becky's.

Tears were flowing down her cheeks. Sam reached over and touched her shoulder. She didn't pull away, but he could feel her tense, so he removed his hand.

"I know you miss him," he said.

"I still have every dime of his life insurance money. It seemed wrong to profit from his death. I thought about doing something good with it—blessing someone, but I couldn't find anything worthy of his memory." She turned her gaze toward him, wearing such a pained expression that he had to look away.

"The best thing you can do now to honor him and your brother is to survive—not only survive but thrive. Use the skills they taught you to teach others."

Her face lit up. She smiled so broadly that her dimples showed. Sam hadn't even known she had dimples. "That's it! That right there is it! I have a purpose now," she said slowly and full of wonder. "Darrel and Billy Joe would want me to share what they taught me to help others survive. They'll live on through me teaching other folks to hunt, fish, shoot and kick ass. I'm going to start tomorrow with Moondust."

Sam chuckled. "You'll turn her into a lean, mean, hunting machine in no time."

≈

As they approached Franklin, Sam was checking out a self-storage facility they were passing when he heard a male voice order them to stop.

Instead of complying, Becky tapped her horse's flank with her heels and took off racing down the street. Sam drew his pistol and tried to do the same, but his horse didn't cooperate. The horse sidestepped and jerked its head. Sam looked for the source of the voice, but the person was well hidden. It wasn't until a gunshot broke the silence and a bullet whizzed past his head and hit one of the storage units that he knew which direction the threat was coming from.

The horse bucked and reared at the sound of the gunfire, and Sam slid backward, but his hand was firmly wrapped up in the horse's mane and he was able to hang on. The horse finally took off down the street with Sam bouncing on its back.

TEN

Lauren
___

Taylor Residence
Unicoi, Tennessee
Day 19

"How's he doing, Angela," Lauren asked, taking off her boots and leaving them in the mud room.

"The same," her father's nurse replied.

Lauren placed a carton of eggs she'd gathered from the chicken coop at the farm on the counter by her parents' non-functioning refrigerator and walked out to the screened porch. Her stomach twisted into a knot as she approached her father's bed.

"Hey, Pop."

Her dad lifted his hand from the bed to give her a wave. "How was…" he coughed, gasped for air, and then continued, "school?"

Her father was growing more and more confused. Lauren turned away and wiped a tear. She had grown accustomed to her mother's mental confusion, but the delirium her father was experiencing now had caught her off guard. He'd declined so rapidly after the EMP. Lauren was sure it was from the stress, both physical and psychological, but Angela had told her it was from sodium levels in the blood.

"Did he eat anything today?" Lauren asked, taking a seat beside his bed.

"I tried to give him some broth, but he only took one sip," Angela said.

Lauren grew quiet as she watched her father sleep. He hadn't eaten anything in five days. He was emaciated, except for his swollen abdomen and legs.

"How was the farm?" Angela asked.

"Good. The tomatoes are looking nice, and the blackberries are just about ripe enough to pick. We might be having cobbler by the end of the week." Lauren forced a smile. "Where's Mom?"

"In the garden. She's picking flowers."

When Lauren left for the farm that morning, her mother had been in the kitchen making bread. Edna hadn't done that in over a year. Although she was still confused at times, she'd seemed much clearer in the last week. She had even helped Angela can cabbage from the garden.

"I have a town hall meeting this afternoon, and then I need to meet with a few department heads. Are you going to be okay here alone with them until I get back? I could ask Millie to come over."

"I think we'll be okay until you get home tonight. You go do what you need to do at city hall," Angela said.

Lauren changed from her musky-smelling farm clothes into clean cargo pants and a pullover shirt. She strapped the Colt revolver around her waist, grabbed her day pack from beside her bed, and headed out the door. Buddy French, her neighbor, came into view as she rounded the back of the house. He was standing over her bicycle in the driveway between the two houses.

"Hey, Lauren. I noticed how bald your back tire was getting. I have a new one in my garage. I could put it on for you."

She wasn't sure what to make of his kind gesture. Suspicious by nature, Lauren questioned Buddy's motives.

"Thank you, but I have to get to work," she said.

"Maybe when you get home then," Buddy said. "Just let me know when's a good time. Better sooner rather than later if you're going to be riding out to the farm and back every day."

Lauren didn't like knowing Buddy was keeping track of her movements. It was normal that everyone knew your business in a small town, but now it seemed more dangerous to be under the spotlight.

"I'll let you know," Lauren replied as she threw her leg over her bike.

As Lauren rode through town, many residents were out weeding their gardens. It would be weeks before they would have anything to show for their efforts and be rough until then.

After making it to city hall, Lauren poured over the latest inventory of food and supplies at her makeshift desk outside the municipal building. The former employees' smoke hole was an unconventional place for a mayor's office, but the temperature inside city hall was nearly one hundred degrees. They were running low on provisions, and hard decisions would have to be made soon. The town was already rationing and distributing only enough food for one meal per day, but soon, they wouldn't even be able to supply that much. Until their crops came in, they'd have to find some way to feed the citizens of Unicoi.

Lauren heard footfalls behind her and turned. "Mayor, there's someone at the north checkpoint to see you. They say they're with the Johnson City Emergency Management Agency and the city manager sent them," Alan said.

Had Corbin sent them?

Lauren looked up from a pile of papers and rubbed the back of her neck. She wasn't in the mood for a confrontation with their northern neighbors. She sighed, threw her leg off the bench, and pushed herself up from the picnic table.

Alan leaned forward with both hands on the table and arched his back. He'd been injured in Afghanistan, and the physical strain of his duties on the security team appeared to be taking their toll, but he had become an integral member of Unicoi's security forces. The subject of the town's defensive posture had led to some very tense council meetings. Benny had been forced to intervene to keep the peace on several occasions. Ralph hated the term "security forces" because he said it implied the town faced a greater threat than he thought was likely.

"I can send them away," Alan said.

She needed to know what Preston Corbin was up to. She'd have to go out and meet this Johnson City delegation. "Did they say what they wanted?" Lauren asked.

"I asked, but they said they'd only speak with you," Alan said.

Lauren frowned and followed Alan to his truck.

Even from blocks away, Lauren could hear the diesel engine of Alford Mitford's fifty-year-old crane and the thunderous crash of a steel shipping container as it was positioned in place near Buffalo Creek at Unicoi's most northern border.

Alan Mayberry steered his truck toward the sound. "I bet Maryann and Gretchen are glad they weren't successful in forcing Mitford to get rid of all that so-called old military junk at his place. All that rusty equipment may just save the town," Alan said.

"Yep, his junk may just save all our lives," Lauren said.

Alford Mitford had owned several companies over the last half-century and adhered to the philosophy of never parting with anything. The town had been in litigation with Mitford on several occasions, attempting to force him to clean up his property and get rid of the old US Army trucks, construction equipment, army surplus, and steel girders and pipes that were piled high on his acre-and-a-half lot at the edge of town. The fact that Mitford was now willing to step up and use that equipment to benefit the town was a testament to his honorable character. With his antique crane, they'd been able to move the semitrailers at the truck stop, and the shipping containers from the moving and leasing company into place, cutting the town off from Erwin to the south and Johnson City to the north.

As they approached, Orlando Lawless, Lauren's high school science teacher, held out a hand to stop them, and Alan Mayberry slowed the truck.

"Hold up here. Mitford is about to pick up another container," Mr. Lawless said.

One rusty steel container had already been wedged between the side of the rock cliff wall and the steep drop-off on the opposite side, completely blocking the roadway near the town limits. The ancient crane squealed and squeaked but managed to lift the heavy box into place. It was a laborious job creating a barrier wall around the town, but they'd made progress, especially to the south, where Lauren feared their greatest threat lay. Sandwiched between Nigel Corbin, who'd set up in Erwin to their south, and Preston Corbin's home base in Johnson City, Lauren wasn't sure which one would be the first to be a problem for the town.

"How many containers do we have left?" Lauren asked.

"Not enough," Mr. Lawless said. He bent down to eye level and leaned on the truck's door. "We've decided to haul boulders from the quarry to block secondary routes into town. It won't stop foot traffic, but no one will be rolling into town in a vehicle."

"Do we have enough fuel for that?" Alan asked.

"Maybe. This beast drinks diesel like my uncle Al used to drink Tennessee whiskey."

The debate surrounding using their available diesel to construct the barrier around the town had been fierce. Lauren wasn't sure the plan was wise either, but what good would it do to plant fields of food if the town couldn't defend them? She sure as hell didn't want all their hard work to go to the Corbins or others like them.

Once Mitford had the container aligned and had moved the crane away, Alan opened the door in the side of the steel box, and they walked into the container. Alan flicked on a flashlight and closed the door behind them. He opened the door on the opposite side and the container flooded with light. Benny poked his head inside. "I'd make this quick. I don't like you being exposed like this, Mayor."

"I will. I just need to know what they're up to." Lauren stepped out of the container outside of the town's cordon. "What can I do for you, gentlemen?"

"We would like to speak to you and the board of aldermen," Glenn Lawson, the head of Johnson City's emergency management team, said.

"What about?"

"Several things. It would be beneficial for us all to sit down and work together to best serve our citizens, don't you think?"

"Is Johnson City proposing to send food, water, and fuel to Unicoi?"

"Um… I don't know what resources Johnson City has to share at this time. What we need is to discuss border excursions and poaching, among other things," Lawson said.

"Poaching? Border excursions? Has Johnson City annexed areas of the county I'm unfamiliar with?" Lauren struggled to keep the fury from her tone. "Are you now claiming the interstate as well?"

"It looks as if you have. Your people are unloading every semi-trailer for miles."

"Not within Johnson City's jurisdiction. We've stayed clear of your territory."

"We arrested three guys just last night breaking into an Amazon delivery van on the interstate."

"They weren't any of ours."

"They came from Unicoi," Lawson said.

"They weren't from Unicoi. They may have been travelers we kicked out of the motel, but they weren't from here. We have a list of everyone who comes and goes from town. We aren't missing three men this morning."

Lawson glanced up at the guard with the rifle standing on top of the container, then took a step closer, shoving his hands into his pockets. "That is something we could discuss—at your office." He stopped, leaned his head slightly to one side, glanced behind her to Benny and Alan, and then down to Lauren's hand resting on the revolver on her hip. Lawson slowly removed his hands from his pockets and took a step back.

"That won't be necessary. If you had intended to provide aid to the citizens of Unicoi, you would have come prepared to do so. Johnson City has over sixty thousand people and much greater resources. Unicoi has less than four thousand residents. What could we possibly have that you want?"

"The commissioners of Johnson City are also concerned with the posture Unicoi appears to be taking."

"Posture?"

"The wall you're building."

"What about it?"

"As if you were planning to go to war."

"War?" Lauren tilted her head slightly and clenched her jaw. "These aren't assault barriers. The EMP happened two weeks ago, and this is the first official visit of anyone from your city. We have a small police force with which to protect our town from the lawlessness now roaming the countryside. The wall is for the protection of the residents of Unicoi."

"I'm not sure you have the right to—"

Lauren cut him off. "The right? We have an obligation to

protect our town in an emergency." She waved her hand in the air. "I think this qualifies as an emergency." Lauren turned her back on Lawson and began walking back to the box's open door.

"Does the board of aldermen agree with you?" Lawson called after her.

Lauren spun on her heels with her hands on her hips. "I wouldn't concern yourselves with the governmental affairs of the Town of Unicoi. You'd be better served by concentrating on your own affairs." Lauren walked back inside the shipping container, and Alan shut the door behind her.

Not all of Unicoi's four aldermen were on board with the plan to secure the town. Maryann Winters still held out hope that things would return to normal and was oblivious to the dangers the town faced. Gretchen and Lloyd were firmly behind securing the town, and at one point, Ralph had been, too. But lately, he'd expressed concerns about the signal it would send. Lauren wasn't sure if they were his concerns or the concerns of his friends, the Corbins.

Mr. Lawless held the door open, and Lauren exited the container. "I have to make a progress report to the board of aldermen today. Do you think you might have time to address them about things here?" Lauren asked.

Lawless straightened, and his gaze shifted to the old crane. "I really should stay here and help Mitford."

"I understand. It was worth a shot," Lauren said.

Alan started the truck's engine as Lauren approached the vehicle. Mr. Lawless raised his hand. "I forgot to ask. Any word on Sam?"

Lauren's stomach flip-flopped as it did every time someone asked that question. She understood they were concerned, and some even genuinely wanted him back home, but answering the question multiple times a day only served to rip off the Band-Aid over the deep wound in her aching heart.

"Not yet," she replied.

She turned to Benny. "May I have a word? They stepped to the side of the road out of earshot of Alan, Mr. Lawless, and the two guards. "I'm going to have to call another town meeting and things could get ugly."

"I need time to round up enough off-duty folks from the security team. I don't want to pull anyone from the wall," Benny said.

"Is tomorrow too soon? We're going to announce we're adding a work requirement to receiving aid from the town and the implementation of the new criminal laws and penalties you and I spoke about."

"That could get nasty. I may need to pull in some of my tier-one team members. You think you might convince Vince and some of his guys to join us?" Benny asked.

"I can ask." Lauren knew her brother-in-law would come to her aid if she asked. He'd bitch about her putting herself at risk, but he'd be there. She had no doubt about that.

"I'll schedule the security team then," Benny said. "It's about to get real in Unicoi."

"I'm headed over to fill Ralph in on the board's decisions."

"You need an escort?"

"I thought I'd take Alan with me."

"Good move," Benny said.

ELEVEN

Becky Shelton

Palmer Street
Franklin, Tennessee
Day 19

As soon as Becky heard the men shouting at them, she rode away toward cover. She yanked the reins and stopped the horse on the south side of an electronics store. Becky slid off the horse and tied its reins to the mirror of a late-model Ford pickup before running back along the front of the store and stopping at the north corner of the building, her rifle in hand.

Sam was bouncing on the horse's back and hauling ass up the street toward her location. She stepped out away from the brick building and waved her hands over her head, trying to get Sam's attention, but he was unable to stop the out-of-control horse. He was going to fall off and hit the pavement.

"Hold on tight," Becky shouted.

A second later, Sam turned the horse to the left, and it ran up the next street. Was he leaving her behind to deal with those men? She slung her rifle over her back and ran to where she'd tied up her horse. Before she could climb on and ride back to the road, she caught sight of Sam. He'd managed to slow the horse and turn it back around.

"Let's go!" he shouted from the corner.

Becky looked to her left to see if anyone was coming. She saw no one, but as soon as her horse stepped onto the pavement, two men moved out from behind a bunch of old cars. One of the men raised a rifle. Becky brought her pistol up and aimed for the man's heart, but her horse lunged just as she went to squeeze the trigger. The pistol went off, and the man dove. She couldn't tell if she had hit him.

She slapped her horse's behind and trotted off toward Sam. He was off his mount and taking cover behind an SUV in the strip mall parking lot on the corner.

"Hurry! Get down!" Sam said.

Becky raced across the street and stopped her horse next to the SUV. Sam rested the barrel of his pistol on the hood and fired in the men's direction as Becky slid down from her mount. Spooked by the gunfire, Sam's horse was nowhere in sight.

"Where did the men go?" Becky asked as she dropped to a crouch beside Sam.

"See that old green Buick?" Sam asked, pointing. "One of them ran behind there."

"I'm not sure if I hit the other one. Spirit lurched as I fired. The man went down, but I don't think I hit him."

"He might have crawled under the purple sedan," Sam said.

"Keep your eyes on the green Buick. I've got the sedan."

That was more than sixty yards. It would be easier with her rifle. She was less proficient with a pistol.

"What do I do if I see them? I don't think I can make a shot this far away."

"Just watch for them. We need to know if they reappear." After a few seconds, Sam moved toward the bumper and looked toward the house up the hill.

"Shooter," Sam said a second before he fired at the man. As he did, the man Becky had fired upon popped up near the Buick. The man leveled his rifle's barrel in their direction, and a second later, the windshield of the SUV shattered. Becky heard the weapon's report and dropped to the ground. Sam moved toward her at the back of the SUV. He fired again and then grabbed her hand. With Becky supporting him to take the pressure off his bad leg, he hobbled as quickly as he could toward the storefront. There they both shouldered open the door, and made their way inside, through the building, and out the back door to a small parking lot surrounded by trees.

"Shit!" Sam said.

They couldn't see the shooter from there. They had no way of knowing where he'd gone.

"This way," Sam said as he hopped toward the east end of the building. He stopped at the edge of the tree line and pushed a branch out of the way for a better look. "There. They're waiting for us behind the retainer wall across the street. We'll go behind that house there to get above and behind them."

They walked as fast as Sam's leg would allow along the back fence behind an older home. Sam kept his pistol trained on the rear of the house while Becky watched for anyone emerging from the houses on the next street over.

At the end of a fence, still blocked by a row of cedar trees, Sam and Becky crept along the evergreens toward the street where the gunmen were waiting to ambush them. Near the road, Sam stopped and slowly parted the cedar boughs.

"Can you see them?" Becky whispered.

"Yeah. They're both still there waiting for us."

"What should we do?" Becky glanced up the street. If they walked the fence lines, they might be able to get away unseen.

Sam slowed, moved toward the street, stepped out, and dropped to one knee. He braced his pistol on a three-foot-high concrete planter at the edge of the driveway near the mailbox. He fired several rounds, striking each of the men at least once. The one Becky had fired at was on his belly, crawling away from the street and toward the house. Becky fired her rifle. The man's body jerked as the round struck him in the back. He lay motionless.

"Follow me. Watch my back," Sam said, struggling to get to his feet. Becky helped him up, and he hobbled across the street and then moved toward the men. Sam kicked the first man's rifle in Becky's direction. "Get his weapon. Point it at his head. If he moves, blow his brains out."

Sam moved to the second man and kicked his rifle away, and it skidded across the pavement for about ten feet. Sam pressed his pistol to the back of the man's skull as he reached down and rolled him onto his back. He checked the man's pulse. "He's dead," Sam said. He walked over and retrieved the man's rifle, dropped the magazine, pulled the charging handle back part way to reveal a round in the chamber, and let the charging handle go, then reinserted the magazine before returning to the first man. "Roll him over and check his pockets for ammo."

Becky grabbed his shirt and pulled, rolling him onto his back. He was wearing a tactical vest. Attached to it were pouches with AR-15 magazines inside. "He had two spare mags." She held them out to Sam. He took them and shoved them into his cargo pants pocket.

"Is that it?" Sam asked.

She felt his front pants pockets; they were empty. "Yeah."

"Go check that guy, and then we're getting the hell out of here before their friends show up."

"Friends? Did you see more of them?"

"Not taking any chances."

The second man had four magazines, but one was only partially full. She was grateful for the ammo but wished it was for her Winchester. She was getting low and didn't know what she'd do when her supply was gone.

"These guys aren't local. Where do you think they got those weapons and all that ammo?"

"Could have brought it with them or might have stolen it. They're common weapons. You could probably break into about any house in the countryside and find one or two."

"True."

"I'm getting mighty low on ammo myself. I'll be hunting with my crossbow before long," Becky said.

Sam gestured toward the street. "We should get going."

"Let's go see if we can spot Spirit or Ghost. We need those horses."

Sam looked south toward the strip mall where she'd left Spirit. "I don't know. All that gunfire will have attracted attention."

"But we need those horses. Just stay here. I'll run down to the road and see if I can spot them. If I can't, we'll go home on foot," Becky said.

He nodded, but his face said no. She didn't wait for him to change his mind and took off running to the east side of the road, then stopped near the back of the strip mall. She edged toward the front and peered around the side. There they were, about a block down, standing in someone's flower bed munching on rose bushes.

Becky gestured to Sam that she could see the horses, and he moved up to her position. "I'll run over there and grab them. You stay here."

"Wait." He moved back to the SUV and placed the barrel of one of the AR-15s on the vehicle's hood. "Okay, but keep your head on a swivel."

Becky ran as fast as she could across the street toward the horses but slowed and walked up on them slowly. Speaking to them in a soft tone, she said their names as she reached for their reins.

Becky and Sam took the long way back to Doc Hammond's, using back streets to avoid going through town. The AR-15 bounced against Becky's belly as it hung on its sling around her neck. Sam gripped his rifle in his right hand, occasionally stopping and peering through the rifle's scope before declaring they could proceed again on their journey. Some folks came out and waved as they rode by, surprised to see horses in town.

After passing through a checkpoint set up at the end of Doc Hammond's road, Moondust and Frank Titus greeted them at the end of Doc's driveway.

"Wow! Where'd you find them?" Frank asked.

"I traded for them. Their previous owner was a barrel racer and trained horses. These are some she picked up to sell prior to the lights going out."

"I meant the rifles. They look aggressive," Frank said.

"We won them," Becky said.

"Won them?" Frank asked.

"Yeah."

"Sounds like a great story."

Becky shook her head. "It's becoming the norm now. It's dangerous out there."

"Glad you made it back safe," Frank said.

They passed some of the Hammonds' neighbors near the barn who were out filling feed sacks with dirt from a recently dug defensive trench. Becky slid down from her horse and put her hand up to stop Ghost so Sam could get off him. She grabbed his halter and steadied him.

While Sam went inside to his sleeping quarters to rest, Becky put the horses in the stalls and gave them hay and water. She didn't have anywhere for them at her apartment. She'd need to speak to Doc about boarding them for her.

Moondust appeared in the doorway of the barn as Becky locked the stall door.

"What happened to Brownie and the cart? Did you trade them?"

"No. He got spooked and took off through the woods. "I'm going to look for him tomorrow when I go out hunting. Would you like to come?" Becky asked. "I can teach you about snares and traps."

"I'd love that."

"You think Tumbleweed would be interested in coming on the hunt with us?" Becky asked.

"I'm not sure he would," Moondust said.

"Are you two together?" Becky asked.

"No! We were trail buddies. Nothing more... but he is handsome, isn't he?"

"He is indeed," Becky said. Tumbleweed was handsome and rugged-looking, but not as good looking as Wolf Ellison had been. "Maybe we *should* ask Tumbleweed if he'd like to go with."

TWELVE

Vince

Wallace Survival Compound
Unicoi, Tennessee
Day 19

Vince removed his headset and placed it on top of his ham radio base station, then put his elbows on the table, resting his head in his hands. He was so grateful he'd kept a twenty-watt radio in one of his Faraday cages along with several other electronic pieces and parts. He could keep the comms going with his solar system that charged three twelve-volt car batteries.

Thankfully, Sam had purchased an extra pair of charge controllers from Amazon about six months before the EMP and stashed them in the Faraday box, because the one Vince had hooked to the batteries was toast. It had literally melted. The compound's security detail was supplied with Baofeng UV-5R handheld radios along with General Mobile Radio Service (GMRS) radios and a Multi-User Radio Service radio (MURS) so they were able to communicate as a unit.

It was weird but reassuring to have some "news" from outside the area, even if none of it was positive. The news coming from outside of Tennessee was as devastating as they'd thought. Enemies of the United States had indeed detonated a high-altitude nuclear device over the nation, resulting in an electromagnetic pulse that had taken down the power grid and wiped out most modern technology. The word was that the US had retaliated, sending nukes into Moscow, Beijing, and Tehran. That could be just a rumor, though, because the government had released nothing official.

Government? If there still was one.

All the chatter on the radio came from sources outside the government. Basically, all that was being reported through ham radio about those other countries was nothing more than rumors. All they did know was that the damage extended throughout most of the continental US. Help was supposed to be coming from Alaska, Hawaii, and the military stationed outside the continental United States. Vince wasn't holding his breath on them reaching eastern Tennessee any time soon. They were on their own. His main concern was still whether foreign troops would attack and when they might wind up in the mountainous Appalachian region.

He had heard another ham operator from down near Memphis, Tennessee, say the governor of Tennessee had fled Nashville and was setting up a command post somewhere between Nashville and Knoxville, Tennessee. However, Vince hadn't heard a peep from them, and he had run up and down the frequencies searching for more information.

"What's the chatter today?" Lauren stepped up beside his chair and placed a hand on his shoulder.

He knew what she wanted to hear. She wanted to know if he'd heard anything about Sam. He hadn't, but he'd heard plenty about the total devastation that had occurred in Atlanta. What little of the city hadn't been burned to the ground in the first week was now controlled by gangs. Thousands of refugees had fled the city, most moving south toward the coast, and some north into the mountains of Georgia, North Carolina, and Tennessee. That was what Vince would have done—moved north—not that he would have ever lived anywhere so populated in the first place. Unicoi had been too crowded for Vince.

"Just more of the same. There's devastation, chaos, fires, roaming bands of desperate refugees," Vince replied.

"Still nothing from the governor?" Lauren asked.

"Not a peep."

Someone near Fort Campbell, Kentucky, said there had been lots of movement of federal military troops into northwest Tennessee. Apparently, people began flocking to the military base as it was the only government entity people could reach out to for help."

"What about FEMA? Are they doing anything?"

"Folks near Nashville and Memphis say they've seen some FEMA and TEMA activity, but anything they set up to provide aid was quickly overrun and then turned into a brawl with people being shot and killed."

"That's what I feared would happen. Too many people are competing for too few resources."

"They had the National Guard surrounding the aid stations and were still overrun," Vince said.

"People are starving and desperate." Lauren turned toward the door.

"Nine meals from anarchy," Vince said.

Lauren stopped in the middle of the room and turned back to face him. "I think we're about two meals away here." She held up a hand. "Don't say it."

"I don't want to have to ride into town, guns blazing, to extract you and your parents," Vince said.

Her gaze dropped to the floor. "I know."

The situation in town was unsustainable. Vince had told his sister-in-law that numerous times over the last two weeks. Sam had foreseen it long before the lights went out. He'd known Lauren would dig her heels in and refuse to move to the compound, and was working on an exit plan for when his sister-in-law finally realized all was lost in town. He admired her dedication to the residents of Unicoi, many of whom were elderly, but no amount of dedication could feed three thousand people who had relied on the grocery stores for their food all their lives.

"I found someone down near Asheville, North Carolina. They're going to ask around their local folks and let me know if they hear anything about Sam. He said fewer people were heading north this week. He has contacts with some of the groups who are running roadblocks on Interstate 26."

She looked up, tears filling her eyes. "He would avoid the checkpoints. We've discussed this. He wouldn't take the chance they'd confiscate the Bronco or his weapons. He planned to take the back roads, avoiding towns."

"I know. I just want to cover all the bases."

There was a commotion coming from the front office. Vince raced across the room. Lauren was out the door and had rounded the firing range's counter by the time Vince pulled the door shut to the office-turned-comms room. Two women were standing toe-to-toe just inside the doorway to the supply hut. Carlos Ramos, a member of the security team stepped between them and held a fiery redhead back with his massive hand gripping her shoulder. "I said, nothing happened. Nothing happened!"

"What's going on?" Vince shouted. This type of thing wasn't something he and Sam had anticipated, but it was bound to happen when you brought men and women into a confined space for too long.

"I want her out. She has to go, or I will," Ramos' wife said.

"Me? If you can't keep your man satisfied, it's not my—"

Ramos' wife slipped around him and decked the red-haired chick, hitting her in the side of the head with a fist. She, in turn, grabbed two fistfuls of Mrs. Ramos' hair and the two women went at it. Vince rushed over to help break up the fight. Carlos grabbed his wife around the waist and pulled as Vince wrapped his hands around the redhead's balled fists. She kneed him in the gonads, and Vince bent over in pain. She attempted to land a punch to his face but was met with the barrel of Lauren's revolver. The redhead took two steps back and flattened herself against the wall with her hands held in the air.

"We do not have time for this shit anymore," Lauren said punching every word. "If you two have the energy to fight over a man, then you aren't pulling your weight around here. Don't you have work you should be doing right now?"

The red-haired woman glared back at Lauren. "You're not the mayor here."

"You better be glad I'm not in charge here. Your ass would be hitting the road."

"You just want to keep everything for yourself like you're doing in town."

Vince slipped around Lauren and stepped between them. "You need to pack your gear and go."

"My brother will have something to say—"

"Your brother can leave with you if he has a problem with it."

"Is that really necessary?" Mrs. Ramos asked.

Vince was dumbfounded. They were at each other's throats a second ago, and now she was defending the woman.

"Emotions are running high. It's hard to adjust to this way of life and the stress of always being on guard, even when you're not on duty," Mrs. Ramos said.

"It's your decision, Vince, but if I were you, I'd show her to the gate," Lauren said, holstering her revolver and moving toward the door. She turned back and pointed at the redhead. "When they throw your ass out of here, don't come to Unicoi. You won't be welcomed."

Lauren had surprised Vince in the last two weeks. He knew she was a tough, no-nonsense woman, but he hadn't expected the strong stance that she'd taken with the folks in town. He feared for her. She'd made enemies. Not everyone was happy with having to work for their food and it wouldn't be easy to rid Unicoi of its freeloaders. There was a storm brewing there, and he needed to plan for it.

His gaze shifted to the love triangle before him. Lauren was right. If they had the energy for romance and fighting, they likely weren't pulling their weight with the chores they'd been assigned. He'd remedy that.

"Carlos, on your way back to work, send Dave back here with the duty roster."

THIRTEEN

Lauren

The Cross Residence
Unicoi, Tennessee
Day 19

Lauren held on to the oh-shit handle in Alan's truck as they drove along John Cross Lane, a narrow one-lane road leading to Aldermen Ralph Cross's home. She closed her eyes, trying to erase the image of rolling off the edge of the road and down the one-hundred-foot drop, should the vehicle leave the roadway. She'd experienced this all her life, living in the mountains of eastern Tennessee, but had never grown used to the hairpin turns and sheer drop-offs like this one.

Alan pulled the truck to a stop and shut off the engine. Lauren closed her eyes and took a deep, cleansing breath, trying to calm herself before walking into the devil's den. Even before knocking on the door, Lauren knew Ralph would be in a pissed-off mood. The news she was bringing would only add to it.

"You want me to come in with you?" Alan asked.

Lauren thought for a moment. Ralph had had a low opinion of

Alan even before the EMP. She needed him to accept Alan's new position of authority with the town's security force but now was not the time. She slid her hand over to her holster. "No. Wait here. If you hear shooting, come help me move the bodies," Lauren said, smiling.

"Vince will have my ass."

"Vince isn't mayor, I am," Lauren said, opening the truck's door.

"I won't be long. I know you need to get back to the checkpoints."

"You go do your magic, Mayor. I'll be right here if you need me," Alan said, patting his holstered .45.

Thanks." Lauren slid from the truck's cab and walked up the driveway to the front door. She knocked and stepped off the stoop.

Ralph's wife came to the door. Her eyes were red and puffy. "Madam Mayor. What can I do for you?" she said.

"I came to see how your grandson was doing?" Lauren lied, attempting to not sound heartless because she was there on business and hadn't had an opportunity to check up on him. No one had time to pay social calls these days.

"Ralph, that lady mayor is here to see you," Ralph's wife called as she turned her back on Lauren.

A moment later, Ralph appeared in the doorway, dressed in a white tank top undershirt and boxer briefs. He looked past her toward Alan's truck, and then his gaze returned to Lauren. "What do you want?"

"How's your grandson?" she asked.

"Cut the crap, Lauren. I already heard you held a council meeting without me today. What's up?"

"I'm sorry, we couldn't wait. There are issues—"

"My people aren't going to go along with your power grab, Lauren."

She backed up a step. Power grab? She so did not want power. She wanted to stay home and spend time with her dying father. She wanted the freedom to jump in Vince's Jeep and keep driving until she found her husband. Power? He didn't know how damn close she was to saying to hell with it all and letting someone else have the "power" he claimed she was "grabbing."

"We can talk about my power grab at the next board meeting if you'd like. I'm here to tell you we've scheduled a working meeting tonight. I'm addressing the town tomorrow."

Ralph looked over his shoulder into the room.

"I understand if you have family obligations and can't attend," Lauren said.

"I'm sure you do. I take mine seriously, unlike you. I hear your dad's on his deathbed," he said, leaning toward her provocatively.

Lauren's hands balled into fists. He did not want to go there with her. She was making the sacrifice she knew her father, a former mayor of Unicoi, would have made under the circumstances.

"I just wanted to let you know what the board had decided and check on you. If you can't make it tonight, I hope to see you at the town meeting tomorrow." Lauren began to back away while still keeping her eyes on Ralph's hands. He wasn't armed, but she wasn't taking chances.

"I'll be there. You can count on that," Ralph said, slamming the door.

Lauren rushed back down the driveway and climbed into the truck. She was shaking as his accusations replayed in her brain. Power grab? That hurt, but most painful was him implying that she should be home with her father—that she was neglecting him in her quest for power.

"Well, that went as expected," Alan said.

"Yep."

"He's going to be trouble sooner rather than later."

"I know." Lauren was quiet on the ride back to city hall, thinking about how she could avoid trouble with Ralph. He was very popular in his district and his constituents liked and respected him. If he started badmouthing her and the efforts of the board of aldermen, it could spell trouble for the efforts to keep the peace.

"Would you mind dropping me off at my parents' house? I'd like to check in on my dad."

"No problem. It's on my way to my assigned checkpoint today. What about your bicycle? You want me to drop it off at your house after my shift?"

"I have to be back at city hall at five o'clock. What time does your shift end?"

"Not until seven."

"I'll walk, Alan. Thank you."

Vince and Lindsay were in the kitchen with Edna when Lauren entered the house. "Where's the Jeep?" Lauren asked.

"Cody dropped us off. He's taking the Jeep up on Buffalo Mountain looking for signs of game. He'll pick us up on his way back."

Cody's experience as a hunting and fishing guide was the reason she'd invited him to stay in Unicoi. Her decision had proven to be a good one. He and the team of hunters he'd assembled supplied over one hundred pounds of meat and fish a day to the residents of Unicoi. It wasn't anywhere near enough though. They'd need seven times that amount to adequately feed the thousands of people in town, but it was something that kept the security team on the town's payroll. Without them, the town would have already collapsed.

"Johnson City is claiming we're poaching their game," Lauren said, removing her holster and placing it on the antique oak kitchen table.

"They would," Vince said. He turned and wiped his hands on her mother's yellow floral apron hanging around his neck.

Lauren looked at the apron and chuckled. She couldn't help

herself. "I'm addressing the town tomorrow. The board has voted on a new set of laws. One addresses restricting the radius of non-sanctioned hunting."

Lindsay put down the mason jar she held and spun to face Lauren. "Non-sanctioned hunting?"

"People can still hunt and fish all they want. They just have to do it on federal or state land."

"Damn! That's going to go over like a lead balloon," Lindsay said.

"It will push residents out of territory that might cause them to be at odds with Johnson City and encourage them to do their hunting and fishing east and west of town to avoid trouble."

"It's not even been three weeks and we're fighting over hunting grounds with other towns?"

"It looks like it."

"As I said, I have to address the town tomorrow."

"And you'd like us there?"

"You should invite Josh," Edna said.

"Josh is in California, Mom," Lauren said.

Edna looked puzzled for a moment. "I know that," she said. "You need to do a better job of keeping in touch with your brother."

"I will, Mom," Lauren knew it was useless to explain to Edna again that the phones were out and there was no way to communicate with anyone in California. Unless he had a Faraday cage-protected ham radio like Vince, anyway.

"I'll round up some guys and we'll blend into the crowd."

"You? Blend in?" Lindsay chuckled. She rubbed his massive bicep, and he flexed for her.

"I'd appreciate you augmenting Benny's security. I have a feeling we're going to have a few unhappy constituents."

FOURTEEN

Sam

Hammond Farm
Franklin, North Carolina
Day 19

Exhaustion had taken over and Sam was down for the count. He wasn't accustomed to sleeping during the day, but his body was still recovering from the blood loss and the injury he'd sustained on the Appalachian Trail. The continued weakness concerned him. How long would it be before he could get back on the road and head home?

When he woke from his nap, Sam lay on his cot, weighing his options for getting home. He wasn't strong enough to fight; the battle he'd experienced that morning was proof. His only option was to travel at night and sleep during the day with hopes of going undetected by anyone who might want to confront him.

On horseback, it could take three days or more to travel the one hundred and twenty miles home. If he took the highways, people might hear the horse's hooves and know he was coming. He'd be ambushed as had occurred that morning. Even if he did everything to avoid towns, traveling that slowly was risky.

The obvious choice as far as safety was concerned was still to travel home along the A.T. He'd encounter fewer people, but the grueling two-hundred-and-forty-mile hike would be excruciatingly painful at this point and take a lot of time. And it just wasn't doable on foot at the moment. With horses, it might take two weeks, given the mare and gelding would need a down day every fifty miles or so.

Two more weeks.

It had already been almost three. His wife, son, and brother had likely given him up for dead by now. Nothing had gone as planned.

Stop it. Stop feeling sorry for yourself, Wallace. Get up and start doing something to get yourself home.

Sam pulled the North Carolina map from under his mattress and spread it out on the bed. He traced several routes, trying to find the one that avoided major towns. It could be done. It wouldn't be easy winding through the mountains on back roads, but he was less likely to encounter trouble. On the other hand, the horse could travel farther per day on the roadway as the gradient wouldn't be as steep or rocky.

Using the horses that Becky had traded her condoms for and taking the highways, he could make it home in around ten days. He'd need ten days' worth of food because there wouldn't be time for hunting.

Ten days or two weeks? Ten days by roadway with danger around every bend in the road, or a rough grueling two weeks on foot on the Appalachian Trail. His mind was saying play it safe and take the A.T. But his heart just wanted to get home.

There was a knock at the door. Sam grabbed his pistol and crossed the room. He pressed himself against the wall on the handle side of the door and eased it open just a crack.

"I'm sorry to disturb your nap." It was a kid around Charlie's age. He was taller and more muscular, but he looked younger than Charlie.

"What can I do for you?"

"My pepaw wants to speak to you," the kid said.

"Your pepaw? Who's your pepaw?"

"Willard Titus. He wants to thank you for saving my cousin, Andrew. He'd come down here, but his knees are bad."

"That's fine. He doesn't need to thank me."

"He has something for you that Doc Hammond said he thought you'd need."

Sam's curiosity was piqued. "Okay, just let me grab my pack." Sam didn't go anywhere without his newly acquired pack—he'd already lost his get-home bag. This one didn't have everything his old one did, but it had the essentials for mountain survival, including water and a day's food.

The kid led Sam up the hill past the Hammonds' place and through a gate that separated the Hammond farm from his neighbor. As they crossed a pasture dotted with cows, Sam asked him his name.

"Isaiah."

"I have a boy about your age," Sam said.

"I'm fourteen. Doc said you were trying to get home to your family when you got injured."

"I was."

The boy pointed to an old wooden barn that was leaning so much Sam wondered how it was still standing. "Pepaw's in the shed off the barn."

"Thanks," Sam said, heading toward it.

The shed was open on three sides and covered in rusty barn tin. Under its roof was all manner of farm equipment, including two old tractors and various antique farm implements—perfect for the non-mechanized farming that was required now.

In the back corner, Sam spotted movement. "Over here, young man," a frail voice said.

"Yes, sir."

Sam stepped over boxes of nails and screws, old inner tube tires, a butter churn, weathered windowpanes, and past several pieces of worn-out furniture before reaching the elderly man. He wanted to ask him how he got back there, but as soon as his eyes landed on the object covered in a weathered car cover, he stopped in his tracks.

Willard Titus pulled back the cover. "It ain't run in twenty years, but I suspect it'll start after a bit of tinkering."

Sam couldn't speak. He just stood there staring at the 1948 Dodge Power Wagon. The red paint had faded and rust showed through in places. There was significant rust on one of the running boards and the seat covers had holes in them and were missing foam. Sam didn't hold out much hope of the old girl running, let alone making it one hundred and twenty miles over the mountain to Unicoi.

"I've got some boys coming to clear out all this stuff in the bay and we'll get her rolled out so we can crank her over and see what she might need, but if you can get her to run, she's yours," Willard said.

Sam walked around the Power Wagon, examining the body and looking at its flat tires. It had seen better days and likely had significant mechanical problems. But it was worth a try, at least to see if it would start. Hope surged in his gut for the first time in weeks.

If he could somehow manage to get this old rust bucket started and on the road, he could be home in less than two hours. That thought was intoxicating. He could barely wrap his mind around it. *Two hours.* He could be holding his wife in his arms in two hours. Sam looked up, tears glistening in his eyes. "I don't know what to say."

"Say nothing. You risked your life protecting my grandson. It's the least I can do to help you get home to your own family."

Mr. Titus' family arrived thirty minutes later. Mark and Martin Titus, along with a teenage boy, began removing all the junk that had been piled in front of the Power Wagon, then they raised the hood and began working on the engine.

Sam leaned over the fender to help the men remove a packrat's nest from the engine compartment. "You think there's hope she'll run?" Sam asked.

"I drove it to high school every day for two years. When I joined the army, Dad parked it in there," Mark Titus said. He was dressed like he had just returned from a hunt and had dried blood stains down the right side of his camouflaged cargo pants.

"Crank her over," Martin Titus said. He was shorter and thinner than the other man and dressed in clean jeans and a short-sleeve plaid button-down shirt.

Mark jumped behind the wheel and turned the key. It cranked over and sputtered for a few seconds before dying.

"It's alive," Mark said.

"Oh, yeah," Sam agreed, high-fiving Mark. But Sam needed it to do more than just start. It had to run—and run well enough to navigate the steep hills and twisting road between Franklin, North Carolina and Unicoi, Tennessee.

"You just give us a day or two and we'll have her on the road for you," Mark said. "I'll have Isaiah come fetch you soon as we get 'er done."

"Are you sure you don't want me to stay and help?" Sam asked.

"Nope, you'll just get in the way," Martin said, nudging Sam away from the Power Wagon.

Sam left them to it and hurried back to Doc's as fast as his leg would allow. He had a route to plan and supplies to gather. Sam had to find Becky to ask whether she wanted to go with him. He found himself hopping along on his good leg, trying to move faster, and cursed his injured leg. He couldn't wait to get home and sleep in his own bed next to his lovely wife. Sam planned to take a day or two to rest and spend time with Charlie and then get to work tightening up any deficiencies in the defenses of the compound and discuss with Vince ways to add to their food supplies.

He hoped he could convince Becky to return to Unicoi with him. She was one badass young lady and would be an asset to the Wallace group.

FIFTEEN

Charlie

Wallace Survival Compound
Unicoi, Tennessee
Day 19

In many ways, the former Wallace Tactical and Shooting Range now functioned like a small town. It was surrounded by a high dirt-filled barrier wall and a steel gate, but inside there were homes and a store of sorts where you could go to barter. Some people made things to trade, others brought things in they found while hunting or scavenging. There were community meetings where people voted on issues, and gatherings around a bonfire at night where the discussions continued. It also reminded Charlie of a campground in many ways with all the travel trailers that had been brought in to house everyone.

The people ranged in age from small kids to the elderly. Charlie and Casey were the only teenagers, and that sucked because Casey mostly kept to herself. He'd tried a few times to talk to her, but she generally ignored him.

The first few days after Charlie had moved to the compound,

everyone was so busy with chores that he hardly had a chance to speak to anyone. He hadn't been assigned a job, so he had gone to the garden and asked if he could help. Mrs. Miller had handed him a basket and pointed him to a row of broad beans. After, they had sat out in front of Mr. and Mrs. Miller's motor home snapping green beans. He'd wound up working with the two of them ever since.

While snapping beans in the shade one afternoon, the Millers shared what their lives had been like when they were Charlie's age.

"When I was coming up, the only things my momma and daddy bought from the store were coffee and salt. We grew, hunted, and made everything else. When Momma ran out of coffee and we didn't have the money to buy more, she'd roast chestnuts and grind them in the coffee mill to make coffee," Mrs. Miller said.

Mr. Miller eased himself into a lawn chair next to his wife. "I expect we'll be doing that ourselves soon. Have you seen how these old boys drink coffee 'round here? Whoa, howdy. They must think they'll just run out to that coffee store in town and buy more when this here runs out."

"Can't you grow coffee beans?" Charlie asked.

"Afraid not," Mr. Miller said. "Coffee needs a tropical climate."

"I heard a couple of the guys talking about checking out some coffee plant in Knoxville. I think that's their plan," Charlie said.

"They best be careful out there breaking into places. Someone's going to get themselves shot," Mrs. Miller said.

After the beans had all been snapped, Charlie followed Mrs. Miller to the firepit in the middle of the circle of RVs and campers. She pointed to a cast-iron pot. "Fill that pot with water for me and then hang it on that hook there."

Charlie stuck the heavy pot under the spigot of a five-gallon water container, filled the pot halfway, and hung it on the hook hanging from a steel tripod straddling the fire.

"Drop these here beans in there to boil." She handed him the pan of green beans, then unrolled a piece of pork fat and dropped it in with the beans along with some baby onions, and sprinkled the water with salt and pepper.

While it cooked, Mrs. Miller continued talking about her childhood growing up in the mountains. He could see why his dad and Uncle Vince had wanted her and Mr. Miller to be a part of their group. She understood how to live without modern conveniences. Mrs. Miller wasn't the most patient of teachers, but she was eager to pass down the knowledge and skills she'd acquired over her eighty years of life.

"These store-bought clothes aren't going to hold up to the type of work folks are doing now. We'll patch them as best as we can, but eventually, we're gonna have to make more. You young folks don't even know how to darn your socks, let alone cut up fabric and sew it together to make yourself a pair of britches."

"Where would we get the material?" Charlie asked.

"We'll I brought some with me, but that won't last long. We're gonna have to piece fabric together from the worn-out stuff or from clothes they found outside the compound until we can get enough cotton grown and a mill built to make our own."

"If the lights don't come back on, everything will have to be made by hand someday, won't it?"

"Near to everything. You young 'uns are going to have to pay close attention and learn the old ways or you're going to be doing without a lot of things you need."

"It's a lot to learn," Charlie said.

"Yeah, that's because they stopped teaching skills to live by in school for one thing, and then the other thing is people had no use for learning how to make stuff that they could just run to Walmart and buy cheap. Now there ain't no more Walmart, so you better pay attention before all us old-timers are gone. From what I hear, folks our age are dropping like flies."

"My grandpa is real sick."

"I heard that. I'm sorry. I offered to make him a tea to help drain off some of that fluid he's retaining but Vince said he still had pills from the doctors. But they ain't working, so I don't know why Lauren wouldn't want to try my tea. It's what mountain folk did long before there were doctors in these parts."

Charlie didn't like thinking about how sick Lauren's dad was. His health had been bad for years. That's why Lauren and his dad had moved from the farm into town to take care of Pepaw and Memaw Taylor.

"How's Lauren holding up? She's got a lot on her plate, taking care of her folks and trying to run the town. I imagine that's like attempting to herd cats."

"I know she's sad about Pepaw, and she's worried about my dad. I think work helps keep her mind off them."

"Well, there's sure enough of that these days. There's not time to sit around stewing about stuff, that's for sure."

The sound of children's laughter got Mrs. Miller's attention. A little girl was carrying a basket and running toward another girl just a little older than her.

"Even the little ones have to work now, just like I did at that age. I was in the fields with my momma from the day I was born until the day she died at forty-five years of age." A sad expression crossed her face. "It's good that they're having fun while they're working. Momma would get on to us if we played before our chores were done."

Maggie Russo ran after Charlotte with her baby boy tied in a wrap on her back. "Charlotte Ann. You stop right there. You're spilling berries all over the ground."

"That's why Momma wouldn't let us fool around," Mrs. Miller said. She was quiet for a moment and then turned back toward Charlie.

"Why don't you run over to the smokehouse now? Mr. Miller could use some help chopping wood. Hopefully, we'll have a bunch of meat to smoke when that Cody and his hunting group get back."

Before the lights went out, Charlie had never liked wild game much, but now, the way Mr. and Mrs. Miller prepared it, he liked it a lot. He hoped Cody's team brought back turkey again. That was his new favorite. He'd never tell his mom he ate wild game though. It wasn't allowed on his no-taste diet. He drew in a quick breath as he rose from his chair. He wiped his brow and put thoughts of his parents and little sister out of his mind. It hurt too much to think of them and he had work to do and new skills to learn if he was going to contribute to this group like his dad would want him to do.

SIXTEEN

Lauren

Unicoi City Hall
Unicoi, Tennessee
Day 19

Today was the day that the board of aldermen was set to vote on the new work requirement and criminal code. Lauren and Benny had worked for days trying to come up with a solution to the growing crime in Unicoi and what penalties should be meted out to deter it.

When Lauren arrived back at city hall, Millie met her at the door, a flowerpot in her hand. Millie placed it on the stoop to block the door from closing. "It's already hot as hell in here. I don't know why they insist on continuing to meet inside," Millie said, stepping aside and allowing Lauren to enter.

She was right. Very little air stirred in the corridor as she continued toward the room where the town board would create laws to address the new world in which they lived.

Maryann, Gretchen, and Lloyd were standing by the open window, glasses of water in their hands.

"Good morning, folks," Lauren said, entering the room.

"Morning," they replied in unison.

Lauren glanced around the room and then checked her watch. "Where's Ralph?" He was usually the first one to arrive.

"His grandson got into some trouble last night," Maryann said.

"Trouble?" Lloyd said. "That's not how I'd describe it."

Gretchen moved away from the window toward the conference table and pulled out a chair. "Levi boy got beat up pretty bad. They said he got caught stealing fish that were smoking in Gary Millard's backyard."

"Justice is what I call it," Lloyd said. "You get up before the crack of dawn to fish before you have to go work in the fields all day so some lowlife can just come take it from you? No, Ralph's grandson got what he had coming to him, if you ask me."

"That's what we're here to discuss today. Things have changed and our laws must be adjusted to reflect that change," Lauren said.

"Not really. Stealing has always been illegal," Lloyd said.

"What has changed is the seriousness—the consequences—of these criminal acts and their effect on the victims. Before, if someone stole your fish, you wouldn't be facing starvation," Gretchen said, taking a seat at the conference table.

"We aren't facing starvation," Maryann said. She pulled out a chair across the table from Gretchen and sat down. "We have a warehouse full of food and the community gardens."

Lauren rubbed her temples. How could this woman not grasp the gravity of their situation? How could she still be blind to it after all they'd seen in the last nineteen days?

"Chief Jameson and I have made a list of activities that he's seeing that might become a problem in the very near future." Lauren handed the piece of paper to Gretchen. She looked at it a moment and handed it to Lloyd. He placed it on the table in front of him and ran his finger down the handwritten list. He nodded. "There's some I hadn't thought of. I'd be interested to know why hunting made the list."

"Allow Maryann to read it and then we can go one by one and discuss them. If we agree they're a problem, we'll need to decide a penalty sufficient to deter the activity."

Lloyd handed the list to Maryann. She read it and looked up with a puzzled gaze. "Really? People are contaminating their neighbors' drinking water? Why?"

"Tensions are high. Former friends are now sworn enemies. The reason isn't as important as the solution."

"That's attempted murder," Lloyd said. "Plain and simple, they should go to jail."

"I agree," Gretchen said.

"We don't have the personnel to guard the jail," Lauren said. "We have one holding cell. We were never equipped to hold inmates. We took them to the county jail."

"We could assign them to hard labor. Make them work extra jobs," Gretchen said.

"That sounds fair," Maryann agreed.

"That would require someone to supervise them and make sure they do what we tell them to do. We don't have the personnel to babysit criminals either," Lauren said.

"What about putting them in stocks like they did in colonial days?" Lloyd suggested. "No one would have to supervise them and the whole town would know they'd broke the law. It would act as a deterrent. I bet we'd probably only have to do it a few times for people to get the message."

"That might be an option," Gretchen said.

"But what about more serious crimes—violent crimes?" Lloyd said.

Maryann stared at him with a blank expression.

"Before, if someone died during the process of committing a felony, their accomplices were charged with murder. If we make stealing food a felony and the homeowner kills the thief, should we charge the thief's accomplices with murder?"

"That seems extreme. I can't support that. People are hungry," Maryann said.

"Stealing food these days is like attempted murder," Gretchen said.

"Let's go down the list one by one and discuss them."

Stealing was fairly straightforward. The board voted to make all thefts a felony punishable by one day in the stocks in public view for a first offense; the second offense punishable by banishment from the city. That penalty had been the subject of heated discussion.

"Sanctioned hunting?" Maryann said. She shook her head. "We're going to ban hungry people from hunting for their food."

"Not a ban on the activity, just where they can hunt," Lauren said. "We have hunting parties that supply the town with meat. They are reporting that it's already getting harder to find any wild game close to town. They propose setting a restricted radius. Residents are free to hunt outside of that."

"How far? I mean, most people don't have the energy to go far," Maryann said.

"We're proposing no hunting within the city limits," Lauren said.

"What? That would mean walking for hours to hunt."

"If we weren't providing game for the entire town, we would never consider such a move."

"In all honesty, we aren't providing meat or food to the town. They have to work to earn it. That's different. If you make it a crime to hunt or fish close to town, you're taking away their ability to be self-sufficient."

Lauren was quiet as she contemplated that. She was a huge proponent of self-sufficiency. That had been her and Sam's goal for themselves when they'd started their homestead. How could the town balance the needs of the people who couldn't hunt and fish against others' desire to make it on their own? She thought of the children that wouldn't get enough to eat once the game became scarce. It was going to happen. No matter what they did, they were only delaying the inevitable. With so many people now eating deer, rabbit, squirrel, and wild turkey instead of beef, pork, and chicken purchased from a grocery store, the population of those animals would dwindle quickly.

"If people want to be self-sufficient, they'll have to abide by the rules and travel farther away from the town to find game. It's about balancing needs," Lauren said.

"We have another matter. As you'll see from your agenda, we need to discuss the dwindling food supply. Our current distribution is not sustainable. I'm told that at this rate, we will run out of food in four days," Lauren said.

The door banged open and Ralph appeared in the doorway. "You started without me?" He strode into the room and took his place at the conference table. No one bothered to answer his question. He was late. Lauren always started meetings on time. Ralph knew that well.

Maryann handed him the handwritten agenda. He stared at it for a moment before tossing it back across the table at her. It slid off the edge and landed on the floor. "What's this about adding a work requirement for getting food?" he asked, glaring down the table at Lauren.

"We'd just begun to discuss that item." Lauren turned to Millie. "Will you note that Alderman Cross was in attendance for this portion of the meeting?"

"Yes, ma'am."

"Now, as I was saying. Our food supply is—"

"Well, I think it's about damn time. We got too many freeloaders is the problem," Ralph said, interrupting her.

Lauren ignored him and continued. "We have too many freeloaders. We have people who are arriving at the distribution center that aren't on the work roster. They haven't planted anything on their own property and haven't assisted with the community gardens."

"I get that," Maryann said. "But how does making them work now help prolong our food stores?"

"We'll be handing out a whole lot less food," Lloyd said.

"How so? They'll still be getting food. They'll just be going to work for it," Maryann said.

Lloyd guffawed. "You think these lazy asses around here are actually going to leave their homes and go work for their food?"

"Yes," Maryann replied.

"You're stupider than you look," Lloyd said.

Maryann looked like she'd been slapped across the face.

"Lloyd. You can't talk to her like that," Gretchen said.

"Let's keep this civil, shall we?" Lauren said. "To answer your question, Maryann, we will have more food because there will be more people growing and harvesting it. Right now, we have hundreds of acres of crops at community farms that need harvesting. Strawberries and tomatoes mostly, but lots of zucchini, beans, and blackberries are ripening. If everyone did their part, we could feed everyone—at least they'd eat *something* every day. Maybe not as much as they'd like, but enough to sustain them another day."

Before the lights went out, many people were used to living paycheck to paycheck. Some mountain residents were accustomed to living day to day like the town was doing now. If they weren't able to find game or catch a fish, they might have cornbread and buttermilk for dinner and they felt blessed to have it.

"It's damn hot in here. Let's just vote on the damn bill so I can get back to my family," Ralph said. He placed both hands on the table and stood. "I make a motion to require people to work at a city-assigned job in order to receive city assistance."

"I second the motion," Lloyd said, rising to his feet.

Millie called the roll and, to Lauren's surprise, the vote was unanimous.

"I would like everyone to be at the town hall meeting in the park tomorrow. It's important that the citizens see we're united and working to try to solve their most pressing issues. I think it would go a long way to encourage their cooperation."

"I'm not sure I can be there," Ralph said.

"I understand. I know you'll do your best and I'm sure your constituents want to see that you're advocating for them."

"I'll see what I can do," Ralph offered.

"Is there going to be security at this meeting?" Lloyd asked. "Because I know some people who aren't going to be happy come tomorrow."

"Yes, Benny will have his security team and I've asked Vince and—"

"The last thing we need is your brother-in-law and his militia showing up and causing trouble," Ralph said.

Lauren rolled her shoulders and stood. "Noted."

"Ralph, if you could stay just a moment longer, I need to talk to you about the other items we discussed."

"I really don't have time."

"We discussed adding new criminal penalties for certain crimes," Lauren said.

"Like what?"

"Stealing."

Ralph clenched his jaws tight. "My grandson wasn't stealing."

"This has nothing to do with your grandson. We've had several instances this week, and it's gotten violent with residents getting hurt. We'd like to deter that activity with stiffer penalties."

"Whatever. Let's vote and get this over with. I have things to do."

The board of aldermen voted to approve the criminal penalties for stealing and set the restrictions for hunting inside city limits and for hunting parties within state and federal lands. Lauren was relieved to have that part over but was dreading informing the residents of the new laws. She knew some would not be happy.

Lloyd hung back after the meeting adjourned and the other aldermen filed out of the conference room. "It's a good thing having Vince and his guys there. Some of the people who might want to cause trouble are scared shitless of them. Just his presence alone might keep some from starting anything."

"That's what I'm hoping," Lauren said.

SEVENTEEN

Vince

Wallace Survival Compound
Unicoi, Tennessee
Day 19

The first few weeks after the EMP attack, Vince hadn't been around much. He'd left much of the organization and operation of the compound in the hands of Dave and the rest of the group. He'd been preoccupied with locating his brother, Sam. He'd been sure Sam would be walking north along the interstate. All Vince needed to do was find him and bring him home, but that hadn't happened. Vince had searched the interstate all the way to the Tennessee/Georgia state line and then from Erwin to Asheville, North Carolina. There was no sign of his brother.

He'd used his mobile ham radio rig in an attempt to reach him, hoping that Sam's handheld radio still worked and his foldable solar panel would be able to charge the battery. Vince hadn't reached Sam, but at least he'd been able to put the word out. If Sam was out there and came across a ham operator, he'd get Vince's message.

The Wagoneer was always fueled, packed, and ready to go in the event Vince learned of Sam's location. Until then, he had to hang out at the compound, monitor the radio, and do his best to run the compound the way he and Sam had discussed.

"We had another attempted breach last night," Dave reported.

Vince pushed his chair away from the ham radio's microphone and spun his office chair to face him. "Were they armed?"

"Yeah—with a kitchen knife," Dave said. He crossed the room and plopped into the chair next to Vince. Dave leaned back and clasped his hands behind his head. Dark circles hung under his eyes. Dave had been pulling a lot of hours, making sure the compound was secure. Vince had put a lot of responsibility on his friend since the lights went out.

Dave hadn't initially planned on joining the compound; he'd had a wife back then. She had been adamantly opposed to anything prepper-related. Even after their separation and divorce, Dave hadn't given up hope of reconciling and had maintained their family home. Vince wasn't sure what had changed Dave's mind, but Vince was eternally grateful that Dave was there to help now, especially since Sam wasn't.

Dave leaned the chair back as far as it would go and looked at the ceiling. "It's sad as hell."

"What is?"

"What's going on out there."

Vince waited for him to elaborate.

A few minutes later, Dave said, "This time it was a chick. She said she had two little ones at home and they were starving. She claims she hasn't eaten in two weeks. Two whole weeks. Can you imagine?"

"That would make you desperate. We talked about this. Desperate people become dangerous people."

"Yeah. I know. It's just…"

They were both quiet for several minutes. Vince wasn't heartless. He'd spoken to Lauren and was aware of how people were struggling to provide even the basic needs for their families. But he had an obligation to the people who had put their trust in him—and the Wallace compound—for their survival. They'd all put in time and money, and planned for an event like this.

"You know what would happen if we helped her, right?" Vince asked.

"I know. I understand. I just don't feel good about it. I mean... you know."

He did know. The group had discussed it dozens of times before the EMP attack. He and Sam knew this day would come. Desperate people would be knocking at the gate and they'd have to make the decision to send them away—to their deaths, possibly.

"This is why we all had to agree to the by-laws," Vince said.

Every member of their group had had to sign an agreement that they understood the rules—one of which was that when people outside their group came begging, they would have to turn them away.

On the face of it, the concept seemed inhumane and cruel, but they only had so many resources. If they helped one person and then they told one other person, soon there would be dozens of desperate people at their gate. After that, there would be someone willing to kill to take what the compound had, and they would be forced to defend it with their lives.

"I sent her into town. I told her to ask for Lauren and tell her I sent her. I didn't know what else to do," Dave said.

"Oh shit! You're going to catch hell from Lauren. They have their own problems to deal with," Vince said.

"It was the best I could think of at that moment," Dave said.

"I know. Hopefully, she'll understand. She just has a lot on her plate."

Dave pointed to the radio. "Heard anything?"

"Not yet."

"He's one tough son-of-a bitch. He's out there somewhere.

Probably playing hero, but he is out there surviving, and he'll make his way home soon."

"I agree," Vince said, glancing back at the radio.

Dave stood. "I have to go deal with an issue with Nick. He's not going to like me much after today. If he comes in here acting like a little bitch, just know I did my best."

"What's up with Nick?" Nick Keys had been with the group since the beginning. He'd been one of Sam's first survival course students. He'd also served three years in the army and understood command structure.

"Well, he needs to stop thinking with his dick, for one thing. That girlfriend of his has him all tied up in knots. He's just sure that she's sleeping with guys while he's on duty. It's screwing with his focus and making him dangerous."

"Not good."

Nick and a few others in the group were single when they'd joined the group a year or so before. They weren't dating anyone seriously, so Vince and Sam hadn't vetted their girlfriends before allowing them in after the EMP. At the time, Vince had been distracted, something Sam would chastise him for later, he knew.

"So, is she sleeping around on him?"

"Oh, yeah. It's almost like she wants him to get mad and get himself kicked out of here."

Vince shook his head. "Maybe she does."

"Or maybe she's just a ho," Dave said.

"Let me talk to him. You have enough to deal with," Vince said, rising from his chair. "It's about time that I straighten a few folks out."

"Okay. Thanks, Vince. I wasn't looking forward to telling Nick that he needed to dump that cheating bitch."

"I'll go talk to Nick now. I'll have a better idea about what can be done after that."

"I hope he listens because the others don't trust working with him much right now. He's on edge and strung too tight, snapping at everyone."

"I'll let you know what I decide after I speak with him."

"Good luck," Dave said, smiling.

Vince didn't have the patience to be dealing with such petty shit. People outside their gate were dying of starvation and disease. The members of his group were stretched thin doing all the things necessary to sustain their compound. This crazy relationship bullshit had to stop. As much as he hated it, this chick had to go before she infected the whole group. It would be Nick's choice if he wanted to follow her, but Vince would not tolerate this type of distraction. Lives were at stake, and one of those was his nephew's. Vince wasn't going to let strife have a chance to take root.

After knocking on the door to Nick's RV, Vince stepped back and bumped into a charcoal grill.

Nick swung the door open. "Hey, Vince. What's up?" He was dressed in the Army Physical Fitness Uniform. The APFU was a black short-sleeve shirt with "Army" in gold lettering and a pair of black shorts with the same gold lettering on the left leg.

"Can I have a word with you?" Vince pointed to a grouping of chairs surrounding a fire ring a few feet from the RV. The set-up looked so normal, almost like they were camping and not in the middle of an apocalypse. The stand meant to hold solar panels to power the RV's appliances sat at the back of the rig, waiting for Nick to have time off in order to install them. Time off wasn't something anyone had much of these days.

"What do you want to talk about?" Nick asked, standing with

his hands clasped behind his back as if Vince were his drill sergeant.

"Have a seat, Nick," Vince said, lowering himself onto one of the chairs.

Nick took a seat opposite him with the fire ring between them. Months before, there had been fifteen guys, including Sam, around a similarly situated fire ring, all drinking beer and talking about the drills they'd run that day. Nick had bragged about his scores in multiple-target engagement, fighting from cover, shooting while moving, and others. He was a great asset to the group. Vince hated the thought they might lose him.

"I've been told that you've been a little on edge—snapping at your team members while on patrol."

Nick was quiet. He stared down at the fire ring.

Vince pointed toward the RV. "You having trouble at home?"

Nick glanced back over his shoulder and then shrugged. He returned to staring at the smoldering ash inside the fire ring. "You know how it is."

Vince had never discussed his own relationship issues with Nick or any of the group members. However, his on-again/off-again status with his girlfriend, Lindsay, was well known in town.

"You can't let that interfere with your duties, bro."

"I'm not. I'm doing my job. I'm out there patrolling the perimeter in a professional manner." His tone was defensive.

Vince slowly rose to his feet, thinking he might cut this short before it got out of hand while reining in his anger at Nick's attitude. "We can't have strife among the troops, Nick. I can't allow it. If you have a beef with someone, you gotta work that shit out before you go on duty."

Nick glanced up at the window of the RV. Vince followed his gaze. Nick's girlfriend stared back at them. "You know how it is when you get deployed and leave your girl on base? You hear rumors that she's sleeping around and find out later that it was with someone in your unit that went home on leave."

"It was a common problem, yeah." Vince returned to his seat but kept an eye on the window.

"I didn't expect to have to deal with that here." His voice was barely above a whisper.

Vince could tell the kid was hurting. This had really jacked up his head. He wasn't fit for duty—not with him suspecting his team members of sleeping with his girl. You have to be able to trust that your battle buddy has your back out there when the shit hits the fan. But what really pissed Vince off was that one of their battle buddies had betrayed them. When he found out who it was, that dude was outta there.

"You know, Nick, I hate to say this but—"

"I know. I know she has to go. I should have never brought her here, but I thought…." He paused and glanced up at the window. His girlfriend was no longer looking back. "I thought maybe she was different."

The RV door opened and a tall, slender young woman stepped out and descended the stairs. She sauntered over, plopped into one of the chairs, and crossed one long, lean leg over the other. She leaned back with one arm up on the back of the chair.

"Do we have a problem?" she asked.

"We do," Nick said. He glanced over at Vince and then turned his gaze to the firepit. "I'm going to need you to leave."

She looked like he'd slapped her across the face. "What?"

"Cindy, you have to leave," Nick said again.

Cindy chuckled uncomfortably. "Are you serious? Why?"

"You're causing problems. I told you if that happened you'd have to go."

"I'm causing problems? For who?"

Nick glared at her. "For the entire group. We have to all get along, and you shaking your moneymaker in front of every swinging dick in the compound is something we can't have. It ain't right," Nick said through clenched teeth.

"Oh, yeah? I thought you liked my moneymaker."

"What you're doing compromises our unit cohesion. So, I'm going to have to ask you to leave—today."

"Today? And where exactly am I supposed to go?"

"Home," Nick said. "Now, I want you to pack all the shit you brought with you, and I will take you back into town."

"Just like that. I don't even get to say goodbye to my friends here?"

"I'll relay the message," Nick said. "Now get your shit and let's go."

Vince wasn't sure Nick taking her into town was a good idea. He was quite angry now, but once she got him alone, no telling how she could convince him to go with her.

"I'm going into Unicoi. I'll take you," Vince said.

She stared at Nick, but he turned his back on her and walked away. "Fine. I'll get my bags."

Vince stopped and waited for the guards to open the gate. Cindy sat slumped in the back seat with her arms crossed over her chest. She stared at him quizzically in the rearview mirror.

"Where you headed, Vince?" the guard asked.

"Into town. I'll be back in about an hour."

"Oh. Okay." The guard smiled at Cindy, but she didn't even turn to look at him.

As they neared the Highway 107 checkpoint, Cindy started to fidget. She twisted the handle to the handbag she held in her lap and adjusted her position several times. She wasn't at all looking forward to going back to Unicoi.

Vince pulled to a stop at the checkpoint. The guard looked into the back seat. "Hello, Cindy. You back to stay?"

Cindy said nothing.

"Your daddy's at the clinic. Your momma was working out in the Smith's farm to the south of here."

Cindy looked straight ahead without acknowledging the man.

"Okay, thanks, man," Vince said and accelerated past the checkpoint into town.

"You want me to let you off at the clinic?" Vince asked. He could have let her nasty ass off at the city limits and left her there, but he was trying to be a nice guy.

"No. You can drop me off at Clay Cross's house."

Vince should have seen that coming. There had been rumors about the two of them, but at the time, Clay was married. His wife had been one of the first to pass away after the lights went out. Without access to her doctors in Nashville and the dialysis that had kept her kidneys functioning, she'd quickly succumbed to her condition and died.

"I'll tell you what. Why don't I just drop you at Smith's farm? It's just up here on the left. I'll let you off at the road and you can go help your momma and the others bring in the tomato crop."

"Whatever," Cindy said.

Vince pulled over and unloaded Cindy's bags onto the shoulder as she got out of the Wagoneer. He drove off without another word.

By the time Vince passed city hall heading out toward Ike's warehouse, he was feeling guilty about bringing Cindy back to town—not because he felt bad for her, but because of the potential problems she might cause for Lauren. He debated telling her, knowing she'd find out eventually, and decided better it came from him than some other way.

Vince turned down Unicoi Drive and nearly ran over Greg Haskins, who appeared out of nowhere, stepping out in front of the Wagoneer.

"Are you trying to get your ass run over, Greg?" Vince said.

"You need to have a long talk with that sister-in-law of yours. She's running the town into the ground. She's refusing to get rid of those thieving outsiders and now she wants to set them up with a prime piece of real estate out at Israel Greenway's old farm."

"What?" That was news to Vince.

"You do know that Johnson City is claiming that territory, right?"

"No. When did that happen? That's way outside their city limits in the county."

"They laid claim to everything within twenty miles east of the interstate."

"Can they do that?" Greg asked.

"They can do anything they have the ability to enforce."

"That means we can't hunt there?"

"That's exactly what that means. I've been warned they're shooting anyone they consider to be poaching."

"You're joking, right?" He rubbed a hand over his greasy hair. "That doesn't leave us much land to hunt. The town already made it illegal to hunt within five miles, and now we can't hunt to the northeast. That bunch down in Erwin is out running the back roads south of here. Our options are getting slimmer by the day."

"I hear ya," Vince said. He knew there was going to be a showdown about hunting rights soon and had hoped to avoid it as long as possible.

"If Johnson City is claiming the Greenway farm, then I say we should send those tourists up there today. Let them deal with the freeloading thieves."

"If I know Lauren, she's two steps ahead of all of us. She's already thought of that."

"I'm on my way to the town hall meeting at the park. Are you coming?" Vince asked.

"I wouldn't miss it," Greg said.

Vince was sure this was going to be as lively a meeting as Unicoi had ever seen, and that was saying something.

EIGHTEEN

Benny

Buffalo Creek Park
Unicoi, Tennessee
Day 20

Benny Jameson climbed the steps to the top of the flatbed trailer currently being used as a stage and stood by Lauren's side. He scanned the crowd of Unicoi residents who had gathered in Buffalo Creek Park to hear the mayor's announcement. Peppered throughout the assembly were members of the newly formed Unicoi Security Force. Their job was to keep the peace and quell any outburst before things could get out of hand. Lauren had overruled a bid by Alderman Maryann Winters to ban weapons from the park. Residents needed to be able to defend themselves, Lauren had said.

The newly appointed police chief's eyes drifted over the hands and waistbands of the people in the first row. Most stood hunched over with their hands in their pockets. They just wanted this over so they could get back to the daily grind of trying to survive.

"Thank you for coming," Lauren said. She cleared her throat

and raised her voice. "I know you have better things to do than stand around in the heat listening to me, so I'll make this short."

The people in the back were talking and not really paying attention.

"The board and I have made a difficult decision. I want you to know this decision was not one made lightly. This decision was made after a great deal of debate and discussion in search of alternative means to deal with a very serious problem.

"Really? Then why was the agenda not posted? Why don't you have open meetings and allow residents an opportunity to speak on things you guys are doing?" Ray Peters said. Benny didn't like Ray much. He ran the wrecker service in town and they'd clashed a time or two over things coming up missing from vehicles he towed.

His brother, Brian, was next to him and stepped forward and pointed a crooked finger at her. "It's illegal what you guys are doing. You can't meet in secret and then hand down edicts like this is some dictatorship."

Benny wanted to turn to see Lauren's expression, but he continued scanning the crowd. People were nodding and talking among themselves. Things could get out of hand very quickly.

"Well, Brian, if you haven't noticed, times have changed. We would love to have the time and ability to post an agenda and take weeks or months to hold town hall meetings and hear everything you have to say on every decision we have been forced to make since the world went to shit, but you know what? Lives are at stake. We don't have time to follow sunshine laws these days." The crowd roared in disapproval. "We're in emergency operations mode," she continued over the crowd. "When lives aren't hanging in the balance any longer, we'll go back to posting the damn agenda and you and your brother can come bitch about anything you want." She took two steps forward and was nearly at the edge of the stage. Benny moved up beside her and glared at Ray and Brian.

Lloyd appeared beside Lauren. Gretchen moved up beside Benny. Benny glanced back to see where Maryann was. She'd remained seated.

The assembly was electric.

"The mayor and board of aldermen have voted to institute a new requirement for receiving assistance from the town's emergency distribution center," Lloyd said. He said something else, but the roars of the crowd drowned him out.

Lauren held up a hand, trying to quiet everyone so he could finish. Lloyd nudged Lauren and she turned to look over her right shoulder. Benny followed her gaze as Ralph Cross entered the stage and wedged himself in next to Lauren.

"We got too many freeloaders in this town. So here's the deal, folks. We've decided that if you don't work, you don't eat. It's as simple as that," Ralph belted over the crowd.

The crowd erupted, some moaning and groaning while others whooped and hollered, and clapped loudly.

Benny's eyes were on those not shouting. He was concerned by the ones in the back who had arrived late. Some crossed their arms over their chests and glared toward the stage. Others shook their fists in the air and, if Benny was reading their lips properly, were shouting obscenities at the mayor and aldermen. They were the folks they needed to identify as hostiles and keep their eyes on.

"Listen! We have a sign-up…" Lauren started to say, but no one could hear her over the raised voices.

The new assistant chief of police, Alan Mayberry, moved across the back of the audience. He was a natural. He may not have attended a police academy, but his time in Afghanistan had trained him what to look for when a crowd got upset. He'd had to look out for Taliban members in every village they visited. They could be anywhere, and at any second, a hand grenade or assault rifle could slip out from under a burqa or an Afghan man's patu shawl.

Mayberry zoned in on a tall man on the eastern edge of the crowd. He walked up behind him, leaned in, and said something.

Trey King spun around and squared off on him for a second before noticing the officer's hand on his pistol, ready to draw.

Benny took a step closer to the stairs, ready to go provide back up, if necessary. Trey backed up, his hands easing into the air. His youngest son stepped around him, attempting to get behind Mayberry. He was met by Vince. A moment later, the King family voluntarily exited the park, escorted by Mayberry and Vince.

Lauren waited until the shouting died down to continue. "After today, in order to receive your food box, drinking water, or any other supplies, you must produce a voucher. For every day that you work, you will receive a food, a water, and a supply voucher given to you by your supervisor. If you do not show up for work, do not show up at the city distribution center."

She was once again interrupted by applause.

"You don't work. You don't eat," someone from the crowd shouted. Chanting of the phrase went on for nearly a full minute.

"If you have not already been given a task, we have sign-up sheets with the jobs that are available. If you are not already assigned to one, Millie has the sheet right over there." She pointed to the picnic table where Millie, Lindsay, and her sister, Maggie Russo, were seated. "I encourage you to sign up today so we can get you on the roster and you can receive your vouchers tomorrow."

Firefighter Greg Haskins stepped out of the crowd and walked closer to the stage. Two of the guards met him fifteen feet from the flatbed trailer. "I just have a question. What happens to those who choose not to work?"

"As I said, they don't receive vouchers."

"And what happens when they steal vouchers from those that do work?"

"It's a small town, Greg. We all know who is working and who is not," Lauren said.

Ralph walked to the edge of the stage. "There's no reason that anyone should go hungry. We have enough work for everyone. All anyone has to do is show up, do their damn job, and they'll receive a freaking voucher. It's not any different from how it was before the lights went out. You don't work, you don't get paid. It's a basic principle of life."

"And just like back then, people still won't work and will steal from others who do. My question is, what will happen to them?"

Ralph glanced back at Lauren. The closed-door meetings where that very thing had been discussed had been loud and lengthy. Some of the freeloaders were family members of the aldermen. They weren't all that sure they could convince their relatives that they needed to contribute or leave Unicoi. In the end, the vote had been unanimous with everyone voting to banish anyone not willing to work.

"Listen up, everyone—you're going to want to hear this," Lauren said. She paused until the attention of the crowd became more focused on her. "The board has voted to exclude any resident who refuses to work. If anyone chooses not to work, they must pack up and leave Unicoi."

Rather than shouts of anger or cheering, the crowd got quieter.

"How is that going to be enforced?" Mrs. King stepped forward. Her son, Trey, and his kids would be the first asked to leave. Benny had no doubt they'd refuse to work. None of them had held jobs before the event and most of the supervisors wouldn't want any of them on their work crew if they did.

Lauren's expression softened. "By force if necessary."

Mrs. King turned and slowly walked away. Others followed her, being in a similar situation with family members who thought the world owed them a living instead of them earning one for themselves.

"As Ralph said, there is no reason it ever has to come to that. There are jobs to suit everyone. We just ask for everyone to do their share. If we all work together, we can make it through this."

"How long is the food even going to last?" asked former bank teller Jenna Norgrove.

Lauren hesitated. She glanced at the aldermen standing beside her. "We are adding to our stores daily. We have teams out searching. We have teams hunting and fishing. We—"

"How long, mayor," someone shouted. "A month? A week? What happens when we've gone through all the food in the trucks on the interstate, the game and fish in the area, and there's nothing left?"

"That's why everyone is required to till their lawns and raise a garden of their own," Lloyd said.

He started to say more, but Lauren raised her hand to stop him.

"In addition to your home gardens, we have the community gardens. Everyone who has chickens is saving their eggs to hatch to make more chickens so that when we run out of canned foods, we have a start on raising some of our own meat."

Not everyone who raised chickens or livestock was willing to share, however. Several farmers along the northern border of town had chosen to keep to themselves even after Benny had told them they were on their own, and they wouldn't be able to rely on his department for security should someone come and take everything they had, and they would not be allowed to receive rations from the town's supply.

One of those residents, Declan Park, had formed an alliance with several of the neighboring farms along his road. They'd blocked the streets and set up their own checkpoints. There had been issues as they'd accused residents of Unicoi of trying to steal from them. A teen had been shot in the ass with an arrow, reportedly as he backed out of Declan Park's chicken coop.

"How we going to keep people from stealing from our gardens if we're all working away from home?" a woman in the back asked.

Lloyd cleared his throat. "In addition to requiring people to work or leave town, the board voted on new criminal penalties for things like stealing. Theft of food or water is now considered a felony. Anyone caught will be placed in stocks outside the police station."

The crowd erupted in gasps. Some of those who had been calling for harsher penalties for anyone caught stealing in Unicoi were shaking their heads. Apparently, they didn't think the punishment was sufficient.

"You really think all this is sustainable? Where the hell is the federal government? Where's the National Guard and FEMA?" Clifford Anderson asked. Until the lights went out, Clifford had worked at the USDA doing inspections.

It was a valid question. One that everyone had asked in the beginning, but it made sense that they were overwhelmed. He shuddered to think what Nashville and Memphis looked like now. From the way Lauren and Vince described the conditions down in Knoxville on just the second day, Benny could see where state and federal personnel and resources would have gone.

"We need to send someone to Nashville. We need help here," said the elementary school's principal, Lewis Waterman.

"The Unicoi County Emergency Manager sent someone to Nashville a few days after the event."

"And? Where the hell is our help?" Hector Ramirez asked. He and his family owned a restaurant south of town. It had been burned to the ground when the mobs from Erwin started looting the Walmart. They'd had to move their family to a vacant home on the north side of town.

"As far as I know, the messenger never returned. I've been informed that Mr. Jones himself was killed while setting up the Unicoi County emergency distribution center, and the county supplies were taken," Lloyd said.

"By those Corbins is what I heard," someone shouted.

"I heard Nigel Corbin took over the grocery store and killed a bunch of people," a man said.

"We've heard that as well, but do not have first-hand knowledge of that fact," Lauren said.

That wasn't exactly true. Benny had spoken to Ronnie Morales, his confidential informant, the day after it happened. Ronnie had joined Corbin and the others at the grocery store and she was still there providing Benny with valuable information.

"I'll let..." Lauren cleared her throat. She placed her hand on her chest. "It's getting hot and everyone has work to do, so I'll close this meeting. I want to thank each of you for all you're doing to benefit the town." Lauren took a deep breath. Her face was flushed. The heat was getting to her.

Benny moved toward her. "Thank you for coming, everyone. Let's move along and get back to what we were doing." He placed a hand on Lauren's back. "Are you alright? Let's get you a drink." He motioned for Officer Neal Wilson and gestured with his hand for him to bring the mayor a glass of water. "Let Wilson take you home, Lauren. You're not looking good."

As Lauren left the makeshift stage with Wilson, a few people began lining up in front of Millie, some of whom Benny knew already had jobs. He slipped down the steps and drew in close to the table.

"I want to pick up extra shifts at the Johnson & Carter Farms," Lorraine Brown said.

"Why, Lorraine? You won't get twice the food."

"But I need it. I have ten people in my family."

"And you should have ten members of your family receiving vouchers," Lindsay said.

Only half of her family members would work. Benny could see a problem coming. One that the board of aldermen would need to address pretty quickly.

"Listen, let me talk with your family members who won't work," Lindsay said.

Lorraine's eyes grew wide. She obviously knew Lindsay's reputation for being aggressive. "It's not that they won't work. Jamie's on disability for his back and Michelle is pregnant."

Lindsay picked up the job assignments book and waved it in

front of Lorraine's face. "We can find them a job they can do. Even little kids are being assigned jobs. They can't stay in town if they won't work."

"I can't ask my family to move out."

"You don't have to do it. When they show up here because they're hungry, someone here will show their asses to the checkpoint."

Lindsay's face was getting red. Benny needed to shut this conversation down before she went off on the woman.

"I'll come talk with them, Lorraine," Benny said.

Her eyes brightened. She placed a wrinkled hand on Benny's arm. "Would you, dear? I think that would help."

Benny wasn't so sure, but he'd do his best to lay out the facts to Lorraine's children. It would be up to them if they followed through or ended up on the interstate, exiled from town.

Raised voices caught Benny's attention. He pivoted to his right and scanned the remaining crowd. To the left of the stage, a very animated Ray Peters was jabbing a bony finger into Lloyd's chest. When Lloyd drew his arm back to take a swing at Ray, his brother Brian jumped on Lloyd's back. All the police officers were busy managing the group who were trying to get their turn to talk to the other aldermen. Vince and Mayberry had followed the Kings out of the park.

Benny sprinted across the front of the stage, lunged, snatched Brian Peters from Lloyd's back, and threw him to the ground, twisting his right arm up behind his back. "You're going to jail now, Brian. You just assaulted a city official."

"Get off my brother. He was just defending me. It's Lloyd that was going to assault me," Ray said, standing over Benny.

Benny pulled his pistol and pointed it in Ray's face. "Get back!" Benny barked. Ray jumped back with his hands raised. "I witnessed you poking Lloyd in the chest. That's considered assault. You're thirty years younger than him. What the hell do you think his response would be?"

Mayberry appeared through the crowd and rushed over to assist. He grabbed Ray and threw him to the ground. "Stupid move, Ray. This will probably land you and your brother in the stocks."

"That's a violation of my civil rights. I request a trial by a jury of my peers," Ray said.

"You'll get a trial and then your ass will be outside the police station in stocks."

"What the heck are stocks?" Brian asked as Benny hoisted him to his feet.

"It's a wooden frame with holes to restrain your hands and head."

"That's a pillory," Mr. Lawless said as he approached. The retired high school science teacher stopped and looked down at Brian. "It's meant to be a form of public humiliation, but I don't think that will work for you two boys. You've been a subject of public humiliation all your life for your behavior and that hasn't stopped you yet."

"Standing on their feet all day bent over with head and hands caught between two rough-sawn boards might make them think though," Mayberry said, hauling Brian to his feet.

"I want a lawyer," Ray said.

"Sure thing. He's right over there. You can shout out to him on your way to the station," Benny said.

NINETEEN

Lauren

Unicoi City Hall
Unicoi, Tennessee
Day 20

"Would you mind dropping me off out at Vince's compound instead of home, Wilson?" Lauren said. She needed to speak with Mrs. Miller, who had offered to make a tea that might help her dad. At this point, Lauren didn't see how it could hurt since the medicines he was taking weren't helping. Angela wouldn't like it, but her father was dying. Lauren was willing to take the risk. Besides, she hadn't seen Charlie since the day before.

She knew Charlie wasn't happy with her for sending him to live at the compound, but she couldn't do her job and worry about the safety of Sam's son as well. Threats had been made against Sam. She wouldn't put it past the Corbins to exact their revenge on his son.

~

The guard at the gate waved them through and Officer Wilson dropped Lauren off at the former office, now turned operations center for the group. She didn't recognize half the people walking by on their way to whatever duties they were assigned.

She pointed and asked Dave, "Are they all new?"

"Family," Dave said.

"Of who?"

"Group members."

"Was that planned? I don't recall children being part of the group."

"They had siblings and kids in tow when they showed up. Vince was off looking for you and they let themselves into the compound." Dave pointed to the rocking chair on the wrap-around porch and Lauren took a seat. "When Vince and I arrived back here, we vetted them the best we could. We've had a few issues, but not like I anticipated. We're working out the kinks, but actually, having more hands to spread out the chores ain't a bad thing —if you know what I mean."

"The reason I came out was to speak with Mrs. Miller and say hi to Charlie. Have you seen them?"

"They were back by the smoke shack tanning hides this morning. Mr. Miller is in seventh heaven having Charlie as his apprentice. They've been teaching him everything from tanning hides with brains to spinning wool into yarn."

"Wow, they're keeping him busy. Those are good things to learn now, I guess," Lauren said.

"Did you see Vince and Lindsay in town?"

"They were at the town hall meeting at the park. When I left, Lindsay was helping Millie hand out job assignments and Vince was escorting the Kings from the park."

"I bet that meeting was pleasant with the King boys there."

"There were a few unhappy residents, but I think, for the most part, everyone went away happy."

~

Lauren found Charlie and Mr. Miller scraping flesh from a deer hide. Several more hides were strung up drying in the sun. The smell made Lauren sick to her stomach. She tried to think about what she'd had to eat that morning but couldn't recall having anything.

"Hey, Charlie Brown. You making some Daniel Boone britches?"

"They're called buckskins. They're for Dave and the hunting party for this winter," Charlie said.

"It'll be here before you know it," Mr. Miller said, looking at her overtop of his wire-rimmed glasses.

"Is Mrs. Miller around?" Lauren asked.

"She's over with Maggie and the children. The little boy has come down with a cough," Mr. Miller said.

~

Mrs. Miller was feeding the baby some type of syrup from a spoon while Maggie held his mouth open. The kid was doing his best to spit out every drop, and his mother was wearing most of it.

"I don't think he likes that much," Lauren said.

"It's not the tastiest thing, but it will get the job done," Mrs. Miller said.

Lauren caught a whiff of it and backed away, holding her nose. Her stomach churned. "What is that?"

"Onion syrup," Mrs. Miller said. "Just onion and sugar. It'll kick congestion like nobody's business."

"No wonder he's spitting it out," Lauren said, doing her best to stay upwind of the concoction.

"I came out here because Vince said you had a tea that might help my father."

"Yes, it's up at my trailer." She handed the boy back to Maggie and wiped her hands on a floral print apron that hung around her neck.

~

"Have a seat, dear. You look like you're getting a bit dehydrated in this heat. You have to drink a lot of water when temperatures get this high." Mrs. Miller poured a glass of water from a glass pitcher on the counter. The curtains billowed out over the small sink in the travel trailer's kitchen, but it was still quite warm inside.

"Thank you," Lauren said, taking the glass from her.

"How is your father, Lauren?"

"Dr. Crabtree came to see Pop last night. He basically said all we could do now is try to keep him comfortable." She choked up. "He didn't even offer him pain meds or anything, so I don't know how we're supposed to keep him from suffering without narcotics."

Without a word, she turned and walked toward the bedroom area. A second later, she returned holding an amber-colored bottle and handed it to Lauren.

"What's in it?"

"Wild lettuce, among other things. I don't like giving out my recipes for these types of things. Some people might abuse them."

"What about the fluid around his heart?"

She handed Lauren a separate bottle. Written on the bottle were the instructions on how to administer the product. "What's in it? Onion syrup?" Lauren wasn't sure she could stomach giving that to her father.

"Foxglove and some other things. Just follow those instructions and don't give him more than what it says."

Lauren hugged her. "Thank you."

"You take this for your stomach."

"Mrs. Miller, come quick!" a young boy yelled as he banged on her door. "My momma said the baby's coming."

"I'll be right there. Tell her not to push till I get there."

"Are you a midwife as well?"

"I've been birthing babies in these mountains since I was fourteen years old. That's a lot of babies," Mrs. Miller said, grabbing a worn leather medical bag from a side table.

∾

As Mrs. Miller went to attend to the pregnant mother, Lauren returned to the operation center. She was hoping to speak with Dave and see if there'd been any news from ham operators outside of Tennessee. Dave wasn't there. No one was there. She sat on the porch waiting for someone to return; she needed a ride back into town. A few minutes later, she heard shouting and shot to her feet.

"Where's Mrs. Miller?" someone shouted. "We need medical care over here."

Lauren stepped off the porch in search of the source of the shouting. Three men, including Dave, were running toward her carrying a very bloody man.

"Who is it?" was the first thing out of her mouth. "I mean, how is he?" As they ran by her, she tried to see who it was, but the man's face was a bloody mess.

"Mrs. Miller went to deliver a baby. I don't know where," Lauren called after them.

Dave stopped. "Let's take him to the ops center, then I'll run and get Mrs. Miller."

"What happened?" Lauren asked as they carried the man up the stairs.

"He was attacked by a bear."

"Shit!" Lauren said. That explained why half his face had been ripped away from his skull. Lauren didn't think Mrs. Miller could fix that. "Someone should ride into town and get Doctor Crabtree. That man is going to need surgery and strong antibiotics." Lauren had known someone who had died from an infection after being bitten by a bear.

Mr. Miller was the first to arrive. Charlie stood by his side. "You shouldn't see this, Charlie," Lauren said, pulling him aside.

"You sure that was a bear that did that?" Mr. Miller asked.

"What else could do that?" Charlie asked.

"I've seen several people who were attacked by bears. My uncle was mauled when I was a kid and I had a guy I was hunting with get smacked by one. Those don't look like bear teeth or claw marks to me."

"Did you see any signs of a bear where you found him?" Mr. Miller asked.

"I wasn't looking. I just wanted to scoop him up and get the hell out of there before it returned to finish the job," the thirty-something man said.

Five long minutes passed as the man moaned and groaned in pain, waiting for Mrs. Miller to arrive. Lauren waited with Charlie outside. When Mrs. Miller arrived, she had blood all over her apron. Lauren imagined she'd stayed to deliver the baby before running over to the operations center.

"Wait here, Charlie," Lauren said, following Mrs. Miller and Dave inside.

"Lift him up here on this desk," she said, clearing papers and water bottles from an old metal government surplus desk. Mrs. Miller wiped the man's face using scraps of fabric that looked to have been cut from old bed sheets.

"That's a shotgun blast," Mrs. Miller said, pointing to several tiny round wounds near the larger gaping wound in the man's cheek.

Dave leaned in close and examined the man's face. "Justin, did someone shoot you?" The man's mouth was partially missing. He couldn't form words. "Squeeze my hand twice if someone shot you."

Justin squeezed Dave's hand twice.

"How many of them were there?"

He squeezed Dave's hand again four times.

"Four. There were four guys. One of them had a shotgun." Dave said, glancing over at Lauren. "How many of the others had weapons?" he asked. "All of them had weapons? Where's your partner? Where is Sean?"

Justin's eyes glazed over and then rolled back in his head. Mrs. Miller felt his neck for a pulse. "He's still alive. He just passed out from the pain."

She wiped her hands and turned toward the door. "I need to get back to the trailer and get some things."

Dave grabbed the arm of one of the men who had found Justin and led him outside as Mr. and Mrs. Miller left to go back to their place. Lauren followed Dave. She wanted to hear what they planned to do about this situation, as it could very well have been someone from Unicoi who had been shot.

"Was there any sign of Sean?"

"Honestly, Dave, I never even thought about him. I assumed Justin had been attacked by a bear. It freaked me out so bad that I panicked and ran him back here with Justin."

"Take a five-man team and go find Sean," Dave said. "I'm going to take Lauren into town and find Vince. He's going to want to know about this right away."

Lauren took Charlie's arm and led him away from the porch. "Charlie, stay inside the compound. Make sure you have your pistol on you at all times."

"I will, I promise, but what happened? I heard Mrs. Miller say he'd been shot."

"Don't you worry about that, Charlie. Your Uncle Vince will be back, and then he and Dave will deal with all that."

"I could come home with you."

Lauren said nothing.

"I could help Angela with Memaw and Pepaw. I won't get in the way."

Despite what had happened outside the wall, the compound was still the safest place for Charlie. She was sure that would be what Sam would want. She placed a hand on his shoulder. "I appreciate you wanting to help, but it's not safe. Your dad wanted you here surrounded by the wall and guarded by these guys."

Charlie hung his head.

"How's your breathing? Is the heat bothering you? Don't overdo it and get too hot. You have your inhaler with you, right?" She realized she sounded like her mother.

Charlie smiled and produced an inhaler from his pocket. Maybe a bit of mothering was what he needed. No doubt the kid had to be distressed and missed his mother, father, and baby sister.

"As soon as I get things squared away in town so it's safe enough, I would love for you to come home. But right now, we have some issues and people are having a hard time adjusting to this new life. Some of them aren't playing nice."

"Are you safe? Don't you need to be safe here too?"

"I have a job to do."

A look of concern crossed his face. Maybe he was anxious about losing another parent figure. "Don't worry about me. I have my own security detail. I'm safe."

"Okay," Charlie said, but he didn't sound convinced.

TWENTY

Lauren

Unicoi City Hall
Unicoi, Tennessee
Day 21

Reports of stealing and an attempted break-in at the food distribution center had Lauren on edge. She was concerned that the announcement of the work requirement had pushed the town into a crisis that would take the security force away from the vital task of securing the border wall against outside threats.

Lauren had spent the morning meeting with citizens who had all manner of excuses as to why they couldn't possibly work. Others appeared to be there to negotiate a higher salary or better position. After she let them know that everyone got the same amount of food no matter what position they held, most went away angry.

"Millie, lock the doors. No one gets in without an appointment. I have to finish up here and get home to do my own chores."

Millie walked around the receptionist counter and across the room. "I'll post a note on the door. They can put their names on the list if they want a meeting. You should have some of the aldermen address their concerns. That's their job, right?"

"*That* is an excellent idea, Millie. Tell them to contact their aldermen," Lauren said, ducking back into her office.

A few hours later, Ralph appeared in her doorway. "Did you tell everyone in town to come to my house with their problems?"

"No. I had Millie post a note telling citizens to address their concerns with their elected alderman."

"Well, apparently Lloyd, Gretchen, and Maryann are unavailable for their constituents because I've had visits from other wards." Ralph jabbed a fat finger in her direction. "You do not want me handling residents' complaints." He turned and stomped down the hall. The rear door slammed and she could hear him cursing her as he walked past her window.

"It's hot as Hades out there today," Benny said, poking his head into her office. "I just came to drop off this updated report from the distribution center. Millie said you wanted to see how many people signed up for work."

"Thanks, Benny."

Millie walked in. "Lloyd stopped by a little bit ago. He said someone broke into his brother's place. He was going there to help with security today if anyone needed him."

Lauren studied the distribution center reports. She used an old-fashioned calculator to add up the totals, but the numbers somehow just weren't making sense. There appeared to be more food going out than coming in.

"Millie, can you check this?" Lauren asked. "I must be too tired. I can't get the numbers to add up,"

Millie took a seat in the chair and began running the numbers. The back door banged open and Lauren sighed, thinking she'd again have to listen to Ralph bitch about doing his job. She sat back down and placed both hands on her desk, as far away from her revolver as possible.

A moment later, Trey King took two steps into her office. The scowl on his face told Lauren he wasn't there to apologize for his family's freeloading.

Millie rose from her seat opposite Lauren and moved to the right side of the desk. "Benny!" she yelled.

Lauren reached into her desk drawer and removed the revolver, placing it in her lap. In the periphery of her vision, she could see Millie backing toward her, a pistol at her side.

Benny rushed into the room and moved toward Trey. Lauren lifted a hand. "Let him have his say." She hoped the man would make his case and she could convince him his family could redeem themselves by volunteering for some of the more labor-intensive jobs, like carrying water to the gardens or chopping wood for the town's winter firewood supply. But as soon as he opened his mouth, that notion flew out the window.

He took another step closer. The smell of his body odor turned Lauren's stomach sour. His clothes were filthy and wrinkled like he hadn't changed them since the lights went out. His shoulder-length hair was greasy and unkempt. His eyes were bloodshot with pupils the size of saucers, leaving Lauren to wonder whether he'd gotten some of Billy Mahon's drug stash.

Lauren's records indicated that Trey King had missed three days of work, but he now expected to get paid anyway.

"I was sick," he said.

"Sick from doing recreational drugs doesn't count," Benny said.

"I've lived in Unicoi all my life. My momma and daddy have lived here all their lives. I got people buried in that cemetery down the road." He leaned in close enough for Lauren to feel his rank breath on her cheek. "Me and mine ain't going nowhere."

Benny bent his knees, lunged, and wrapped his arms around Trey's skinny waist. Twisting, Benny threw him to the ground.

Before Trey even knew what had hit him, Benny had the man's arm twisted behind his back and was reaching for his handcuffs.

Lauren got to her feet, revolver in hand, and rounded her desk. Millie emerged on the opposite side, pistol gripped in both hands and pointed at the floor.

"Stop resisting, Trey."

"What are you gonna do, Benny? Put me in jail?" Trey taunted as he continued to thrash about in an attempt to keep Benny from cuffing his hands behind his back.

"No. No, I am not. If I put you in jail, I'd have to feed you. What I'm going to do is escort your sorry ass to the border."

"You can't do that. I own a home here. I pay my taxes. My taxes pay for your salary."

"Not anymore. I haven't been paid since the lights went out," Benny said.

"I bet you got a house full of food though. You probably took yours before anyone else."

Benny didn't reply to the man who'd done nothing but take from the town even before the lights went out. Finally managing to get Trey's left arm twisted around to his back and the cuffs cinched tight, Benny stood, hoisting Trey to his feet. "Let's go, tough guy. You're done here."

"You can't just make us leave Unicoi. We have a right to be here," Trey shouted over his shoulder.

"You had an obligation to the community to contribute and not take what you didn't earn. You and your boys sat on your asses smoking weed and eating the food others worked to supply. That ends today. In this town, you work or you don't eat," Lauren said.

When she'd made that proclamation at the last town hall meeting, she'd received a big round of applause from those working hard to contribute, and scowls from the small population of free-loading residents. There had been threats made against her and the board of aldermen. She'd received visits from grandmothers concerned their lazy grandkids would be sent away. Parents had offered to work double shifts to ensure their children could remain within the walls of Unicoi. It made Lauren sick to see parents still coddling their children instead of preparing them for the harsh life that lay ahead for everyone, but especially those unwilling to work hard to save themselves. She was sure every generation contained elements who could not be bothered to pull themselves up by their bootstraps, but the EMP had made such behavior downright dangerous. No one had extra to give.

"If you can find another community willing to share their food with you while you do nothing, you should stay there."

Trey dragged his feet as Benny pulled him toward the door. "What about my momma and daddy?"

Lauren pointed her finger at Trey and wagged it. "Your momma is one of the most hardworking women I've ever met. She's been down at the church cooking for the elderly and disabled in the nursing home since the day after this happened. All her life, she's contributed to this town while you boys just sat back and watched. Shame on you."

"Who's gonna look after my daddy if you kick me and my family out?"

"Frankly, Trey. I don't care," Lauren said. Edward King was a drunk. He'd always been a drunk. The fact that he was on his death bed now was his own fault.

Well, that won't work—I don't have the heart to just let the old jackass die—but I don't have to tell Trey that.

"You bitch. You self-righteous, heartless bitch. I'm going to…"

Grief suddenly ambushed Lauren, and her thoughts of how her father's last moments might go played in her head. Her vision tunneled, and she heard no more of Trey's insults. She bent forward. Placing both hands on her desk, she drew in deep breaths, trying to rein in the overwhelming rush of emotions. Anger replaced grief. Hot anger bubbled to the surface. Then rage that her father would be taken from her, fury that she had no idea whether her husband was dead or alive, and wrath that she had to deal with a piece of shit like Trey King on top of everything on her plate at the moment.

"Are you all right, Lauren?" Millie's hand was on Lauren's back. Bile rose in Lauren's throat. She bolted from her chair, ran down the hall, and threw open the door. She vomited at the base of the old oak tree.

"Let me take you home," Millie said.

Trey was still cursing her as Benny dragged him toward Alan's truck. Trey reared up and Alan clocked him across the jaw with the butt of his rifle. Alan helped Benny throw the cuffed man into the bed of the pickup and hopped in with him. The truck started, pulled out of the parking lot, and disappeared from view.

Lauren felt a cool cloth being placed on the nape of her neck.

"I'm fine. I just needed some cool air. That smell was just too much."

"What smell?" Millie asked.

"Trey's body odor."

"I didn't notice."

"Really?" Lauren straightened, wiping her mouth with the damp cloth.

"Everyone smells these days. Who has time to wash laundry? It takes too much water anyway."

Drawing water from the North Indian Creek to wash clothes wouldn't have been as difficult if, after a long day working in the community gardens, they weren't so exhausted from getting firewood for cooking and tending to their home gardens.

Lauren rubbed her face with a cloth and handed it back to Millie.

"You need to drink. You don't look good. You're as white as a bed sheet," Millie said

"I'll just work here at the picnic table the rest of the day. The breeze will help. It's already scorching hot inside," Lauren said, lowering herself onto the bench and throwing her legs over it. She checked her watch. It was barely ten o'clock. It shouldn't have been so hot already. She longed for air conditioning. The heat and humidity had taken their toll on her father and she was sure it was the reason for his rapid decline. His damaged heart just couldn't take it.

"I'll get you a glass of water and bring you the folders from your desk."

"Thank you, Millie." Mille had been a godsend. She'd been an exemplary city clerk even before the event, but Lauren couldn't keep things on track now without her. She was a rare, dedicated public servant and invaluable not just to Lauren, but also to the town.

Millie turned to go, but Lauren called after her. "Millie? Do you think I'm doing the right thing?" It wasn't as easy to banish people as it was in the fantasy novels she'd read as a kid. They were people she had grown up, played soccer and softball, and attended church with many times. She had no idea how they would survive cut off from the rest of their families and the resources of the town.

"I don't see you have any other choice. Their freeloading has the hardworking residents angry as hell. They're the ones who are demanding something be done. It's a much more compassionate solution than some have demanded. If you let it go on much longer, there's going to be blood in the streets, and innocent people could get hurt or even killed."

"I know. I know you're right. It has to be done. I worry though."

"You fear they'll join up with Corbin's gang and come back for revenge?"

"Sort of, but they'd have to work there too. I can't see Nigel feeding freeloaders. They're more likely to get killed in Erwin than here. And who knows how long they'd last in Johnson City with that civil war brewing between Corbin's lackeys and the rest of the town."

"That concerns me more than Nigel, honestly," Millie said.

"I think it's only a matter of time. My sources say people are starving there now, and the Corbin-backed side of town has gobbled up every available morsel of food for themselves. The city is divided and something is going to happen. Parents are going to watch their children starve to death while the wealthy stay fed in their gated communities."

"I just hope it doesn't spill over to here."

"We have the wall."

"And not enough people to guard it. Two teenagers hopped over it just yesterday."

"They were caught."

"What about the ones we don't know about?"

Lauren stared off in the direction of the interstate. "We're doing all we can."

"I know."

"You can move out to the compound, Millie. No one would fault you. You've gone above and beyond for the town."

Millie lowered her head. "I couldn't do that. Steve was the one who invited me and he's…"

A stab of guilt jabbed Lauren in her now empty gut. Steve had lost his life coming to rescue her and Charlie the day of the EMP.

"You know you're always welcome there. Lindsay, Maggie, and the others would love to have you."

"Vince wouldn't. He can't even look at me."

"What? No. That's not true. Steve was his friend. Why would he think like that?"

"Because the last words I said to him before they left to go find you were for him to not get my boyfriend killed."

Lauren hadn't considered that Vince might feel guilt over Steve's death.

"Besides," Millie continued. "I'm needed here. This is where I belong."

"I do appreciate…" A wave of nausea sent Lauren racing back to the old oak tree.

Millie followed her out to the tree and said, "You need to go home, Lauren. You need rest, at the very least."

"It will pass in a minute."

"How long have you been feeling this way?"

Lauren retched, and then straightened. "About a week. It's worse in the mornings, but it goes away by the afternoon. I'll be fine. I'll just sip some water and it'll pass soon."

A broad smile spread across Millie's face. "Lauren, could you be... you know?" She gestured with her hands, making a circular motion over her stomach.

"What? No!" Lauren scrunched her face and moved back to the picnic table. "No way I'm pregnant. That's not possible."

"I bet I could find you a pregnancy test at the birth counseling center."

"No! I'm not pregnant." Lauren slowly lowered herself onto the bench. "I can't be."

TWENTY-ONE

Benny

Unicoi Police Department
Unicoi, Tennessee
Day 22

In the forty-eight hours since the mayor's announcement of the new work requirement and penalties for certain types of crimes, Benny had been busier than he'd ever been in his entire career. Fights had broken out within families about having to work to eat, and others were stealing their neighbors' food and other things that they thought they had some right to, in broad daylight. One vocal group even complained freeloaders were taking food from their children's mouths right after everyone had been told that they'd be given rations if they worked, as well as about the use of the stocks and banishment to enforce the no work/no eat requirement.

After he thought things had quieted down, Benny returned to city hall to give Lauren an update. "We're handing out so many citations that I'm running out of paper. People are complaining about the hunting regulation. Judge Hanes sentenced three men to thirty hours of extra labor for hunting inside the town limits."

"They have to abide by the laws or pay the price," Lauren said. "They've been going to Ralph to complain."

"That won't do them any good. We voted. It's settled."

"Maybe not. Ray and Brian Peters have been trying to rile people up to bring it back before the board for a new vote."

"Why can't they see these laws are for the good of the community?" Federal land was within two miles in any direction. It wasn't an unreasonable distance, considering. The hunting was much better up in the mountains anyway.

"They're complaining that after working sixteen-hour shifts, they don't have the time or energy to travel to federal land to hunt or fish in a group."

"Why're they pulling double shifts?"

"Because they have fines to pay for breaking the law."

"Wait!" Lauren held up a hand. "The judge has sentenced people to double shifts for offenses other than theft of food. That wasn't the purpose. That was to be used for the most extreme cases."

"We have to have some penalty for the other crimes. We can't put them in jail, you know that. What are we supposed to do with them?

"Take away half their ration cards or something, but pulling sixteen-hour days on the food we provide isn't healthy."

"That will only lead to them stealing," Benny said.

"If they steal, put them in the stocks. It's not going to work as a deterrent if you're using it for everything," Lauren said.

"I'm not the judge. You need to tell him that."

Lauren closed her eyes and clenched her jaw. She exhaled slowly and then opened them. "Okay." She pulled out a piece of paper and started to write Judge Hanes a letter, but was interrupted by a pounding on the main lobby door.

Millie ran into Lauren's office. "Ray Peters is at the door demanding to address the aldermen."

Lauren waved her hand in the air. "Let him in. We'll let him rant, then maybe he'll get it all out of his system," Lauren said.

"Why let him put you through that?" Benny asked.

"Because of the rest of the yahoos that he's riled up. We might be able to convince them we're doing everything we can to provide for people."

"Okay. But you've been warned," Benny said.

Benny walked through the lobby, unlocked the door, and yanked it open, putting Ray off balance and causing him to stumble forward. "The mayor has agreed to meet with you, but I'm going to need to search you for weapons first."

"Search me? Why?" Ray asked.

"I'm not letting you bring weapons inside city hall. Certainly not after the threats you've been making against the mayor and town council."

Ray lifted his shirt and allowed Benny to remove his holstered pistol. "I want that back when I leave here," Ray said.

"Sure thing."

Benny considered confiscating it. A hothead like Ray shouldn't be allowed to carry one these days. Ray stomped through the lobby and down the hall toward the council chambers.

"She's in her office. Second door on the left," Benny said.

Millie stepped out and stood in the corridor next to Benny.

"It's not fair, Mayor. We're just trying to provide for our families in the way we always have, and you're making it impossible," Ray said. His tone was loud and angry.

Benny stepped inside Lauren's office and moved up behind Ray, ready to take him down to the floor if he made a move toward Lauren. Ray's hands clenched as he stepped toward Lauren's desk. Benny rushed around Ray, stepping in front of him. He bumped his chest into Ray's shoulder, pushing him away from the desk. Benny stood a head taller and had at least forty pounds on the man, but he wasn't in the mood for a fight. He hoped the guy backed down so he didn't ruin one of his last good uniforms.

"I pay my taxes. I've been a law-abiding citizen all my life. I have a right to be heard just like everyone else."

"You need to calm down, Ray, or go home."

"Screw you, Jameson. I'm a free citizen. I go where I want and do what I please. You can't tell me what to do."

Benny grabbed his arm, spun him around, and twisted it up behind his back.

"I think you've had your say. Now you need to leave." Benny turned Ray toward the door.

"Wait, Benny," Lauren said. She stood and stepped out from behind her desk. She stopped for a moment and placed one hand on her desk to steady herself before continuing to the middle of the room. "Tell me something, Ray. What do you propose we do when all the game animals close to town are gone? How will we supply meat to the town and those who are unable to hunt for themselves?"

"If you weren't feeding a bunch of freeloaders, you wouldn't need as much and there'd be plenty for everyone."

"The ladies at the church are helping the town produce food or provide clean drinking water," Benny said. "They're earning their keep."

"I'm not opposed to them helping. I just think they shouldn't be treated like Unicoi citizens. They didn't ever pay no taxes around here."

Lauren never understood those who viewed anyone not born in Unicoi County as an outsider and someone to be suspicious of and dislike. Wasn't that something from a bygone era?

"Neither have a bunch of your relatives, Ray. Should we treat them like second-class citizens too? Exactly which services would you deny them, anyway? Should we restrict their access to the only source of meat there is?"

"I just don't like all these people here that don't belong."

"What about that cousin of yours?" Benny asked. "He and his wife aren't from here."

"Um..." Ray stammered.

"You have several people at your house who aren't from here and haven't been pulling their weight. It's fine if you want to share your food and water with them, but you can't complain when people who've earned food vouchers get them and your family members don't," Lauren said.

"Me and my family are growing a garden. My boy and I hunt and fish. We're trying to take care of our own, but your stupid regulations are making it impossible."

"You receive rations just like everyone else who works to earn them. If you need extra food to feed family members that won't work, then you'll have to go out beyond the boundary set by the ordinance. Work off your fine and then abide by the law, Ray," Lauren said.

"Ralph said you passed those laws without citizen input and they should be brought back up for debate—let the residents decide."

"Ralph said that?" Lauren asked.

"At the meeting last night."

"Meeting?"

"At his house. Several of us in his ward wanted to know why he voted for this crap."

"The entire board voted on the new laws. If you don't like them, you can be escorted to the checkpoint and you can find a new home elsewhere," Lauren said. "You can tell the rest of your neighbors trying to cause trouble the same thing."

Ray stomped out in a huff and slammed the door.

"Ralph is behind this mess. Instead of explaining that the new rules are for the good of all, he's agreeing with them and encouraging this rebellion," said Lauren.

"I should go talk to him and let him know the trouble he's causing," Benny said.

"It won't do any good. Ralph has always stirred the pot and pulled this crap. He has his own agenda that he's working on and it is not about what's good for Unicoi."

TWENTY-TWO

Lauren

Taylor Residence
Unicoi, Tennessee
Day 23

Lauren hadn't been able to keep down her breakfast. Stress often did that to her and she recalled the morning she took her bar exam when she'd thrown up three times. *It's just nerves.* She took a sip of mint tea, trying to settle her stomach. She had work to do and needed to be focused.

The herbal medicine that Mrs. Miller had given Lauren had provided her father with some relief, but he still struggled to breathe and was confused at times, becoming combative. It was difficult for Angela to see to his needs and make sure Edna didn't wander off or burn down the house with a candle. Lauren had been trying to work from home so she could sit with her father and spend as much time with him as possible.

"Lloyd, you know Mitford's just going to sue," Bill said. He was delusional again, talking like he was still the mayor of Unicoi.

Lauren placed a hand on top of her father's. "What, Dad?"

"Josh left the gate open and Ranger got out and bit the postman again."

Lauren didn't know how to respond to her father's babbling, so she just sat there, her heart breaking. She needed him lucid. She desperately needed his wise advice on how she should deal with the situations at city hall and with the residents of Unicoi. She needed him to tell her what he would do about Ralph Cross and that whole mess.

Bill started coughing again, and she rolled him onto his side. He was gasping for air, and there was nothing she could do for him. Nothing. She'd never felt so absolutely helpless in all her life. A part of her wanted him to let go and move on to a better place so he'd be out of this pain, but she knew she was nowhere near ready to let him go. How could she be? He'd been her rock all her life; the one person on the planet who she knew would never, ever let her down.

Was she failing him now? Her attentions were divided. She spent so much time and mental energy trying to save the town that she'd barely been there for him. Thank God for Angela, but his nurse wasn't blood and her mother was in and out of reality and needed constant supervision.

At times, Edna understood how sick Bill was and was attentive and loving. Other times, she was lost in her own world, reliving bygone days when life was simpler. In a crazy, bizarre way, Lauren sometimes wished she could join her mother and escape the reality of the present. She would love to go back to a time when Sam was by her side and her father was still strong. Lauren really needed to be with her parents full time, but how could she do that?

Bill cried out and then gasped. He stopped breathing. Lauren froze, not knowing what to do. "Angela!" Lauren screamed. "Angela, come quick!" Lauren began shaking uncontrollably and clutched her chest. "Please, Daddy! Please breathe. Don't..."

Bill sucked in air and then began to cough again.

Angela ran into the living room and turned up the oxygen

flowing to the attached mask on his face. Her father calmed again and settled back into sleep.

It was too much. Every single time he stopped breathing, Lauren died inside. It was excruciatingly hard to watch. She was so tired. So very, very tired.

Sam, I need you so badly.

Sam wasn't a miracle worker, and she knew there was nothing her husband could do to save or extend her father's life, but somehow just his presence made her feel better. But he wasn't here for this and she had no idea where he was. If she were honest with herself, she had no idea if he was even still alive. Her breaths came in rapid gulps, her hands began to tingle, and she felt as if she was suffocating.

Lauren ran from the room, through the kitchen, and out the back door. Falling to her knees, she dug her fingers into the dirt in her mother's flower garden. It felt as if her heart was being ripped from her body and there was nothing she could do to stop it. She felt Sam slipping away. It was as if he was getting farther and farther from her instead of closer. She wanted to hold on to hope, but the pragmatic, analytical part of her brain would not shut up. Three weeks and still not home, her brain repeatedly told her. Twenty-three days to make it two hundred miles. An image of Sam's face down against the dirt flashed through her mind. She couldn't breathe and she fought to regain control. She leaned back with her butt on her heels and looked at the sky.

"Sam!" she cried, sitting up and hugging herself. "Oh, Sam!"

"Lauren!" Charlie said. "Are you okay?"

Lauren grabbed Charlie and pulled him into an embrace. She wept and wept until there were no more tears to cry. He patted her back, and when she was done he produced a bandanna for her to dry her tears.

"I miss him, too," Charlie whispered.

"I'm sorry, Charlie. I'm so very, very sorry."

"You have nothing to be sorry for. My dad is going to be so proud when he gets home and sees all you've done."

"I'm sorry I couldn't protect you from Billy Mahon. I'm sorry you had to do that."

"It wasn't your fault. He was an asshole."

Lauren stared at him, wondering if she should scold him for cursing. Would Sam? No, she finally decided.

"What are you doing here?" she asked, getting to her feet.

"Vince brought me. He and Lindsay are inside."

Vince met Lauren in the kitchen while Charlie continued through to the living room. Lauren's attention was divided between listening to what Charlie was saying to her father and what Vince was saying.

"We found Sean." He let that statement hang in the air for a moment as Lauren pulled herself together. She leaned against the sink and placed both hands on the counter to ground herself to the present. It wasn't working as well as she'd hoped, but Vince was patient. He crossed the room and stopped in front of her. Bending down, he looked into her eyes. "Are you okay?"

"It's been a rough few days with Dad."

"I'm sorry, Lauren. I wish there was something I could do."

"I know. You were saying you found Sean. Is he dead?"

"They hanged him, Lindsay. They strung him up and tacked a note on him that said, 'Stay off our land,'" Vince said.

"Where was he found?"

"On the east side of Stone Mountain, along the creek bed. We believe he was tracking the people who killed Justin."

"Justin died?" Lauren asked.

"Yesterday."

"I'm sorry."

"Justin was shot in the face at close range."

"Any idea who might have done that?"

"The note was written on Corbin Industries stationary."

Lauren balled her fists and pushed away from the counter. She wanted to punch something. Wasn't life hard enough? Survival alone was almost impossible. You'd think Corbin and those who support him would be too busy trying to find food and obtain water and other supplies to be out on Stone Mountain killing Wallace compound sentries.

"What do you plan to do?"

"That's why I'm here. Whatever I do will have an impact here in Unicoi. If we retaliate, they may do something to the folks here, thinking they're involved."

"What would you do if that wasn't a concern?" She knew they had to respond. Johnson City was sending a message that Unicoi was claiming territory that wasn't rightfully theirs. They had to be dealt with or no one would want to leave Unicoi or the compound.

"I'd take my sniper team and take out a few of their leaders," Vince said.

Lauren thought about it for only a moment before responding. "Then that's exactly what you should do."

Lindsay put her hand on Lauren's arm. "You don't look so good. Why don't you go lie down? I'll stay with Bill for a while. Rest, Lauren. You're doing too much."

She was doing too little. Too little for the town and too little for her family. There were just such great needs that she struggled to prioritize them all. If the town fell to the likes of the Corbins, or Ralph somehow wound up in charge, Lauren knew she'd have to take her parents and go to the farm. That would kill her mom for sure, and her father was too weak to move.

"I need to deal with something at city hall if you could sit with Pop for a couple of hours."

"Not a problem. Take as long as you need, but Lauren, this is all going to catch up with you. What happens when you get sick?" Lindsay asked.

The look on her best friend's face was concerning. Did she look that bad? Lauren glanced down at her clothes. They were clean—Mrs. Miller's team made sure of that, but they hung off her. How much weight had she lost? She couldn't remember when she'd last been able to keep anything solid in her stomach.

Lauren knew her friend was right; she needed to take better care of herself. She vowed to do better—right after she dealt with Ralph. She had to head off whatever it was he was planning before it got out of hand.

TWENTY-THREE

Sam
―――――

Hammond Farm
Franklin, North Carolina
Day 23

Under the shade of an old hickory tree in the Hammonds' backyard, Sam and Shane Montgomery, aka Tumbleweed, split firewood and stacked it by the firepit where Mrs. Hammond was stirring a pot of rabbit stew.

"If I don't start now, there's no way we can make it to Moondust's home in New Hampshire before winter," Tumbleweed said.

Tumbleweed and Sam had been discussing him and Moondust traveling north with Sam and Becky if they took the Appalachian Trail route. Now that Sam possibly had a vehicle to get him home, Tumbleweed and Moondust were planning to spend a day or two gathering supplies once they got to Unicoi and then strike out northbound on the A.T. for their homes in New England. Sam had offered to let them take the truck, but Tumbleweed was afraid of driving it through all those towns. "It'll take longer, but we'll be safer on the Appalachian Trail."

"When we finish here, do you want to go with me over to the Titus farm and take a look at the truck?" Sam was anxious to see what progress the Titus family had made with the vehicle.

"You really think that old thing will run?" Tumbleweed asked.

"I'm praying it does."

∼

As soon as Sam and Tumbleweed started across the pasture toward the barn, they heard the engine roar to life. Two seconds later, gunshots rang out and echoed through the hollow.

He and Tumbleweed picked up their pace, with Sam literally hopping through the field. He drew his pistol and searched for the shooter.

As they rounded the corner of the barn, where days before he'd been so elated to be offered the Power Wagon, he hoped someone wasn't trying to steal it before he ever had a chance to get behind the wheel.

There was shouting near the front of the home. A female screamed, followed by more shouting, but Sam couldn't make out the words. He recognized Mark Titus' voice.

"My boy has been here with me the whole night. Ain't no way he touched your daughter. No way. We were out here in the barn working until two in the morning."

Tumbleweed put his arm around Sam's waist and helped him move toward the commotion. As they entered the front yard, Mark was helping Isaiah up off the ground. Next to him were a man and woman in their late thirties. Their hair was dirty and their clothes hung off them like they hadn't eaten in a long while. Behind them stood a girl about Isaiah's age, maybe a little younger. She, too, was extremely thin and dirty.

"Isaiah was in his bed—the one he shares with his brother—from two until five thirty when I got him up to go hunting with me. We were gone hunting until midday. We just got back and have been working in the barn ever since. He ain't left my sight so your girl is lying or something cause it weren't my boy who touched her."

The man spun around, drew his fist back, and struck the young girl across the cheek. She fell to the ground and her mother ran to shield her from further blows. As the man prepared to land a boot in his wife's side, Mark Titus tackled him, throwing him to the ground, and proceeded to pound him in the head with massive fists. "You never, ever hit a woman in my presence, you piece of shit. Ever! You got me."

Mark's wife ran over to him and fell to her knees, getting in his face. "Don't, Mark. You're gonna kill him and then who will provide for Erin and Julie?"

Mark glanced up at his wife and then down at the abusive, bloodied man. "They're better off on their own than with this man."

"That's not your decision to make. He's her husband, and that's their family business."

"What?" Sam couldn't restrain himself. "They're better off with someone who beats them?" Sam had experienced his share of domestic violence cases. During his first two years on the police force, they were the bulk of his cases—that and drunk drivers. He'd always tried to convince domestic violence victims to leave their abusers.

"Things have changed. You wouldn't understand. You aren't from here. There ain't no abused women's shelter no more. If they don't have a momma and daddy to take them in, they're gonna starve to death," Mark's wife said.

"It looks to me like they're already on their way to that. He ain't provided enough food to make it worth them getting beat on," Mark said.

"If you think you can do better, you take them. I'm done with them." The man got up and took off walking. When the woman and girl tried to follow, he stomped his foot at them like they were dogs. "Get! I told you I'm done with you two. Now get! Leave me the hell alone."

The mother and daughter stood in the roadway holding each other. Sam took a step toward them, but then realized he wasn't a cop any longer, and Mark's wife was right, there was no battered women's shelter to refer them to.

Mark's wife ran to them. She put her arm around the woman's shoulder. "You got people nearby?"

"No," the woman said.

"Where they at?"

"In Spartanburg, South Carolina." The woman broke down in tears. "All I got here is him and his kin."

"We can go to Memaw and Papaw's house, Momma," the young girl said.

She nodded and took her daughter's hand. Before leaving, the young girl turned to Isaiah. "I'm sorry my daddy did that. I told him it wasn't you, but he said you were the only boy on this road, so it had to be you."

"I'm sorry that something bad like that happened to you," Isaiah said.

"I wasn't raped. After Daddy came into our barn and caught me with Darin, Darin took off running across the field so fast Daddy couldn't get a good look at him in the dark. I love him and he loves me, but his daddy says he's too young to get married. I couldn't tell my daddy who he was, or he'd kill him."

"I hope it works out for you two," Isaiah said.

All that because she couldn't be honest with her father, thought Sam.

Mark walked back toward the barn, wiping blood from his knuckles. "Anyway, I had just gotten the old Power Wagon started before all of that."

"I heard. I can't believe you got her running."

"I ain't said she's roadworthy yet. I just got the engine to run smoothly. I gotta find some new belts. She's gonna need some tires and someone willing to give up diesel—that's gonna be even harder to find."

"Can I show her to Tumbleweed?"

"Tumbleweed? What kind of name is that?" A look of recognition crossed Mark's face. "Oh, you're one of those A.T. hikers."

"I am… was," Tumbleweed said.

"We'll let's go take a look at the old Dodge, Tumbleweed."

Becky and Moondust were plucking feathers from a turkey when Sam and Tumbleweed returned from the Titus farm.

"You ladies bagged a turkey," Tumbleweed said. "We should dry some for our hike."

Becky looked at Sam.

"Mark Titus got the Power Wagon started. He still has some work to do before it can make the trip to Unicoi though."

Becky looked away.

"I still want you to come with me. I know we haven't talked about it in a while, but you'd be more than welcome to come stay with my family in Unicoi. You all would."

Becky pursed her lips. "I've been thinking about going home. I'm worried about my momma."

"We're planning to take Interstate 26. You said it was just before the border with Tennessee, right?" Sam asked.

"About fifteen miles from the interstate. I can't ask you to go out of your way. I know you want to get home to your family," Becky said.

Sam took her hand. "Don't be ridiculous. After all you've done to keep me alive and fed, I owe you a ride home to your family. It's settled then. We will drop you off at your momma's near Shelton Laurel Creek."

He owed her his life. If she hadn't come along when she did, he would have bled out right there in the forest, and he would never have made it to Doctor Hammond's place.

"I need to go back to my apartment and get some things before we leave," Becky said.

Tumbleweed and Moondust filled their water bottles and went through their hiking packs, going over what they might need for their hike from Unicoi to New England.

"I really wish we could hit one of the outfitter stores. I could use a new sleeping bag. The one I have is rated for forty degrees. I mailed my winter bag home after we hit Virginia. It's going to be cold as hell sleeping on the ground once we get farther north this fall," Moondust said.

"You really should consider taking the Power Wagon. Months on the trail without the ability to resupply is just suicide. How will you feed yourselves?" Sam asked.

"I know how to hunt now. I got that turkey with the crossbow. Becky said I could take it with me," Moondust said.

"I wish you'd change your mind. I understand you want to get home to your families—I do too. But that's a long way to hike," Sam said.

Sam recalled all too well the starvation they'd all experienced on the trail, and he was an experienced hunter. They would have to spend the majority of their time looking for small game to have enough food for that leg of the hike.

"The offer stands for you all. We have a nice, safe compound at my place in Unicoi. There are trained security personnel, gardens, plenty of water, and lots of game in the mountains to sustain us all."

"Sounds very nice, but like you, we miss our families," Moondust said.

Sam understood. He ached for his family and the knowledge that he was getting close to being able to go home to them had his stomach doing somersaults.

TWENTY-FOUR

Lauren

Buffalo Mountain Medical Center
Unicoi, Tennessee
Day 23

After stopping at city hall, Lauren had learned through Millie that Ralph and his family were all at the medical center. It seemed his grandson had taken a turn for the worse, and Doctor Crabtree was treating him at the clinic.

Lauren opened the front door slowly and peeked inside. She could hear voices coming from one of the exam rooms. She paused, second-guessing as to whether now was the right time to approach Ralph about him stirring up discontent among some of the residents in his ward.

She was just about to close the door and return home when Ralph exited the exam room. His face was flushed. It was then that she noticed how much weight the man had lost. His blue Dickies work pants were bunched up at the waist where he'd cinched them. Somehow, they had to find a way to provide more food for those who couldn't hunt and fish to supplement what the town could provide.

Ralph's sons had been keeping his family supplied with fresh meat and fish, but the whole family was suffering with Levi's son at death's door.

"What's wrong?" Ralph asked as he entered the lobby. His eyes were red-rimmed.

Despite the animosity she and Ralph had experienced over the years since she'd been elected mayor, she felt genuine sympathy for the man.

"Nothing, well, nothing immediate. I'm sorry. This is a bad time. I'll talk to you later," she said, backing out the door.

He crossed the room and stopped the door before it closed all the way. "Lauren, what did you want to speak to me about?" He paused. "I need to feel useful; you know what I mean?"

She did. She very much did, though she mostly felt like nothing she did was enough. She was watching her town die, her father die, and all hope—die. She knew exactly what Ralph meant. It was why she was there instead of at her father's bedside.

"I had a visit from Ray Peters. He was quite upset and said he'd attended a meeting at your house, but we can address that later. You should be with your family."

Ralph stiffened, but it was barely detectable. He was good but not good enough. If Lauren hadn't had experience with body language from her time as a defense attorney, she wouldn't have noticed he was trying to hide something.

"I've had residents in my ward and all the other wards climbing up my ass ever since we voted on those new criminal laws." He stepped outside and let the door close behind him.

"He said you were proposing raising the matter again and retaking the vote after allowing citizens time to comment. Normally, I'd be all for that. You know I've always advocated for the people to be heard. But this time, well… it's too critical. The vocal minority cannot dictate the rules here. This is about the survival not only of the town but of individuals and families."

Ralph looked back over his shoulder. "Some are having a hard time seeing it that way."

Lauren stepped closer, and threw her shoulders back and chin up. She was four inches shorter than Ralph, and there was no way she could physically intimidate the man, but she wanted him to know she wasn't afraid of him.

"Whatever differences we have, whatever power play you're attempting, this is not the time. You want to be mayor. I get it. As soon as we get through this crisis, go for it. Run against me. Hell, I may step aside and let you have the damn job. But, Ralph, turning citizen against citizen at a time when we need to be united is dangerous for us all."

Ralph's brow creased into deep furrows. He worked his jaw before responding. "I'm not the one acting like a dictator here, Lauren Taylor."

"Wallace."

"Huh?"

"Wallace. Lauren Wallace. I'm married to Sam Wallace."

Ralph smirked.

"Let's work together, Ralph. No one benefits from a civil war."

"A civil war? Do you think that's what's happening here? This is democracy. You and your lackeys in the police department are the ones subverting the will of the people." His expression darkened, and his eyes narrowed. "I'm not going to stand idle while you and your brother-in-law rob this town blind."

Lauren's hands balled into fists, and she took two steps closer. "I'm robbing the town blind? I am. I…" She decided Ralph Cross was not worth it. He knew she wasn't taking anything from the town's food and water supply. He was trying to bait her into a fight. Why? What did he have to gain?

"Is that what you're telling your constituents? Is that the bull-shit you're feeding anyone who will listen? You know well and good that I have taken nothing from the town. My salary, such as it was, always went back into the town budget. I haven't received a single morsel of food from the distribution center. Not one noodle. Not one can of corn."

"How is that, Lauren? How is it you have presented no vouchers at all to the center? Are you taking yours and enough for your brother-in-law's militia when the center is closed for the night?"

Lauren glared at him. She heard her father's voice in her head. "Don't give in to bullies, Lauren Michelle. Be the bigger person and walk away."

She had. When she was younger, and her father was mayor of Unicoi, she'd done just that—even when Lindsay got her involved in a fight with the popular girls in middle school. She'd walked away because she hadn't wanted to tarnish the family name and embarrass her dad.

Bill wasn't the mayor of Unicoi now, she was, and after leaving Tennessee to attend college, she'd discovered her voice and stood up to grown-up bullies like Ralph—in college and her law career. She wasn't about to back down and leave Ralph Cross to destroy the town. Not on her watch.

"There is an inventory done every single day. Every day. There are guards posted at the doors. No one ever goes in after hours. Never!"

He'd know all that if he ever showed up at the meetings.

"The foxes are guarding the hen house."

"Then bring in your people, Ralph. Let them do an audit. Let them be there when the jars of pickles are counted. Let them track who gets rabbit and who gets squirrel for their rations that day. I'm sure the folks at the distribution center would love to have volunteers help with the ledger and counting vouchers."

He stammered at the challenge.

"Show up yourself, Ralph. Show up and see what comes in and what goes out. There's not much left. It should be easy to count.

You personally verifying that the process is fair would go a long way to settle those rumors."

"I don't have time. I have family issues here that—"

"My father is dying, Ralph. I'm here talking to you. I'm here because this town needs someone to lead it, or it will fall." She stepped back and uncurled her fingers. "We aren't enemies. We're on the same side. We do have enemies though. Unicoi is in Corbin's crosshairs. We must be united if we intend to repel or defeat them."

"I heard you had a visit from the Johnson City manager," Ralph deflected.

"They're claiming more territory than they're entitled. They insinuated we were poaching game from within their borders."

"Were we?"

"Not Cody and the official hunting team, but I don't doubt our residents are going wherever they can to find food. I can't control that."

"Wars have been fought over less."

"I understand that, but we have no jurisdiction to tell them they can't hunt or fish outside city limits."

"What about the ranger?"

Lauren considered it. Did he? Did the forest ranger have the authority to regulate hunting in the mountains outside Unicoi? That would solve the issue for those who still respected the rule of law, but would hunger outweigh that?

"I'll make a note to talk to Jack about it," Lauren said. With his law enforcement background, Jack, the ranger, had joined the security team. He'd abandoned the ranger station a few days after the EMP.

"I want us to work through our issues, Ralph. I welcome your honesty. Talk to me if you have an issue with how I'm handling things. Let's come to some understanding. Let's have a working meeting like we used to and hash it out. Yell if necessary. You did before. We both want what's best for the town." She didn't fully believe that, but she was holding out the olive branch, angry as she was, so she went with it.

Ralph glanced through the medical center window toward where his grandson lay dying. He was a devoted family man—that was plain to see. Somehow she had to get him to understand that working together was vital to his family's survival. She wished she could settle once and for all whether he had ties to the Corbins and if he was the source of the leak to them. If Ralph was working with the Corbins to destroy the town from within, Lauren wouldn't hesitate to end him. Doing so without proof would likely cause a split that could kill the town.

She needed Sam home. He would know how to find out if the Cross family were spies for the enemy.

"I'll talk to Jack and see if there's anything he can do about people hunting within Johnson City's limits. I'll also tell Millie to open the food bank's books to you and any of your constituents who want to view them."

"I'll send Heather Michaelson from the bank over to city hall. She's done audits before. I'll have her do a report and address my folks. I can't guarantee that will satisfy them though, Lauren. They're hungry. Some children are going to bed hungry. You wouldn't know what that is like, but as a parent and grandparent, it's devastating."

Lauren didn't know. She had Charlie, but he wasn't going without. He might not have extra food, but Sam and Vince had ensured that those who took refuge inside the compound boundary would not starve.

"I am doing all this for the kids, Ralph. If there's more we can do to provide for them, then tell me—please tell me. I will do it. I'll do whatever it takes. I just don't know…" Lauren choked up and turned away, not wanting her adversary to see her cry.

Why am I so freaking emotional all the time?

It was so unlike her. She had never before been one to not have control over her emotions. She chalked it up to the apocalypse, her father's illness, and not knowing where her husband was.

Suck it up, Lauren. Pull yourself together, girl.

"Honestly, Lauren, I think some of these people just won't be saved."

"What?"

"They're too soft."

"Everyone is working so hard to survive. What do you mean, too soft."

"Not everyone. They're the problem. I heard that only about ten percent of the laborers in the fields are actually doing a full day's work. You've got people taking breaks as if they work for the union."

Lauren had been too busy to police the folks in charge of the community gardens. She'd left that to people with much more experience in the area. The Johnson & Carter Farms and the Stephens' Farm Market had managed migrant workers to pick their crops and deliver them to markets all over the United States for nearly fifty years. Why would she suddenly doubt their managers' ability to supervise field workers now?"

"I'll address that with the agricultural manager. I'll go out there now and check on things. I can tell you this: if people are slacking off and skirting their duties in the field, they will be docked and lose vouchers. We can't have that—not when lives depend on productivity."

TWENTY-FIVE

Becky

Becky's Apartment
Franklin, Tennessee
Day 23

What to take and what to leave behind was an enormous decision. It was almost too difficult. How do you pare your life down to what will fit in a suitcase? Becky knew for a fact that she would never return to the apartment she'd once shared with the love of her life. Never. Whatever she could pack into a suitcase or her backpack now was everything that she would be able to keep from her former life. Until that moment, staring into the closet where Darrell's clothes still hung, she hadn't realized she was stuck in place. She'd stayed in Franklin because that was where they'd lived and loved. Leaving Franklin was like losing Darrell all over again; the man she'd loved with all her being was never coming back.

Becky removed things from drawers and then put them back—they weren't practical to bring with her. Becky removed one of Darrell's long-sleeved white shirts from the closet, wrapped it around her shoulders, and breathed in deep, hoping for his smell. He'd worn it to church the day before he left for Fort Hood and then on from there to Afghanistan. Becky had slept in that shirt for two weeks after she'd received the news he'd been killed in Afghanistan.

Darrell's scent was gone from its fabric now. She could dash a splash or two of his favorite cologne onto it, but would it be the same? Becky reached out and stroked down the length of her husband's old, worn ACUs. He'd kept them to wear hunting. Below them were his old jungle boots, worn out from road marches and months of zero-dark-thirty PT while stationed at Fort Campbell, Kentucky.

How could she leave all of Darrell's things behind? They were all she had left of him. Becky lowered herself onto the bed they'd shared.

Maybe I should stay.

The Hammonds needed her, after all. They were in their seventies. They couldn't hunt, fish, and forage for wild plants. Could she leave them?

That was the first time Becky truly missed home since leaving Shelton Laurel. Her mother was sixty-nine. What about her? What about Aunt Sylvia and her disabled cousin Marcus? Didn't they need her?

Home. She was going home. She had to go home.

Becky closed the closet door. None of what was inside would help her or anyone else survive what they were experiencing now. Mementos were from another time. She'd have to carry her memories of her life with Darrell in her heart because there wasn't room for all his belongings in the old red Dodge the Titus family was giving Sam.

Her thoughts turned to the cabin in the woods of Shelton Laurel where she'd grown up. She imagined life there wouldn't be much different than now. Her family had always struggled for enough to eat. That's where she'd learned to hunt, trap and fish.

Electricity was a luxury her folks couldn't afford, so their water had always been drawn from the spring out back. She'd known lots of mountain folk without indoor plumbing. She was the one who had grown soft with her internet, flush toilet, and fast food.

Becky inhaled deeply and let it out. She was no longer ashamed of where she came from. She was going home, and for the first time in years, she was looking forward to returning to her roots.

Becky came from a long line of survivors. She'd return to folks who knew how to live in the mountains and provide for their families. They'd come to the Blue Ridge Mountains from Maryland. They'd carved their way through the forest, built cabins, planted crops, and eked out a living from the land.

After finally selecting a few items from her apartment and gathering what clothing she needed, Becky backed out the door, locked it, and pocketed the key. She turned and came face to face with a man twice her height.

"Hey, there, little lady. What's in the bags?"

The man's breath was rancid, and Becky almost vomited.

"Clothes," she said, fingering the KA-BAR in a sheath attached to her right thigh. Normally, Becky would have given the man the bag and run away, avoiding confrontation. But these weren't normal times, and the things inside her suitcase and the pack on her back were the most precious items on earth to her. Were they worth dying for? She thought about that as the man ran his hand down her arm and toward her breast.

"Sir, I would advise you to remove your hand from my person and step away."

He chuckled and looked back at his companions, who were waiting at the bottom of the stairs.

The railing around the small landing leading to her garage apartment was loose. Becky knew if she shoved the man hard enough, he'd fall right through it to the ground, but she'd still have to contend with his three friends below.

Four against one. She'd have to lessen the odds somehow—starting with the perv stroking her arm.

Slowly, she removed the knife from its sheath. Becky smiled as the man ran his fingers up her neck and wrapped them around the hairs at the back of her skull. As he pulled her close, their eyes locked. That's when she drew her knife and pushed it into his gut, just under his rib cage, twisting and driving it up into his heart. He barely made a sound.

Becky peered around him to his friends at the bottom of the stairs. They had their backs to her, looking off toward the outfitter store where she'd once been an employee before the lights went out.

Twisting the knife and driving it deeper into the man's chest, Becky whispered in his ear as he slumped forward, putting all his weight upon her. "See you in hell, prick." He slid down her leg and crumpled to the floor of the landing before his friends even noticed.

A tall skinny dude in shorts and a T-shirt pointed and then poked the guy next to him. "What the hell happened?" the second man asked.

"I don't know. I think you should go get help. He just passed out. He might need a doctor or something."

It didn't work. The three men started up the stairs. Becky was trapped. She could unlock the door and run inside, but what then? She'd have to jump out a two-story window to escape them. She couldn't run. She had to fight. She had to kill these men before they killed her.

Becky swung her rifle around from her back and fired at the first man coming up the stairs. He slumped onto the fourth tread blocking the progression of the other two men, giving her time to set up her second and third shots. After firing a second time, the other two men returned fire, forcing Becky to dive toward the railing, suitcase in hand. It wobbled a second before it gave way, sending her crashing to the ground. Fortunately, she landed on top of her luggage.

The wind was knocked out of her, but she grabbed her suitcase, tossed it under the stairs, and rolled into the space underneath the men. She got to her feet, grabbed her bag and stumbling twice, she ran behind the bushes along the side of the garage to the corner of the building. Crawling on all fours, Becky dragged her suitcase as she followed the back of the garage to the corner of the house. She crouched and then ran to the house next door.

She was sprinting across the adjacent street by the time the two men rounded the garage. She ducked out of sight behind the check cashing store. Becky pressed her back against the brick building, inhaling and exhaling quickly, but trying to catch her breath. The realization of what had just happened to her began to sink in. She reached down and touched her scabbard. She'd lost her knife. It was still lodged in the man's chest.

She leaned her head back against the wall and closed her eyes. Fury rose in her. Her brother had given her that knife. He'd taught her to skin rabbits and squirrels with it. Becky closed her eyes. Was it worth risking her life to go back to retrieve it?

Maybe.

As Becky walked up the Hammonds' driveway, she thought about all the violence she'd seen since the lights went out and imagined what her brother and husband must have experienced when they deployed to shit holes like Afghanistan. Her husband had been different after his first deployment. Now she knew why. Killing a man changed you. In some ways, she imagined it made it easier to kill again. She resolved that she would react much more swiftly the next time someone threatened her like that.

Sam was seated outside the barn with his leg up on a crate. She'd seen how quickly he reacted when threats arose. She hoped that whenever the time came again, she'd be able to do the same.

Becky put her suitcase, containing the two folded flags that had once draped her brother's and her husband's coffins, along with pictures of the two men in uniform, down on the ground and took a seat next to Sam.

"Are you okay?" he asked.

"Fine as frog hair," she replied. She was a survivor. Becky knew that now. She knew she would survive when others didn't, and even if one day it came down to it and she lost, Becky would know that she had never given in to fear. It wasn't in her DNA. She was a Shelton, after all, and they never backed down from a fight.

Sam pointed to her shoulder and stood. "You're bleeding."

Becky glanced to her left. Her blue top was stained with the man's blood. "It's not mine."

"What happened? Are you sure you're okay? Maybe we should have the doc look at you," Sam said, taking Becky's hand.

Becky looked Sam in the eyes. "I killed two men."

At first, Sam didn't say anything, but then he stood, bent down, and wrapped his arms around her shoulders. "I'm sorry."

"I had to."

"We do what we have to do."

"I didn't recognize them. They weren't with that group of tourists or any of the other bands that have formed since the lights went out. These guys were new in town. What do you think that means?"

"It might mean people are coming out of the cities into the mountains looking for food," Sam said.

"I thought that would happen eventually," Becky said. "They best stay away from Madison County is all I can say."

"They might find quite a few folks on these rural roads not very welcoming," Sam said.

"It's a shame that now every stranger you meet is to be eyed as dangerous. That kinda narrows a girl's chances of finding a mate."

Sam chuckled. "Might not be a bad thing since you traded away your condoms."

Becky smiled. "True, dat."

Sam lowered himself slowly back into his chair.

"So, you're all packed and ready to go?"

"I'm so ready," Becky said.

Home. The word had new meaning for her now; home was no longer just where she lay her head at night. It was a place of safety and belonging. She knew that even though they'd fought before she left Shelton Laurel; under the circumstances, all would be forgotten.

Her kin would rally around and die to defend her, if necessary, and she would do the same for them as well. She relished that support in a way she'd never imagined before. She'd never known how rich she really was. She had a family.

TWENTY-SIX

Lauren

Stephens' Farm Market
Unicoi, Tennessee
Day 23

Lauren smiled as she passed by crates of zucchini, peppers, half-runner beans, yellow squash, cucumbers, broccoli, cauliflower, peppers, tomatoes, okra, and onions ready to be put on the horse-drawn wagons and taken to the food distribution center. They were blessed. Outside the guarded perimeter of Unicoi, many, many people were starving to death. That fact wasn't lost on her as she walked on in search of the field manager.

Stephens' Farm Market had been a commercial farm for over fifty years, employing hundreds of locals. As they grew, migrant workers from places like Honduras and El Salvador were brought in to help grow, harvest, and ship produce all over the United States.

Lauren located the Stephens' Farm Market field manager inside the old packinghouse building. He peeked out from behind a door to a storage room. "Mayor, what can I do for you?"

"I have a couple of questions, but finish what you were doing there."

"We're running low on crates and boxes. I'm improvising with plastic storage totes, but it's still not enough. We're emptying them as fast as we can to get them back out to the fields. With so much being harvested at once, we have some people using pillowcases and anything else they can find, but that risks damaging the produce."

"Too much produce is a good problem to have." Lauren moved toward the roll-up doors to get some air. "I think you just answered the question I came to speak with you about. Ralph Cross had a complaint about people standing around in the fields. I knew there was a reasonable explanation. Please try to come up with something quickly so Ralph has nothing to complain about—at least as far as idle workers are concerned."

"I'll do my best, Mayor," the field manager said.

Lauren stepped outside the packinghouse, stopped, and wrapped her ponytail up into a bun, relishing the fresh breeze on the back of her neck. How she longed for the return of air conditioning. As she stood there, she listened to the workers in the nearby field. Their chatter warmed her heart. They were talking about their families and how their gardens were growing—not about how hungry they were or who had died the night before. Lauren had expected many of them to perish in the first couple of weeks after the lights went out, but they turned out to be more resilient than she had thought. What a difference a week made.

Several piercing screams brought her back down to earth with a thud. Lauren ran as fast as she could toward the sound of the cries for help. They appeared to be coming from the direction of the former produce market's parking lot. After rounding the corner of the building, Lauren stopped in her tracks at the sight of a mound of tangled people on the ground.

"Stop! Stop! You're going to kill him. He's bleeding. Stop, please!" Marie Morales yelled.

The man on top wasn't listening. Marie grabbed the back of his shirt and pulled, but the man swung back and landed a blow to the side of Marie's face, knocking her off balance. As he did, Lauren got her first glimpse of the person on the ground beneath the attacker.

"Benny!" Unholstering her revolver, Lauren closed the distance between her and the fighting men. "Stop. Let him go or I will shoot you!" Lauren shouted.

"Lauren! No!" Benny yelled.

The man released his grip on Benny's uniform shirt and straightened, his right hand still balled into a fist above his head. "Come on, Madam Mayor. Shoot me. I dare you. Shoot me and see what happens."

Is he stupid? Does he have a death wish? She was pointing her revolver directly at him. *She had a clean shot, yet he taunted her?* He lunged for her weapon.

Lauren squeezed the trigger, the revolver thundered, and a bullet struck the man in the chest mid-stride. He stood there with a look of shock on his face as the others dispersed. For a moment, Lauren thought maybe the bullet hadn't hit him. He reached and touched the wound in his chest. "You just unleashed the hounds of hell," the man said as he dropped to his knees.

"Lauren!" Benny shouted. "We need him alive!"

Lauren focused on the man's hands. As his right hand moved back toward his boot, Lauren fired again and again until the guy fell face first to the pavement. Lauren rushed over and placed her foot on his wrist just inches from the stub-nosed revolver he'd pulled from his boot.

"If you move so much as an eyelash, I'm putting a bullet in your brain," Lauren said. She watched for several seconds. The man didn't move.

Lauren moved toward Benny. He was standing now and searching the ground for something.

"We were fighting over control of my service pistol. He knocked it from my hand, and I kicked it."

"Who the hell is he? I've never seen him before," Lauren said.

Benny spotted his pistol at the edge of the parking lot and rushed over to retrieve it. After he inspected the weapon, he holstered it and returned to the body on the ground. He rolled him over onto his back. "He's one of Corbin's men."

"Which Corbin?"

"Nigel Corbin," Marie said.

"What's he doing here?" Lauren asked.

"He thought he could blend in with the workers," Marie said.

"As a spy?"

"He was asking too many questions," Marie said. "One of the workers got suspicious."

"What did he learn, and what did he mean that I was unleashing the hounds of hell?"

"I don't know. The field workers didn't know much sensitive information to tell him. They aren't on the security teams. He asked where all the food was going and how much produce they were picking in the other fields around town."

"Sounds like a spy to me," Lauren said.

"Yep!" Marie said.

Lauren pulled Benny aside and whispered, "Ronnie didn't say anything about Nigel sending this guy?"

"She knew they'd sent spies to try to breach our defenses but hadn't learned if anyone made it through," Benny whispered back.

"We need to find out how many more of them are in town. I think it's time to turn the tables on Nigel," Lauren said, walking back over to the dead man.

"I'll have Mayberry and his team do a search of the workers and the people at the warehouse to see if they can spot anyone they don't know," Benny said.

"You should go to the clinic and get checked out first," Lauren said, pointing to the cut above Benny's eye.

"I'm fine."

"Yeah? You don't look fine. Let Marie drive you to the clinic. I'll get someone to deal with this body," Lauren said.

"Really, I'm fine. I have a first aid kit in the truck. I need to speak with Mayberry and get him started looking for more spies, then speak with my guys about how this asshole got into town," Benny said.

"I'll ride with you. I want to see how things are proceeding along our northern border. We may have to pull people off there and have them work on making the southern border more secure," Lauren said.

They all knew that the perimeter was porous and would be next to impossible to secure against a single person coming in by foot.

TWENTY-SEVEN

Lauren

North Unicoi Drive Checkpoint
Unicoi, Tennessee
Day 23

As Benny drove through town, Lauren waved to residents walking to work in the fields. She took note of how thin they were, even though much more produce had been coming out of the fields lately. Could someone be taking it before it reached the distribution center? She'd need to talk to the field managers and find out how their inventory was kept. From what she saw being loaded, there shouldn't be any shortages. She needed to pay closer attention to people's physical condition. If someone was stealing produce before it reached the distribution center, they'd look different from those poor workers trudging off for their day in the fields.

"Benny, could you spare Officer Bradshaw for a special mission?"

He looked at her quizzically. "I can," he said questioningly. "What do you need him to do?"

"I want to know if someone is stealing food from the cargo wagons that take food from the fields to the warehouse."

"You have reason to suspect that's happening?"

"It's merely a hunch at this point, but what I saw coming out of the fields and onto those wagons was enough that..." She pointed at Melanie Porter and her three preteen children on the sidewalk as they passed them. "That they should not look like that. There should be more than enough to feed everyone."

"I'll have him start by checking the inventory coming out of the farms and then matching that to the one at the distribution center."

"That would be a good place to start. Could you have him check the cashed food vouchers? If I'm right, someone isn't cashing in the ones for produce, but they're in line for their meat and water rations."

"That's good detective work there, Lauren. You picked up a few things from..." Benny stopped as if saying his name was taboo.

Sam.

Yes, it hurt to hear his name, and it reminded her he wasn't there with her, but she didn't want to erase him from everyone's memory.

"We used to discuss his cases at the end of the day. It helped him to transition from work to home." She and Sam would go over anything that was troubling him about whatever case he was working on at the time. Most often, just saying it all out loud was enough for the pieces to fall into place, and he'd know what he needed to do next.

Benny cleared his throat. "He'll be home soon."

Everyone said that. But, as the hours and days passed, it became harder and harder for Lauren to believe.

∾

When the truck neared the checkpoint, one of the guards waved frantically to catch their attention.

"What is it?" Benny asked.

"We have a car coming this way."

Benny jumped out and began barking orders at the guards posted on top of the container wall. Lauren exited the vehicle and took cover behind one of the concrete Jersey barriers along the street.

"They've stopped about two hundred yards out from the wall."

"You got the shot, Sid?" Benny called up to the man lying prone on the top of the container with his rifle aimed at the car.

"I got it, but they're waving a white flag out the driver's side window," Sid said.

"Any weapons?" Benny asked.

"Wait one," Sid said.

"A trick?" Lauren asked.

"Could be," Benny said. "We're not taking any chances."

"They're holding their hands out the windows showing they're not holding weapons," Sid said. "I think State Senator Phelps is in the passenger seat."

"You know that for sure?" Lauren asked.

"Not one hundred percent. I only met him one time. He lives in Johnson City, and he brought his wife's car into my shop for repairs," Sid said.

State Senator Ryan Phelps had only visited Unicoi a handful of times. The last time was a year before when he was promoting new legislation in an attempt to make human trafficking a Class A felony with mandatory sentencing requirements.

"I'm surprised he's still alive and kicking," Benny said.

"Me too. He wasn't exactly one of Preston Corbin's favorite people," Lauren said.

"I'd be interested to know how he managed to avoid the same fate as District Attorney Coleman. They worked together to change the law specifically to go after the Corbins."

"I'd like to find out myself, but what if it's a trick?" Lauren asked

"Sid, do you still see the security team?" Benny asked.

"No. If he has security, they must have fanned out before the car came into view." A second later, he said, "Wait, Richardson and Simpson are working their way up behind the vehicle."

A moment later, Simpson radioed that State Senator Ryan Phelps wanted to speak to the mayor.

"Where's the bull horn?" Lauren asked.

Benny and Alan Mayberry opened both doors to the container, and Lauren stood to one side, concealed from the sight of the vehicle's occupants.

"You in the vehicle. Keep your hands out the window. Do not move a muscle," Benny said.

"You still got them, Sid?" Alan asked.

"I've got a clear view of the passenger and the driver."

"Bravo Team, secure the vehicle," Benny said into the bull horn.

Lauren could hear Richardson shouting but not what he was saying.

"The driver is out of the vehicle," Sid called down. There was more shouting, and then Sid said, "The senator is out." A moment later, Sid called down, "The vehicle is clear, and the subjects have been searched."

Benny stepped into the shipping container's doorway. "Simpson, bring me the senator."

He smiled. "Hello, Mayor."

"What do you want, Phelps?" Lauren asked. "I don't have time for pleasantries. I have a lot of work to do. Why are you here?"

"We have a mutual enemy."

"Corbin. I know. What about him?" Lauren moved in closer so

she could see his face better. She needed to evaluate his body language to tell if this was a ruse.

"As you may know, I, along with District Attorney Coleman and others, have been working for some time to take down the Corbins."

"I'm aware of your work on the human trafficking laws. As the mayor of a town directly dealing with the issue, I was very supportive."

"I spoke to your husband, Sam, about the issue. I know you were frustrated with the speed at which the case was moving. Putting the new law and penalties in place was an important element. Otherwise, Coleman could have the Corbin family arrested, and even if convicted, they'd only be sentenced to a few years in prison. They deserve to spend the rest of their lives behind bars for what they've done."

"Nigel is free. Did you know that?" Lauren asked.

"I had heard."

"He killed Coleman," Lauren said.

"I know." Phelps hung his head. "May his soul rest in peace."

"How is it you've avoided the same fate?" Benny asked.

Phelps glanced up and briefly made eye contact with Benny. He looked him up and down and then turned his gaze to Lauren, addressing his answer to her. "I've been in hiding since the lights went out. Corbin sent his goons for me the second day. A member of my security team was killed, but I slipped away."

"Where have you been since?" Lauren asked.

He licked his bottom lip and shifted his weight. He was about to lie. "With a friend."

"Where is that?" Benny asked.

"A cabin up on Watauga Lake."

"What do you want from Unicoi?" Lauren asked.

"Help."

"What kind of help?" Benny asked.

Phelps turned his back on Benny and stepped toward Lauren. His disrespect for the chief of police was pissing her off.

"I'm sorry, maybe you haven't met. This is Benny Jameson, our new chief of police," Lauren said.

Phelps' eyes shifted from Lauren to Benny. "What happened to Avery."

"Our resident human trafficker, Billy Mahon, killed him. It seems that was how he handled internal personnel problems."

"Avery was working for Mahon?"

"He was working for the Corbins. We found evidence in his office after his demise," Benny said.

"I misjudged him. So did Coleman."

"That was the plan," Lauren said.

"What kind of help do you want from the people of Unicoi, Senator," Benny asked.

"To join forces. Sort of a mutual aid arrangement."

"I'm tired of talking in circles, Ryan. What do you want?" Lauren asked.

"We want to hit Corbin and his compatriots and take them out."

"Who is this we?" Lauren asked.

"Some of the Johnson City folks, a group from Elizabethton, and a small faction from Jonesborough."

"How many?" Benny asked.

"Seventy-five or so."

"How many does Corbin have supporting him?"

"Two hundred, but not all are fighters. A lot of them would avoid a conflict."

"Let me see if I understand you correctly. You want Unicoi to send fighters to join you in a war against Corbin and his army on his home turf?"

"War? No!" Phelps said as if Benny was accusing him of treason. "This will be a proper police action. I don't want him killed if we can avoid it. I still want him to stand trial. We need to stop his reign of terror in our region."

"Police action? What agency is leading this operation?"

"Mark Sever with the Tennessee Bureau of Investigations and members of their SWAT team."

"Why are you recruiting if TBI is conducting the raid?"

"They're a little short on personnel at the moment."

Benny and Lauren looked at one another.

"How many trained officers do they have with them?"

"Twelve."

"Twelve? You plan to go into Corbin's gated community and drag him out with twelve officers?"

"No, not just twelve." Phelps turned to Lauren. "We also have volunteers who are willing to join under the direction of the TBI's SWAT team. He has secured his neighborhood with under three dozen armed men and women."

Lauren's mind swirled, considering a world without the threat from Preston Corbin. She'd go after him herself if she could, but she had Charlie to think about.

"I can ask for volunteers, Phelps, but I'm not sure how many will want to leave the safety of their homes to join you," Lauren said.

"I'd appreciate it if you'd let them know how important it is to neutralize Corbin and his henchmen. They haven't directly challenged Unicoi yet, but they will—and soon. They're running out of resources. Corbin will become desperate. When he runs out of food to feed the people protecting him and stealing for him, he's going to want what you have here."

Phelps didn't know that day had already come—and that she and Benny had just taken out one of Nigel's spies. Convincing Unicoi citizens to join in Phelps' battle when they and their families had yet to be affected would likely be a hard sell. "I'll make the pitch," she said.

As Phelps turned to leave, Lauren grabbed his arm. Ryan, have you heard from Nashville? FEMA? Anyone?"

His face was sullen. "Nashville is mostly in ashes. FEMA tried to roll out something resembling a recovery center at the Expo Center, but they were quickly overrun. There weren't enough workers to efficiently handle the number of people needing help. The center in Knoxville lost all food and supplies in less than four hours, and when it was all gone, the crowd was so angry they burned down the building and then moved south to downtown. Knoxville, too, is in ashes now."

"I was there the first two days. People were in shock for the most part," Lauren said.

"Good thing you got out. It got really bad about that second week when people realized after waiting that long for help, even FEMA couldn't do anything."

"That's what I thought, but I still had a thread of hope the feds would be doing something," Lauren said.

"The governor is trying to put something together, but they're focused on the big cities at this point. He flat out said the rural areas were on their own for now."

"You talked to him?"

"I was in Nashville at the capitol building the first few days after the lights went out. We were trying to figure out what the hell had happened and trying to reach the feds and get guidance. Then the mobs and rioting started, and we had to flee. I came home," Phelps said.

"Your family?" Lauren was almost afraid to ask. She'd heard what Nigel had done to Coleman's wife and children.

"Thankfully, they made it to our lake house. My father-in-law got them out within hours after the EMP took down the power grid."

"That's good," Lauren said.

"And your family?"

Lauren's throat tightened. She swallowed hard and looked away. "They're fine," she lied. She didn't want to give away any information in case this was some trick by Corbin.

"Great! Great! Good to hear." Phelps turned to face Benny. "How about your family, officer? Is your family alright?"

"My family's fine."

Lauren detected a small hitch in Benny's voice. He had no idea how his family was. They were all a thousand miles away from Unicoi.

Phelps nodded, then turned to Lauren. "So, you'll put out our call for volunteers?"

"I will. How will they contact you?"

Phelps reached into his back pocket and produced a small Tennessee flag. He held it out to Lauren, and she took it. "Hang this on the outside of this shipping container, and my folks will know you have volunteers. Mark Sever with SWAT will contact you, Chief." He turned to Benny. "We need to take out Preston Corbin. No one's safe until he's gone."

Lauren agreed. She just wasn't willing to order her people to put themselves on the line without more information—information she intended to ask Vince to gather. If there was going to be some tactical operation against Johnson City, Vince was the one who could ascertain whether it was a fool's errand.

TWENTY-EIGHT

Lauren
___

Wallace Survival Compound
Unicoi, Tennessee
Day 23

Vince listened skeptically to Lauren explaining State Senator Phelps' visit, then shook his head. That was about how she had expected him to react.

"You know how I feel about politicians," Vince said.

"I'm a politician. You're painting with a pretty broad brush. He's still the enemy of our enemy," Lauren said.

"Doesn't mean you can trust him."

"But it's in our best interests if Corbin and the group protecting him are brought down. That will leave only Nigel and his henchmen to our south to worry about."

"I agree it would be good for Corbin to be taken out. What I'm saying is, I'm not sure this senator and whoever he's rounded up to do the job are capable of executing such a mission."

Lauren smiled.

"No!" Vince said.

"What? I didn't ask anything."

"Yes, you did. You just didn't use words," Vince said.

"You're mind reading?" Lauren studied his face. He and Sam looked a lot alike. She wondered whether Charlie would look just like them when he got older.

"You want me to volunteer. You want me to say I'll go talk to this senator and help plan their operation. I won't. I won't do that, Lauren. I have an obligation here—to these people—the people Sam and I recruited."

"What if you just advised and didn't get involved in the actual attack."

"You are seriously thinking of sending a group from Unicoi?" Vince asked.

"Maybe—if you were to help with the planning. Mark Sever is leading this operation with a small SWAT team. That could be done, right? Like the SEAL team that took out Bin Laden?"

Vince leaned back in his chair and ran a hand over his growing beard. "Lauren, you're killing me." He adjusted his ball cap several times, finally removing it and placing it on the desk next to the list he was compiling of ham radios still operating around Tennessee, North Carolina, and Georgia.

"I'll talk to Mark and the leader of his special weapons and tactics team. After meeting with Sever and the SWAT team leader, I'll be able to tell pretty quickly whether this mission stands a chance of succeeding."

Lauren walked over and threw her arms around his neck. "Thank you, brother. It means a lot to me."

"I'm not committing to do anything other than to talk to Mark. He and Sam were friends. If he thinks there's a chance and wants to talk tactics, I might offer up a few suggestions."

"I love you, Vince. I appreciate this," Lauren said, turning to go. She stopped at the doorway. "Thanks for looking out for Charlie."

"My pleasure. I love spending time with my nephew."

After leaving Vince with all the wheels in his head turning, Lauren headed back to Alan's truck. Passing by the garden, Lauren stopped to watch Maggie Russo sitting with her two children on the edge of the garden picking beans. Her little boy was strapped to her back with some sort of cloth wrap. Lauren was mesmerized by the interaction between this mother and her children.

Lauren's childhood memories came flooding in about the times with her mother in their backyard garden. Edna was always so patient, kind, and soft-spoken back then—so different from Lauren.

"When will we see Memaw and Papaw Reynolds?" the little girl asked.

Maggie placed her hand on her daughter's shoulder. "I don't know, Charlotte. But what I do know is they love you so, so much, and when we do finally make it to Georgia to see them, they're going to be so very happy to see your smiling face."

The mention of Georgia sent daggers through Lauren's heart. This child's father may have harmed Sam down in Atlanta but in her heart, Lauren knew the little girl wasn't responsible for what her father had done. Lauren studied Maggie's face. The pain was evident, not unlike how Lauren had felt when discussing Charlie's concerns about his mother and sister.

Charlie rarely spoke of Sam. Lauren tried every chance she could to keep hope alive in Charlie's heart that Sam would come home, and that somehow he would see his mother and sister again.

Her stomach churned, and her breakfast threatened once again to force its way out of her stomach. Lauren couldn't imagine bringing a new life into this craziness. If it turned out that she was pregnant, how could she be there for a child and do what she needed to do to make sure everyone around her survived this awful apocalypse? It was as she had always known. She would not make a good mother—certainly not like Maggie Russo or Edna. Despite her best efforts, she lost the battle with her stomach's contents and raced over to a bush.

"Lauren?"

She spun to see Lindsay standing behind her.

"Are you alright?"

"Fine," she said. "It's just a little warm today." Lauren unclipped her water bottle from her pack and took a sip. "I think I'm a little dehydrated, is all."

"You want me to ride back to town with you?" Lindsay asked.

Lauren smiled. She was considering saying no, but Lindsay looked so eager. "Sure, Mom and Dad will be thrilled to see you."

She glanced back over her shoulder before sliding into the driver's seat of Alan's pickup. Maggie was on her feet now, her daughter's hand in hers. Lauren pictured herself and Sam walking through Buffalo Creek Park, each holding the hand of their little girl or boy. Sam was an amazing father.

Maggie waved. Little Charlotte smiled a huge smile, and her tiny arm swung back and forth. Maggie picked her up and kissed her cheek. For the first time since Lauren had learned Lindsay's little sister was a Russo, hate didn't fill her heart. She remembered the little girl who had pestered her and Lindsay when they were having sleepovers, working on their cheer routines, and when they were on double dates. Lindsay's parents had insisted they drag Maggie along. Now Maggie was a wonderful, loving momma. Lauren smiled and returned the gesture.

On the ride back to town, Lauren had been so deep in thought about her visit with the state senator and his plan to take out Preston Corbin that she hadn't seen the men on the side of the road.

"Lauren!" Lindsay shouted.

"What?"

Lauren stomped on the gas, intending to speed past them, but the taller of the three men ran into the roadway. Lauren reacted by swerving into the opposite lane, and her left tire slipped off the blacktop and onto a narrow gravel shoulder. As Lauren eased it back onto the asphalt, the other two men stepped into her pathway.

Lindsay had her pistol unholstered and was leaning toward the window. "Wait, Lindsay. That's Tom Christy and his boys."

Lauren slowed the truck to a stop five feet in front of the old mountain man. He stuck his left hand inside the pocket of his hunter's overalls. On the right, he held his rifle, the barrel balancing on his shoulder.

"Howdy, Mayor," Tom said.

His eldest son bobbed his head in her direction. "Morning." Dangling around his knees were two dead rabbits.

"You caught breakfast, I see," Lauren said, climbing down from the truck. She glanced back at Lindsay. "Stay with the truck and watch our six."

"We didn't see much this morning," his youngest son said.

"Game's getting scarce already. Too many people have to rely on wild game to survive now. It puts a lot of pressure on animals in the area," Lauren said.

"It doesn't help none that those Johnson City folks keep stomping through our woods shooting at anything that moves."

"Have you seen them?"

"They're everywhere."

"Cody and his team were going up by Lost Cove to see if they can find anything there," Lauren said.

"He likely won't see much there either. I'm telling you; it seems like every person up in Johnson City with a gun is out hunting," Tom said.

"That is concerning."

"Not just for the loss of game, but for our safety. Those idiots shoot into a moving bush without even knowing what's in there," Tom said.

"We had an old boy shoot our beagle a few days ago," Tom's son said.

"It's dangerous out there for sure," Lauren said. This was a concern Cody had already shared with her. They'd been talking about pushing farther toward the border with North Carolina, away from the cities. But it would be a very long haul to bring the meat back. They risked getting attacked by bears and mountain lions, and there was a possibility the meat would spoil before they could get it home.

"You coming from the gun range?" Tom asked.

"We are. I was visiting my stepson. He's visiting out there for a few days." She lied. She couldn't tell him about the state senator's visit or the attack that was being planned on Corbin and his men.

"We've been thinking about going up there and talking to Vince about ways we can secure our place and maybe work together."

Tom's place was across the hollow from the Wallace property. There was extremely rough terrain between their farms. Lauren imagined it would be good to know in advance if there was trouble on the ridge that might threaten the compound.

"Vince and his guys know their stuff. I'll let him know you're interested the next time I come out." She didn't want to tell him she visited every day to care for her garden and animals, not that she had any particular reason to believe they posed a danger to her. She wouldn't be standing there talking to them now if she had, but if they said anything to the wrong people, it might be bad for her.

TWENTY-NINE

Charlie

_____

Wallace Survival Compound
Unicoi, Tennessee
Day 23

"Are you avoiding me, Charlie Brown?" Startled, Charlie spun around to face Casey. They hadn't spoken much since their first meeting in Knoxville the day of the EMP. They'd traveled together back to Unicoi, and he'd been at the compound for almost a week, but they'd barely seen each other.

"No," Charlie said. His palms started to sweat, and he wiped them on his jeans.

"Could've fooled me."

"I…" he stammered.

"I saw your mom the other day."

Charlie knew she meant Lauren, but the word mom caused an uneasy feeling in the pit of his stomach. His mother was in Ohio with his little sister, and he wasn't sure when he'd see them again. After Dad gets home, he'll take me. He kept telling himself this.

"I was going to ask her how things were in town, but she looked busy," Casey said.

"Yeah, she's pretty busy. As far as I know, things are pretty good, considering. Of course, they don't tell me much. I'm hoping to get to go see my grandparents again soon. Maybe you can come if you'd like."

"That would be nice. I haven't left the compound since I got here." Casey cupped her hand near his face and leaned in close to whisper in his ear. He could smell the shampoo in her hair. It was nice.

"It's boring here. I'm not ungrateful—I'm very glad to have been allowed to be here, but all we do is work or listen to the grown-ups play the fiddle and sing bluegrass music."

"I know. I miss movies, music, and video games myself. I have some books from home if you'd like to borrow one."

She flipped her ponytail over her shoulder and stepped back. "No, I don't have the energy to read. When I sit down, all I want to do is sleep."

"Charlie boy," Mr. Miller called.

"I have to go. I have to help skin rabbits or something."

"Gross," Casey said.

"It's not that bad," Charlie said.

"If you say so, Charlie Brown," Casey said, turning and running in the opposite direction.

"Yes, Mr. Miller. You needed me." Charlie was surprised at how tired he was just from running a hundred feet or so. He coughed, took out his inhaler, and took a puff from it. He'd been trying to conserve it since he only had a few left. Charlie drew in a deep breath and let it out slowly trying to keep the medicine in his bronchial tubes and lungs. He coughed and coughed until he had to sit. "What can I help you with?"

Mr. Miller walked over and put a hand on Charlie's back. "You okay, Charlie boy?"

Charlie nodded, but he wasn't really sure.

"Betty!" Mr. Miller yelled. "Betty, come quick. Charlie is having one of his asthma attacks."

Charlie didn't want to be a problem. He held up a hand. "I just need to sit a second." He coughed. "And let my inhaler work." Charlie took another puff of albuterol.

"Come inside, Charlie. We need to get you cooled off. I have something that will work alongside your inhaler that will help," Mrs. Miller said.

Charlie scrunched his face. He had smelled some of Mrs. Miller's herbal concoctions and wasn't looking forward to her treatment. She led Charlie to the tiny kitchen and pulled out a chair from a small table. "Sit. I'll go grab it."

The door to the travel trailer opened, and Maggie, Charlotte, and Ian entered. "I heard you were having another attack, Charlie boy," Maggie said.

He nodded as he coughed and wheezed, unable to respond verbally. Charlotte ignored him and walked right past, heading straight for the brownies cooling on a rack.

As she reached for one, Maggie yelled. "No!" She put Ian on the loveseat and rushed to her daughter. "Don't. Those aren't brownies."

"They smell like brownies," Charlotte whined.

"They're not. That's medicine for grown-ups. You can't take them. It will make you feel funny."

If Charlie could breathe, he would have chuckled. Medicine for grown-ups? Medical marijuana had been growing in popularity, and one of his mother's friends had even suggested the remedy to his mother to treat his allergies and asthma. Of course, even though his mother was super committed to the all-natural approach, she was vigorously opposed to mind-altering substances. His mom wouldn't even consider CBD oil, citing the lack of scientific evidence that it was more effective than the pharmaceutical drug his doctor prescribed.

Mrs. Miller returned with one of her amber bottles that Charlie had grown accustomed to seeing her bring out to treat everything from a cut to diarrhea from drinking bad water.

"No. No. Charlotte, they're for Mr. Miller. His arthritis has been acting up something fierce lately," Mrs. Miller said, moving the rack of pot-laced brownies to a shelf over the sink.

"Okay, Charlie." She opened the small vial, and Charlie's stomach lurched from the smell that instantly filled the room.

Maggie plugged her nose. "What is in that?" She picked up Charlotte and sat down across from Charlie.

"My special anti-asthma intervention. It's based upon a traditional Chinese herbal remedy. It's quite effective."

"It smells bad," Charlotte said, holding her nose.

Charlie was too afraid of offending Mrs. Miller to refuse, but he wasn't sure whether the treatment would help or hurt him. After giving Charlie her "special treatment," Mrs. Miller gave him a spoonful of honey. It helped rid his tongue of the taste of the awful remedy he'd just swallowed.

"Mrs. Miller, I dropped by to see if you'd mind watching Charlotte and Ian for a little while. We have so many veggies coming out of the garden the last few days that we need to get some of them into jars for the winter, but the kids have been super fussy today, and I can't get anything done," said Maggie.

"Well, I... um."

"I can watch them," Charlie said. It wasn't like he would be able to do much else today. He'd been through this enough times to know it would take some time for his breathing to return to normal.

Maggie stared at him. Her gaze bounced between him and her children. "How old did you say you were?"

"I'm thirteen. I used to watch my baby sister for my mom when she had to run to the store and stuff." He could see his sister's little round face. She was such a happy baby. Not fussy like

Ian. But he was sure he could cope with two little kids for a couple of hours. What could go wrong?

Charlie played hide and seek with Charlotte for over an hour. It was difficult to pretend he didn't see her in the tiny RV. The baby slept on the sofa as they drew pictures at the table in the kitchen. "Charlotte, I need to use the outhouse. Can you sit with your brother for just a minute?"

Charlie swatted wasps away as he rushed to the outhouse, twenty-five feet from the RV, to do his business. Five minutes later, as he was rounding the corner of the motor home, a strange man exited the RV with the baby under one arm and Charlotte under the other. His hand was over the little girl's mouth, and she was kicking her feet, trying to get away from him.

"Stop!" Charlie shouted. He drew his pistol from its holster, took aim, and yelled. "Stop! Put those kids down."

The man turned. A look of surprise crossed his face, but he kept moving down the steps.

"I said stop!" Charlie yelled. He couldn't shoot the man without hitting the kids. The man knew that. He took another step, and Charlie screamed. "Help! Someone help! Stranger! Stranger! Help, someone!"

The man's eyes narrowed. He was armed, but his pistol was still in its holster on his belt. He'd have to put the children down to draw on Charlie. Charlie took up an isosceles shooting position, gripping his pistol in both hands just like his dad had taught him. He leaned forward slightly, made sure his knees weren't locked, and tried to calm his breathing. He would be ready to squeeze the trigger the moment the children were out of his shot.

"Put those kids down, and I will let you leave." He lied. He wasn't letting this kidnapper take another step.

The man glanced to his left and then back to Charlie. A second later, the man suddenly took off running. Charlie ran after him yelling for help. He knew he couldn't keep up. He could feel his lungs closing already.

Cody and Casey had heard Charlie and each of them ran toward the man from opposite directions. In her hand, Casey carried a garden hoe. She raced up to the side of the man and landed a blow across his back. He stumbled and caught himself, nearly dropping Charlotte in the process.

Casey launched herself onto the man's back, and as Cody and Charlie reached them, she dug her fingers into the man's eye sockets. He let go of the children, and Charlie dove to catch the baby. Charlotte hit the ground, but Cody scooped her up and handed her to Charlie before landing a blow to the side of the man's head.

Maggie's screams pierced the air. "My babies! My babies!" She ran up to Charlie, swooped her children into her arms, and held them to her chest, then dropped down on one knee, inspecting them for injuries. "Are you okay?"

"I told him no, Mommy," Charlotte said. "He didn't know the secret code."

"That's my girl. You're safe now." Maggie was sobbing.

"Charlie boy saved us, Mommy," Charlotte said.

Maggie opened her right arm, inviting Charlie into the group hug. Charlie resisted. He hadn't saved them. He'd left them alone.

"Get to your feet," Cody barked at the kidnapper. "How did you get in here?" He spun the guy around, and Maggie turned as white as a ghost. She shot to her feet and took two steps back, pointing at the man with her mouth open.

"You know him, Maggie?" Cody asked.

She stammered. "He works for my father-in-law."

THIRTY

Vince

Wallace Survival Compound
Unicoi, Tennessee
Day 23

Before his sister-in-law had shown up with a mission for him, Vince had been flipping through the pages of one of five binders he and Sam had compiled with information and instructions on everything survival-oriented in a post-apocalyptic world. He opened the rings of the binder and removed the section for unconventional warfare. It was time to break out the incendiaries, explosives, and guerrilla warfare tactics. There was no end to the responsibilities of running a survival compound in the apocalypse.

If Unicoi fell to the Corbins, defending the compound would be much more difficult. He had to find a way to make it too costly for them to breech Unicoi's perimeter.

Vince planned on convincing Benny and Mayberry to task teams with digging the pits necessary to carry out his plans.

~

Vince keyed his handheld two-way radio and asked Dave to come to the communication center.

"On my way," Dave replied.

"Stop and pick up Nick on your way," Vince said.

Five minutes later, Dave and Nick joined Vince on the porch outside the comms shed.

Dave's face was flushed from the heat, and his shirt was soaked in sweat. None of them were used to the heat that northeastern Tennessee was experiencing that summer, and doing so without the benefit of air conditioning was compounding the difficulty.

"Tangerine or lemon-lime?" Vince asked, holding up two glasses of water enhanced with Liquid I.V. Hydration Multiplier.

Nick scrunched up his face. "I'll take lemon-lime. I can't stand tangerine." He took the glass from Vince and tipped it up, drinking it all in fast gulps.

"You shouldn't be that thirsty, Nick. There's plenty of potable water stashed along the perimeter."

There were six fifty-five-gallon drums of fresh spring water in various places around the perimeter wall. The spring had been one of the major factors Vince and Sam considered when selecting the range as the place for their compound.

Sam and Vince's farms each had three water options: ponds, streams, and wells, but this twenty-five-gallon-an-hour spring, along with the sheer bluff on the back side, made the gun range an ideal spot for a survival compound. They had originally planned to enclose all the land the Wallace family owned on the ridge with a Hesco barrier wall, but they'd simply run out of money and then time.

"So, what's up, boss?" Nick asked, placing his glass on the round wooden table next to Vince.

Vince pointed to the rocking chairs opposite him. "Take a seat, guys. This may take a minute. I need to explain the situation."

Vince didn't need to lay out the activities of Preston Corbin and the folks he'd recruited in Johnson City that had previously been discussed at one of their daily security briefings. His guys were plenty aware of the situation. Vince had called Dave and Nick to share the news Lauren had brought him about the attack that the senator and Mark Sever were planning. He also wanted to begin discussing their part in the raid as well as the security improvements he intended to implement on their compound.

"She can't be serious about sending fighters. You told her that, right?" Dave became more animated, waving his hands in the air. He took off his boonie hat and dropped it into his lap. "You told her a move like that would leave our compound and the town wide open for Nigel Corbin to attack, didn't you?"

"We never got that far. I only said I'd talk to Sever and his SWAT leader about the operation. I can't advise Lauren until I've spoken to them and determined what exactly they're asking or needing from us. They may only require intelligence or resupply or comms or something."

"You really believe that?" Nick asked. Vince was a little concerned Nick might be holding a grudge about his girlfriend, sensing Nick's tone held a hint of disrespect.

"Lauren said they'd rounded up two hundred bodies to go against Corbin's men. I think that's more than enough if they're well trained and armed. Hell, a couple of guys experienced with a hunting rifle could probably take down their guards. Sending two hundred fighters inside Corbin's gated community seems like overkill to me from what we know about the situation on the ground there."

"Cody and his guys last reported on their activities sometime last week."

They'd lost a man on that reconnaissance mission and Vince had been reluctant to send Cody's team out again. It shouldn't have happened. They were supposed to keep their distance and observe while out there hunting for food—not get involved. The guy who got captured had broken protocol and gone down into Johnson City to rescue a family member.

"Hopefully, Sever's intelligence is fresher than ours,' Vince said.

"So, when are we going?" Nick asked.

"I'd like to leave at first light tomorrow."

Dave stood. "We'll be ready."

Nick nodded his head, stood, straightened his posture, and said, "Yes, sir."

Nick had been a good soldier. He'd worked harder than anyone during their survival drills and training. Vince had trusted him completely until the thing with his girlfriend. Vince knew how a chick could mess with a guy's mind but Nick would shake it off, and when the brass started flying, Vince was sure Nick would have his six.

Vince had his gear all laid out on his bed, readying for his trip to Watauga Lake to speak with Mark Sever when Melissa Brower poked her head inside the door. "Going somewhere?" she asked.

Mel Brower was a former drill sergeant. She'd been tasked with training the civilians and preparing them to defend the compound. Vince liked her no-nonsense style, but she could be a little abrasive at times.

He filled her in about Lauren's visit.

"She asked you to go?"

"I volunteered to speak with Sever to find out what he's planning. We need to know in case it spills over this way. We need to be prepared."

She was uncharacteristically quiet. At first, Vince thought she might be upset about not being asked to join them on the mission.

"Dave and Nick are going with me, so Emilio Ortega will be in charge."

She huffed.

"You got a problem with Ortega now?"

"Not particularly, but if something happens and you don't come back, he's not the one I'd want making the decisions around here."

"I'll be back."

"You can't guarantee that. There are no guarantees in life. You know that."

"Thanks for the vote of confidence."

"It's not that. I know how capable you are, but shit happens. No matter how much we train or how well we plan, things can still go wrong out there. That's reality."

"I got you. I understand." He did. They'd both lost friends in Afghanistan. They had been well-trained and well-armed, but they didn't make it back.

"We have a continuity plan, remember—a line of succession. You're on the board. You and Lauren, along with Dave, Nick, Emilio, and Lindsay. Everyone has a role to play. I don't run this place all by myself. It wasn't set up that way. Everyone has their areas of expertise. Everyone will follow the plan and continue."

"Roger that. I just came in to tell you that I have another group of recruits ready for inspection, but I guess it can wait until you return," Mel said.

Vince would have preferred to have Mel with him when he met with Sever, but he needed someone to stay behind and take charge should something happen while he was gone. He knew that the compound would be in good hands with Mel and the others running it in his absence.

As she exited the building, a member of the security team pushed past her, rushing into the room. "We have a problem."

Vince shot to his feet and grabbed his rifle. "What now?"

"Someone tried to break into Mr. and Mrs. Miller's trailer."

"What?" Vince moved toward the door.

Mel spun back around. "That took nerve."

"He's not from here," the guard said. "He works for the Russos."

Vince felt a rage he'd never experienced in all his life. According to Maggie, the Russos had been sent to kill his brother and Tara Hobbs. Maggie had been forced to shoot Stuart Russo to get her children and bring them to the safety of the compound. Vince had promised his girlfriend's little sister that she and her children would be safe with him.

"Where is he? Take me to him," Vince said.

After hours of interrogation, Russo's henchman hadn't given up any useful information, despite taking a pretty bad beating. Vince's knuckles were raw. He needed a new tactic to extract information from this piece of shit.

"You want me to take a go at it?" Mel asked.

"I don't think so. We need him alive," Vince said, wiping blood from his hands.

Mel flipped him the bird and headed toward the door. "He ain't going to give up anything useful. He's had training. Anyone can see that."

"Watch him. I'm going to find Mayberry. If anyone can make him talk, it's Alan."

Alan Mayberry had experience interrogating insurgents. He'd been brought up on charges but fortunately for Alan, he'd avoided a court martial. Seemed the Army just wanted the incident to go away.

Dave followed Vince to where the Wagoneer was parked. "What about going to check out the SWAT team?"

Vince stopped and turned. He chewed his lip.

"Let one of the team go get Mayberry. He'll have the answers for you by the time we get back," Dave said.

"I need to know what the Russos are planning. They didn't send that guy after the kids just because they miss them."

"You know whatever's planned has something to do with the

Corbins. The best way you and I can find out what's going on is to see this SWAT leader and find out what they know about Corbin's movements."

Vince struggled to put aside his anger and see the logic of Dave's reasoning. Dave was objective and rational, whereas Vince was reactive. He trusted his friend's tactical acumen.

"Okay, but we need to make this quick just in case they have an attack planned or something. I don't like being gone with this new threat lurking."

THIRTY-ONE

Lauren

Unicoi City Hall
Unicoi, Tennessee
Day 23

With Lindsay helping Angela care for Bill and Edna, Lauren slipped away to address a few things back at city hall. It was hard to put what was happening at home aside, but there was so much going on in the town that she had to do her best to focus. She never thought there'd be so much paperwork to do in the apocalypse. Her hand was tired from signing official documents all morning. A knock at the door was followed by Millie poking her head inside.

"You have a visitor. He said Benny sent him."

"Okay, let him in," Lauren said.

Police Officer Everett Bradshaw entered the office. He was new to the Unicoi police force, but Benny spoke very highly of his qualifications. Bradshaw entered and stood in front of Lauren's desk with his hands behind his back like a soldier. Lauren glanced down at the paper on her desk that listed his qualifications. Benny had been thorough in vetting the members of his security team.

After the betrayal of the prior police chief, John Avery, and that of Officer Owens, Lauren understood Benny's diligence and appreciated it.

"You were a special agent in the Army Criminal Investigations Division?"

"Yes, ma'am."

"Bradshaw, I have a job for you. I need to find out if someone is taking produce from the wagons after they leave the fields and before they reach the distribution center."

Bradshaw's eyebrows raised. He looked so young, barely old enough to be out of high school. Lauren glanced down at his resume again. Twenty-six. He had to be lying about his age. Lauren felt ancient, especially lately.

"If there's a discrepancy between what's being reported from the fields and what's inventoried at the distribution center, I need you to find out who the culprit is and how they're accomplishing it. Can you do that, Bradshaw?"

"Yes, ma'am. I may need assistance with access to the inventories. I'll need to know who prepares them and how. Are they prepared contemporaneously or—"

"I don't need to know how you will accomplish your mission, Bradshaw. Just talk to Millie. She'll get you whatever you need. Tell her if anyone gives you any problem and she'll straighten their asses out. Okay?"

"Yes, ma'am." Bradshaw just stood there.

"You can start now," Lauren said.

"Yes, ma'am. I'll have a report for you by the end of the day."

"By the end of the day?" She hadn't expected results so fast.

"I'm very good at my job, ma'am."

"That's good to know."

Bradshaw left and closed the door. Two seconds later, it flew open again, but this time Benny and Alan rushed into the room.

"We have a problem," Benny said, plopping down in the chair opposite Lauren's desk. Mayberry stood with his hand on the second chair. Lauren pointed, gesturing for him to take a seat as well.

"I'll stand. My back can't handle your hard-backed chairs."

"What's the problem now?" Lauren asked.

"I've been asking around about that fella you shot at the market," Alan said.

"He attacked Benny," Lauren said.

"I talked to the manager at the distribution center. No one has ever seen the man come through there," Alan said. "He didn't have a voucher for his work either."

"So no one in town knows this guy?" Lauren asked.

"Someone knows him," Alan said.

"Are you going to tell me, or do I have to guess." Lauren recognized how snarky that sounded. She couldn't let her fatigue and level of stress cause her to snap at people.

"Sorry. The guy you…" Alan stopped to rephrase his statement. "The man Benny tussled with was seen leaving Ralph Cross's place two days ago."

Lauren slapped her hands down on her desk and leaned forward. "What?"

"Ralph's neighbor, Debbie Layton, said she saw a Hispanic male leaving Ralph's place just before dark. This neighbor was out tending the garden in front of her house, and the stranger left Ralph's place and walked right through her yellow squash plants. He stopped and picked a tomato and was eating it when Debbie confronted him. She says the man said something to her in Spanish, pointed a gun in her face, and then backed out of the garden, disappearing down the street toward downtown."

"This spy was at Alderman Ralph Cross's house two days ago?" Lauren inhaled deeply and let it out.

"What do we do now?" Alan said.

"I think it's time I confront Ralph and find out if he's working with Corbin and against the town," Lauren said.

"You think that's wise? He'll just deny it. He'll call Debbie a liar. They've never gotten along. She didn't vote for him, you know," Benny said.

"I wouldn't tell him who connected him to the man. I say, Benny, you should go to Ralph's house, tell him there's an urgent issue at city hall, and take him to view the body of the spy. He will either give a reasonable explanation as to why the man was at his house or pretend he doesn't know him," Lauren said.

"What does that prove, though? It will just let Ralph know we're watching him," Benny said.

The door banged open, and Ora Sellers, the security team training coordinator from the Wallace compound, ran into the office. "Mayor." He stopped in the middle of the room. "Oh, good. Glad you two are here so I don't have to repeat this."

"What's wrong?" Benny said, rising from his chair and turning to face Sellers.

"Something happened at the compound. Someone slipped in and tried to kidnap Lindsay's niece and nephew."

"What the hell?" Lauren was on her feet, heading toward the door.

"Charlie alerted help, and Casey and Cody were able to stop the kidnapping. Vince worked the bastard over pretty well, but the guy didn't give up much. Vince sent me to fetch you, Mayberry. He thought you might have better luck."

Mayberry glanced over at Benny with a half smirk "Spies, kidnappings, embezzlement. What kind of town have we become?"

Lauren didn't find it at all amusing. "Where's Vince?'

"He…" Sellers' gaze bounced between Benny and Alan. "He went to do that thing you asked him to do."

"It's okay. They both know about State Senator Phelps' visit," Lauren said.

Sellers' shoulders relaxed. "He and Dave were going to take the Wagoneer and run up to Watauga Lake to talk to Mark Sever about the SWAT operation and what he knows about Corbin's movements in the area.

"Mayberry, if you want to go deal with the kidnapping investigation. I'll go handle our spy issue," Benny said.

"Be careful, Alan," Lauren said. The only people who would risk something like that to take Maggie's babies would be her husband and his family. If the Russos are involved, who knows how many more of them have infiltrated our town.

Somehow, Lauren knew it was all connected. It was possible the spy could have been searching for the whereabouts of Maggie and her children. But why was he at Ralph's house and asking about the production of Unicoi's vegetable fields?

"Millie, I'm running home for a bit. I'll be back in an hour."

"I'm locking the freaking door then. This place has been busier than a one-toothed man in a corn-on-the-cob eating contest."

THIRTY-TWO

Sam

Doctor Hammond's Farm
Franklin, Tennessee
Day 23

Becky looked forlorn as Sam, Moondust, and Tumbleweed went through their packs one last time before leaving Franklin. She'd been quiet after the encounter at her apartment. She'd done what she needed to survive, but from her demeanor now, Sam could tell the incident had messed her up. It was never easy to take someone's life—even if they deserved it.

"How long will it take Mark and his son to put the new tires on the Power Wagon?"

"Thirty minutes maybe, unless they encounter a problem getting the old tires off."

"So, we leaving today?" Moondust asked.

"Yes, as soon as the beast is ready," Sam said.

"I wish there was a way to quiet the noise of the Power Wagon. That beast is going to echo through the hollows and announce our arrival long before we get there," Tumbleweed said.

"The echoing is both good and bad. The sound will travel a good distance, but it's hard to pinpoint where the engine noise is coming from—and where it's going," Sam said.

Doc Hammond exited the house through his rear door and followed the sawdust path to the fire ring in the center of his back lawn. "You young folks preparing to head out?"

"If all goes well putting on the newish tires," Sam said. "I cannot tell you how grateful I am to you and your wife for all you've done to help me. I would have died if not for you two." Sam turned his gaze to Becky. "And you too, Becky. I will never forget the kindness and generosity I've found here in Franklin."

"That's just how we were raised here in Macon County," Doc said. He took a seat across from Sam. "How's the leg today?"

Sam's leg ached because he had been moving a lot lately, going back and forth between the Hammonds and the Titus barn and checking on the progress of the old Power Wagon. He had helped Mark put in new fluids and fill the fuel tank with diesel. Finding enough diesel for the trip had been a challenge. Mark and Martin Titus had taken up a collection from the farmers along the Hammonds' road and gathered enough diesel to fill the tank and one five-gallon fuel can to take with them. It should be enough to get the truck to Unicoi, but Sam was concerned about how much fuel their route might actually take, given the hills on the back roads they had to climb.

"You planning to go up through Asheville and get on the interstate to Tennessee?" Doc asked.

"I've routed us on a few back roads to avoid Waynesville, Asheville, and other populated towns where possible. It will add time and miles to the trip but lessen the risk of a confrontation over someone wanting the truck."

"Seems sensible to me," Doc said.

"I'm sure going to miss you young folks around here. You've been a blessing to the missus and me. I guess I'll be the one splitting wood tomorrow." Doc smiled. "I'm glad you can finally get on the road to your families though. That's what's important these days."

"I agree," Sam said.

"Sam," Isaiah called as he crossed the field and approached the Hammonds' back lawn. "Hey, Sam. Uncle Mark wanted me to tell you he found the tires and could use a hand unloading them from the wagon."

"Tumbleweed, can you give me a hand?" Sam asked.

Getting the old tires off the Power Wagon and the better tires onto the rims wasn't easy, even with three people to do the work. Once they were on and Mark backed the Power Wagon out of the barn, Sam stepped back and looked at her. She didn't look any better. Her paint was still faded, and rust still showed through, but the tires looked good, and the paisley print seat cushion over the driver's seat was a nice touch. The engine sounded amazing. The exhaust was loud, but the noise was music to Sam's ears, not only because this machine was his ticket home, but because it had been three weeks since he'd driven a vehicle. Part of him had honestly believed that he'd never drive again. Sam enjoyed being out on the road.

"I'd like to leave it here until we're ready to leave. I don't want to attract too much attention before we're ready to pull out," Sam said.

"Not a problem," Mark said.

Becky had returned empty-handed from one last hunt before leaving Franklin. "There's not much stirring today. I'm sorry, guys." She handed Tumbleweed a canvas bag filled with wild greens she'd picked. "They'll be a little bitter this time of year, but they're still nutritious."

Tumbleweed stared into the bag and then handed it to Moondust.

"They'll do great. Thanks, Becky," Moondust said.

Sam handed Tumbleweed the shotguns that had been recovered from the shootout with the group that had attacked the Titus kid five days earlier. Becky had traded the horses for a box of shells and bullets for her .30-30 Winchester. It wouldn't be much if they ran into a group with guns, but Sam hoped by avoiding towns they wouldn't need to fire their weapons.

"Tumbleweed, make sure you keep that extra box of shotgun shells in your pouch on your belt," Sam said.

Moondust was the only one not armed with a gun. She clutched a canister of bear spray in her hand and wore a knife inside a scabbard on her belt. She was prepared to take on a bear, but Sam knew none of what she carried would do anything to stop a shooter's bullet.

"Well, are we ready?" Sam asked. His stomach was in knots, not just because of what they might face over the next one hundred miles, but because he'd be in Unicoi in a few hours. He'd learn the fate of his family and that of the town. He pushed aside any pessimism and thought about his reunion with his wife, son, and brother.

After Sam had thanked the Titus family for the truck for the hundredth time, everyone mounted up. Moondust sat in the middle of the bench seat and Becky sat next to the door with the AR-15 rifle poking out the open window. Tumbleweed hadn't been thrilled to ride in the bed of the truck, but Sam was glad to have someone who could watch for anyone coming at them from behind.

The Hammonds came over to the Titus farm to see the group off and the whole Titus clan showed up. After what Sam had seen of these fine folks, he liked their chances of surviving the apocalypse and being part of the rebuilding process. They were all hardy, resilient folks, and that was what it took to make it during rough times.

Becky waved goodbye to them as Sam backed the Power Wagon out of the driveway, put the old girl into drive, and turned toward Highway 23.

THIRTY-THREE

Sam

Main Street
Franklin, Tennessee
Day 23

Driving the beast would take some getting used to. The major challenge driving the old Power Wagon was double clutching. The downshifting was tricky, but upshifting was no problem. There was no shift pattern on the knob or elsewhere and Sam tried to recall Mark's instructions as he ground the gears. When he finally found the right gear and sped up, he felt he needed ear plugs due to the exhaust and engine noise inside the cab.

Moondust pointed to a sign along the road and then covered her mouth. "We stayed at Chica and Sunsets Hostel on our south-bound hike," she shouted. "Professor had struggled to get the miles in, so we took an extra day in town before getting back on the trail. I miss him."

Sam was quiet as he recalled Professor's last hour on earth. The older gentleman had made the two thousand-mile journey, and the strain on his body in attempting a return trip with little to no food had been proving too much for him. But had those hunters not attacked them, Sam thought he would still have had a chance of getting Professor to Unicoi with him. The hunters killed Professor over something of little value to them. Neither Professor nor Sam had had any food with them, and the hunters already had whatever they would have found in their packs. Sam would have been home by now if not for that encounter and his resulting leg injury.

"I'm sorry for your loss," Becky said to Moondust, her voice raised over the sound of the engine. "I'm sorry I didn't get to know him."

"Thank you. He was a wonderful man."

Coming up on Franklin's Main Street, Sam began to slow as they approached a curve to get a look at the intersection. If anyone was at this end of town, they would hear the truck coming. After grinding a few more gears and finally getting the beast down-shifted, he scanned the intersection ahead. The westbound lanes were clear, so he crossed over and continued into the eastbound lanes.

In the parking lot of the farm and garden store on the right, fifty-pound bags of lime and fertilizer were strewn about and split open, their contents spilled on the asphalt. All of the adjacent stores and restaurants had their windows and doors smashed.

They passed the automotive shop where Mark Titus had obtained the used tires they'd put on the Power Wagon. An older gentleman sat in a lawn chair in the open bay, a wrench in one hand and an old carburetor in the other. He waved as the Power Wagon passed by.

After crossing the Little Tennessee River, Sam slowed again at the sight of a jumble of cars, trucks, and SUVs blocking the next intersection. He was trying to determine if that was how they'd stopped the day of the EMP or if someone had placed them there as a roadblock or ambush point. Bollards in the median would prevent most vehicles from crossing over into the westbound lanes. Yellow and black traffic barrels had been placed near the guardrail. Cars also blocked the parking lot of the shop on the corner.

He could use the ten thousand pound winch to move the vehicles so they could pass, but that would mean getting out of the Power Wagon and exposing themselves and would take time— enough time for someone to hear them and come try to take the truck. The only way around was through the sand or water-filled traffic barrels, or over the concrete bollards. Sam knocked on the back window to catch Tumbleweed's attention. "Hold on!"

Tumbleweed gave him a thumbs up gesture, and Sam turned the wheel to the left and nudged the front bumper up against the barrels, trying to push them out of the way.

"Watch out!" Becky shouted as a group of men ran out from between the two buildings across the street. She leaned out her window and began firing her AR-15 at the men.

A second later, Tumbleweed was standing in the bed of the truck, taking aim at the men approaching them, making himself a target.

"Get down!" Sam yelled, but Tumbleweed couldn't hear him over the roar of the Power Wagon and the boom of Becky's rifle.

The men began returning fire with rounds striking the front of the truck. Sam yanked the wheel to the right and crossed back into the eastbound lane knocking Tumbleweed off balance and causing him to fall into the truck bed.

"Hold on, ladies. It's about to get bumpy."

Sam gripped the steering wheel with his left hand and shifted with his right as he swerved around the mass of cars blocking the intersection and drove up onto the curb along the right-hand lane. Tumbleweed was kneeling in the bed and returning fire at the men, causing them to duck for cover behind a newer model pickup.

That's right, just keep those assholes pinned down a few seconds longer.

Sam rammed into a mid-sized sedan, mashed the gas pedal, and pushed the sedan into the intersection, out of the path of the Power Wagon. The beast never even slowed down. Bullets whizzed by, striking the windows of the cars lining the road, but the truck was too far away now for the shooters to be accurate.

Tumbleweed moved back to his position with his back to the cab of the truck. Until that moment, Sam had feared Tumbleweed and Moondust weren't up for what they'd face on the road, but Tumbleweed had just proven himself. When things got real, he did what was necessary for their survival. He'd seen Becky in action. Although she didn't have tactical training, she was a good marksman.

"That was crazy," Moondust said. "Is that what's going to be out there on the road all the way to Unicoi?"

Sam glanced over at her. She was grinning from ear to ear. He'd expected her to be frightened, but her reaction showed she might just be an adrenaline junkie.

"From my experience. That's why I always say we have to keep our heads on a swivel. I tried to warn you."

"It's like the movies. The way you jumped the curb and plowed into that car with bullets flying. That was intense," Moondust said.

"It's not the movies. Those were real bullets they were firing. It could have very easily gone sideways for us," Sam said.

"I wish I had a gun too. This bear spray isn't going to cut it."

Sam considered for a moment. They had the second AR-15 and Becky's .30-30, but Moondust had no weapons training. It was more dangerous for her to have a weapon that she didn't know how to use.

"Hopefully that will be the last encounter we have. Sam has planned a route that should avoid most populated areas," Becky said.

That was Sam's plan. He only had to avoid trouble for one hundred more miles.

Sam swerved to avoid a collision with a delivery van sitting in the middle of the road, and then shifted gears and punched the accelerator, steering the Power Wagon toward Highway 23 North and the Blue Ridge Parkway.

THIRTY-FOUR

Sam

Highway 23 North
Savannah, North Carolina
Day 23

Although the Power Wagon's top speed was only forty-five miles per hour, Sam wasn't able to consistently keep its speed that high. Mark and Martin Titus had done their best to get her back on the road, but that didn't mean she ran smoothly or efficiently. On the steeper climbs, the engine bogged and slowed. Thank goodness for the equally steep descents, which helped with getting the ten thousand pound beast up the next hill. At this rate, it was going to take three or four hours to make it to Unicoi. They had just passed the Savannah, North Carolina's fire department when they encountered their second roadblock issue.

The line of vehicles, Jersey barriers, tractor-trailers, and other obstructions stretched across all six lanes of the highway and into the parking lot of a Dollar General store. Again, at first glance, Sam couldn't tell whether this was another attempt to ambush folks or whether the vehicles had just been left where they were when the EMP took them out. He saw no guards and no one stepped out as they approached. However, they had to have heard the truck's loud engine.

"Get ready, Becky," Sam said.

"Again," Moondust said, grabbing the dashboard.

"Scoot over, Moon. I need room," Becky yelled. Due to the gear shift placement, both of Moondust's legs were in the passenger-side footwell, making it difficult for Becky to pivot in her seat.

Sam eased forward, looking for a soft spot through the maze of vehicles where he might drive through without potentially damaging the Power Wagon and making it inoperable. He could barely make out the edges of the barricade three hundred and fifty feet ahead.

He'd hoped there would be a way to cross over into the southbound lanes, hop the ditch, and drive around the west end of the roadblock, but on closer inspection, a shipping container had been wedged between a tree and a hill, making that passage impossible.

Examining the east end for a moment, Sam thought he had found a way around the barricade. He switched back into the right-hand lane, steering toward the ditch, intending to drive across the grass and parking lot on that side, through a line of bushes, and make it back onto the roadway on the opposite side.

As soon as the right tires left the pavement, Sam spotted movement ahead. Two men in police uniforms holding rifles appeared from behind the barricade and stepped into view. Sam didn't want to get into a shootout with fellow officers. He could pull over, explain that he was attempting to get home, and possibly they'd let them pass without confiscating the truck. However, Sam wasn't willing to risk losing the Power Wagon.

Sam knew the officers would likely shoot at them if they tried to keep driving past them, but he didn't see any other choice. He had to get the vehicle closer to the checkpoint. He needed the officer to think he was going to stop and comply, and then he'd attempt to maneuver the truck around the checkpoint and race away before they could open fire—that had been the plan anyway.

Sam slowed to about ten miles per hour, trying his best to downshift without stalling the vehicle. If that happened, he might not be able to get it restarted before the officer rushed the truck. "Let off gas, clutch down, shift into neutral, clutch up, rev the engine to get it to the right RPMs," he said out loud, repeating what Mark had shown him. The gear ground and the truck stalled.

"Shit! Shit!" Sam said as he attempted to get the vehicle started again.

"Out of the car!" the taller of the two officers yelled, stepping into the open and pointing his rifle at the truck.

"What should we do?" Moondust asked. She wasn't smiling anymore.

"Becky, do not shoot. Lower your rifle out of view and tell Tumbleweed to lay the shotgun in the bed between his legs out of sight. We don't want them to open fire on us." Becky knocked on the back window and relayed the information to Tumbleweed as Sam kept trying to restart the truck.

The second officer joined the other as the Power Wagon's engine cranked over and roared back to life. Sam smiled at the officers and made a questioning gesture. He pointed to the shoulder of the road as if this was a normal traffic stop. The cop was motioning for him to stop.

"Stop right there. Shut off the engine and put your hands outside the vehicle," the taller officer shouted.

When Sam didn't comply, the second officer began shouting and moving toward them.

"Let me see your hands. Stop the vehicle and let me see your hands."

"We aren't armed," Sam yelled out of the driver's window. He kept rolling but slowed to around seven miles per hour, maintaining eye contact with the second officer even as he eased the Power Wagon toward the shoulder. They were reaching the point where he had to act.

"I'm pulling over, officers. I'm pulling over. We aren't armed." The vehicle was now within one hundred feet of the checkpoint and well within the range of the officers' rifles. Sam mashed the accelerator.

The officers began to fire, and Sam upshifted, yanked the wheel to the right, and pointed the beast into a strip mall parking lot. There was no way to get past them without risking getting shot. Sam swung wide and drove between two of the stores, making a hard left and racing along the back service drive as fast as the old beast would run.

"Hold on, ladies."

Sam glanced into the rearview mirror. He could no longer see Tumbleweed. "Becky, look back and tell me if we lost Tumbleweed," Sam said.

Becky pivoted in her seat and peered through the glass. "He's on the floor of the bed with his hands over his head."

The service drive behind the shops ended next to an eight-foot-high chain-link fence. Sam mashed the accelerator again and crashed through the gate, causing it to fly up and over the cab of the truck. The sound of the fence smacking and scraping against the truck was deafening.

More shots rang out, and some found their target, striking the roof of the cab. One round pierced the driver's side mirror, shattering it. Sam punched the accelerator, drove down into the ditch, and crawled up the other side then looked back over his left shoulder and saw the two officers were pursuing them on foot. The Power Wagon bounced across someone's lawn, plowing through the long grass until the front tires finally hit a gravel driveway. Sam yanked the wheel to the left and steered the truck back onto Highway 23.

They'd made it without getting shot and without having to fire upon the officers. They had been on the road less than an hour and had twice come close to getting killed or losing the truck. Sam's knuckles were white from gripping the steering wheel so tight.

"We're close enough still that you guys could walk back to the Hammonds," Sam said as they bounced down the highway toward Sylva and their turn onto Highway 74.

"And miss all this fun?" Moondust laughed.

"Check on Tumbleweed and see if he's still alive," Sam said.

Becky rapped on the glass. "Do you need to put on clean drawers now?"

"I need clean everything after that," Tumbleweed said. "I almost bounced out of the bed and took a swim when you hit that ditch back there."

"Sorry," Sam shouted over his shoulder out the open driver's window. "I couldn't go any slower."

When they reached Dillsboro, they cautiously weaved through the remains of a roadblock before crossing over the Tuckasegee River and turning east onto Highway 74.

Sylva looked deserted. No one came out of their homes to check out the sound of the engine and Sam was relieved.

Continuing northeast, Sam kept his head on a swivel, looking for potential threats and for their turn onto the Blue Ridge Parkway, which would bypass Waynesville, North Carolina, a town of over ten thousand people before the EMP event. As the miles passed by, the pit in Sam's stomach moved into his chest. Could he get these people to Tennessee in one piece? The last time he'd driven through dangerous villages, he'd been in an up-armored HMMWV with fellow trained soldiers, all wearing twenty pounds of body armor and carrying M4 rifles. Still, it had been nerve-racking driving through villages where the enemy could be around every corner.

Part of him wished he'd left the hikers back at the Hammonds' place. But if he'd had any doubt about his chances of making it home without them, the shootout back on Main Street in Franklin had settled that. If not for Tumbleweed and Becky, he might not have made it any farther than that.

THIRTY-FIVE

Lauren

Taylor Residence
Unicoi, Tennessee
Day 23

Edna was in the kitchen attempting to make dinner. She turned the knob on the now non-functioning stove and then opened the empty refrigerator. "What happened to the pastrami I put in here this morning? Joshua Michael! Get your butt in here. You better not have eaten a whole pound of lunch meat again."

"Josh isn't here, Mom. He's in California, remember?" Lauren didn't know why she chose that moment to correct her mother. A look of confusion spread over Edna's once round, plump face. "Let me help you, Momma. The meat is in here." Lauren opened the cabinet and took out a jar of ground deer meat she'd canned from Sam's hunt the previous fall.

"Let's make some deer chili. You always make the best chili on the planet."

Edna leaned in close to Lauren's ear. "It's the beer. I use a can of beer in my chili. Don't tell your father. He'd never eat it, thinking he'd go to hell for consuming alcohol." Edna snickered.

Lauren chuckled. "Beer? Really, Mom? I'm shocked." She could picture her mother at the liquor store purchasing one can of beer and trying to sneak it into the house without Bill finding out.

"I had to taste it first, you know. Just a sip here and there," Edna said through a toothy grin.

"You're a rebel, Mom."

Lauren had so missed her mother's sense of humor. Edna Taylor had once been a lively, cheerful, generous, and amazingly funny woman. She had dozens of friends and often hosted parties in her home. Dementia had stolen her life. If her mother realized or noticed her loss of memory, she didn't express it to Lauren.

"Well, we don't have beer today. What else can we add to the deer meat to make a good pot of chili?"

Edna moved nearer the screen door and stared toward the backyard.

"Mom?"

"I have to get the laundry in. I think it's gonna rain."

And that quick, she was back in her own world.

There was a knock on the door and a moment later, Lindsay poked her head into the kitchen. You have a visitor. Someone from city hall. I'll stay with Edna."

Natasha Serediuk stood in the foyer. She was fourteen and tall for her age, so she looked older. She'd been helping Lauren with all the paperwork and running messages back and forth between Lauren and the aldermen. "Ma'am, Everett Bradshaw is at city hall. He needs to speak with you."

"Already?" Lauren said, grabbing the leather gun belt holding her Colt revolver, and putting it on.

"Lindsay, I have to run back to city hall for a minute."

"I've got this. Go do your thing, Madam Mayor."

~

Buddy French was pulling weeds from his front garden as Lauren threw her leg over her bike and followed Natasha down the driveway. Buddy tossed a hand over his shoulder. "Have a nice day!"

He'd lost so much weight that Lauren barely recognized him. She hadn't seen his name on the food voucher redemption lists. Lauren knew Buddy had a bad back, but there were other things he could have done to earn vouchers. Had he been relying solely on what he grew?

She didn't have time to worry about her neighbors at the moment. She had things to attend to and then get back home to help with her parents' care. With Vince and Dave gone, Lindsay would be needed back at the compound, not as a nurse to Bill and Edna.

"Is there a problem, Everett?" Lauren asked as she entered the municipal building.

Everett gestured toward her office. "In private?"

"Sure. Millie, please don't disturb us unless it's an emergency."

Lauren unlocked her office and took a seat behind her desk. Everett stood.

"Ma'am, I discovered a discrepancy with the inventories."

The door opened, and Ralph walked right in without knocking. "I just had a visit from Benny."

"Can it wait, Ralph? This is important," Lauren asked.

"If it's about city business, then I should hear it too, and then we're gonna discuss what just happened with that new police chief of yours." Ralph pushed past Everett and dropped into the chair across from her. "Carry on."

Lauren was stuck. She couldn't order the alderman out of her office when this was the investigation he'd inquired about. "Go ahead, Officer Bradshaw."

"I examined the inventories from both the field managers and the distribution center. I interviewed"—he flipped through his notes—"a Toni Barbieri, the field manager at Stephens' Farm Market. He keeps copious records, by the way. He produced an inventory of the last two weeks' harvest written in legible penmanship. I compared his record with that of the one delivered to the distribution center, and it appears the record Millie received there was altered."

Ralph slapped his knee. "See, I told you. Folks have been saying something was off with the accounting. I knew someone was sticking their dirty little fingers into the cookie jar when no one was looking."

"Go on, Officer Bradshaw," Lauren said, giving Ralph a dirty look for interrupting him.

"Who's stealing from the shipments?" Lauren asked, cutting through all the steps he'd taken to investigate the matter.

"I can't say who yet. I can say the issue arises with the last wagons of the day. They arrive after dark—after everyone's shifts in the fields have ended. The distribution center is closed to residents at that time, and the staff has all gone for the day, except for the two guards assigned to watch the center overnight."

"So it's the guards? I knew it," Ralph said.

"I can't confirm that. They don't have access to a vehicle to remove the amount of produce being taken. They would have to sign out a team of horses and a wagon. That would draw suspicion immediately as they have no reason to make such a request."

"So it's the drivers. It's someone from the teams tasked with taking the produce from the fields to the center," Lauren said.

"If it is, it's quite an elaborate scheme. There are different driver teams nearly every day. It's random. No one knows who will be the last drivers of the day. And it's happening every day."

"So, who is taking food from the wagons."

"No one."

"No one? But you said that there was a discrepancy between

what was coming from the fields and what was making it to the center to be distributed."

"The wagons are driven inside the former school bus barn. The wagons are left inside overnight until the distribution center employees arrive and begin their inventory."

"What about the horses? Couldn't the guards just take the wagon somewhere else?"

"The horses are unhitched from the wagons and ridden back to the pastures near the fields so they can be used to haul the wagons the next day. Bradshaw stopped to flip through his miniature notebook again. "A neighbor who lives across the street from the back of the elementary school—I mean distribution center—this neighbor claims to have seen a truck back up to the bay around eleven pm two nights ago. They opened the doors and drove inside. A few minutes later, they pulled back out with their headlights off."

"Did they recognize this truck?" Lauren asked. It wasn't like there were hundreds of trucks on the roads these days. The town had four altogether. Vince had one that he'd converted to run on wood. It was old, from the 1940s. A couple of farmers out past the city limits had 1970s model pickups.

"She said it was really old and smoked like a chimney."

Ralph shot to his feet. He leaned over Lauren's desk and jabbed a finger near her face. "I knew it! I knew it. You and that brother-in-law of yours think you're slick, but we're on to you now." He turned to Bradshaw. "I want her arrested. I want her, Vince Wallace, and everyone out at the survivalist militia compound put behind bars."

Bradshaw moved closer, and for a moment, Lauren thought he was actually going to try to take her into custody. Lauren's hand moved to her revolver even as Bradshaw stepped in front of Ralph.

"Alderman Cross. I'd like to complete my investigation before making any arrests. I would like to interview Vince and the members of his group. I'd like to talk to the chief and see who was authorized to access the distribution center building after hours. I need to talk to the guards that were on duty two nights ago when the witness said she saw the truck there."

"You do that." Ralph spun around and raced to the door. "And then I want her in handcuffs by the morning."

He stormed out of the office, nearly knocking Millie to the floor as he did.

"I overheard. I didn't take food from town, Lauren. I'd never do that," Millie said.

"I know, Millie. No one is accusing you of anything like that."

"Your records are meticulous. No one has any reason to think you're involved," Bradshaw said. He smiled at Millie.

"Who then?" Millie asked.

"I didn't want to say anything in front of the alderman, but I have reason to believe the smoke was from an engine burning too much oil. The neighbor said the smell hung in the air after a loud truck pulled away, and she had to close her windows. Ralph's son owns a 1963 Chevy Dually, but he said it hasn't run in a long time. It's parked in Ralph's garage."

"Are you saying Ralph is taking food from the center and blaming my brother-in-law and me?"

"I need to confirm whether that truck runs. I have to go back and talk to Ralph's neighbor. She would have heard the truck coming and going that time of night."

"Please do that as fast as possible and report back," Lauren said. "Millie, I need to talk to Benny. Could you raise him on the radio and have him come right away?"

THIRTY-SIX

Sam

Haygood County Line
Waynesville, North Carolina
Day 23

Any other time, Sam would have enjoyed the drive along the Blue Ridge Parkway with its stunning views of the mountains and the Appalachian Highlands. But not this time. The winding, twisting road had him white-knuckling it for miles, watching for threats around every turn.

"I will never get tired of these views," Moondust said. "You almost forget there's an apocalypse. The mountains look like they have for ages. The world may have changed, but the views remain the same."

"It is pretty," Becky said, a hint of sadness in her voice.

Sam glanced out over the breathtaking landscape. Somehow the view of the mountains calmed him. It was comforting that at least something hadn't changed. The towns may be full of desperate, dangerous people, but the Blue Ridge Mountains, part of the larger, still stood tall and majestic, untouched by what the enemies of the United States had unleashed on the nation.

Sam was lost in thought recalling a similar drive with his parents as a boy. He and Vince had been bored with the scenery as kids. Having grown up in the mountains, they had failed to comprehend its beauty. His father had pulled the car over once and had everyone get out. He had made Sam and Vince look out over the Blue Ridge Mountains without speaking as he told them the story of how their ancestors had made their way through those very mountains to make their home in Tennessee. He and Lauren had stopped in that same spot to show Charlie and told him the same story. At the time, Sam could never have imagined the nation reverting to the age his great-great-grandparents knew.

After cresting a hill and rounding a sharp curve, the Balsam Gap overlook came into view. Sam slammed on the brakes, stopping a few feet from a hunter crossing the road with a string of squirrels hanging from his belt. The elderly man must have been deaf not to hear the beast approaching. He raised his rifle, pointing it at the truck. Without a word being spoken, Sam and Becky aimed their weapons back at him. The hunter lowered his weapon and backed away until he disappeared into the forest on the opposite side of the road.

"That was close," Moondust said as Sam put the truck into gear and pulled away, leaving the hunter behind.

Sam slowed, coming out of the rest of the curves, not wanting to be caught off guard like that again. Coming around a tight curve, Sam slowed the vehicle again. Two hundred feet ahead was a tunnel through the mountain. "What the hell?"

Sam flicked on the headlights and mashed the accelerator, racing toward Pinnacle Ridge Tunnel. Seven hundred feet later, after cutting through the mountain, they emerged back into the sunlight.

"I've never driven through a mountain before," Moondust said.

"That would have been really cool if I hadn't been anticipating being shot dead somewhere inside there."

"Watch out!" Becky shouted, just as the Power Wagon rounded a tight curve.

Sam stomped on the brakes and stopped inches from a giant boulder. Beyond it, a rockslide had blocked the roadway.

"What now?" Moondust asked.

Tumbleweed twisted his body around the cab and poked his head in Sam's window from the truck bed. "Should we turn around and find another route?"

"Let me take a look. You and Becky watch our six."

"Our what?" Tumbleweed asked.

"Watch for bad guys coming from the tunnel."

"Oh."

Sam walked around the ten-foot wide boulder to the rest of the rockslide. There was no way through unless they did some serious off-roading. On one side was the rock face of the mountain. On the opposite side was a sheer drop-off just five feet from the edge of the pavement.

Sam climbed over a boulder and stood on the edge overlooking the valley below. He studied the ground beneath him. It appeared fairly solid, but the earth narrowed significantly before they would clear the rockfall. Half the ten thousand pound truck would be hanging over the side of the cliff and the risk of rolling was great.

Having to backtrack five miles and find an alternate route around Waynesville made Sam's stomach sour. He'd expected complications—it was the apocalypse, after all. He wasn't naive enough to think he'd hop on the interstate and be home in two hours like he would have a month prior. Living in the mountains all his life, Sam had driven up on rockslides before.

Think, Sam. Think.

He walked around some medium-sized rocks along the edge. If they were able to get the Power Wagon around the large boulder in the middle of the road, he might be able to drive over the rocks along the left-hand lane without going over the cliff.

"Okay, folks, this is what we're going to do," Sam said, climbing back over the rocks and returning to the truck. "You three are going to carefully make your way to the other side and wait for me well away from the rocks."

"You're going to try to drive around them?" Becky asked, her voice high-pitched.

"Not exactly around. More like over them, just the smaller ones on the edge. If all goes well, I'll have two tires on the ground at all times."

After his companions had made it safely to the opposite side of the rockslide, Sam climbed behind the wheel of the Power Wagon. His goal was to keep all four wheels touching the surface and providing forward traction.

It's now or never, Wallace.

After slowly edging the truck past the boulder with barely an inch of clearance, Sam touched the accelerator and made the right front tire of the beast crawl up onto the first few one-foot-high rocks. The Power Wagon climbed over them with ease. Then came the tricky part. The next section had multiple rocks of various sizes and only three feet of clearance between the pile and the sheer drop.

Keeping the left-side tires on the ground, Sam crawled over three more feet of rocks with his body feeling every jolt and vibration as the heavy vehicle bounced up and down and back and forth. He gripped the steering wheel so tightly that his hands were cramping. The right front tire slipped down into a gap between two larger rocks. Sam applied more power and the beast climbed up and over the next rock. At one point, he was at an angle where his body was shoved up against the driver's door for several seconds. The right front tire dropped off a larger rock and crashed down onto the road, and the inertia threw Sam back toward the middle of the vehicle. By the time the vehicle was clear of the rockslide, Sam's body felt like he'd been run over by a Mack truck.

"You did it!" Becky ran up to the driver's door and held her hand up for a high-five. They slapped their palms together, which caused pain in Sam's shoulder. His neck muscles were so stiff from the tension he'd maintained crossing the rockslide that moving his head was painful.

"That looked like so much fun. I always wanted to try off-roading," Moondust said, a huge grin plastered across her face.

"It was awesome, man. I thought for sure you were going to roll that beast over the side of the mountain at one point," Tumbleweed said.

"I thought so, too." Sam gestured toward the bed of the truck. "Let's get loaded in and back on our way."

With everyone back in the Power Wagon, Sam looked into the rearview mirror and smiled. In hindsight, he had to admit, that had been kind of fun.

THIRTY-SEVEN

Sam

Blue Ridge Parkway
Waynesville, North Carolina
Day 23

The Blue Ridge Parkway was beautifully scenic, but Sam was ready to leave the twists and turns and put some miles behind them. He exited the parkway at Beech Gap heading north toward Canton and drove around Lake Logan, where several people were camped in tents. An elderly man stopped and stepped off the roadway. In his hands was a nice string of fish. He waved as the Power Wagon passed. "Nice truck!" he said.

"Thanks," Sam replied.

They crossed the Pigeon River and continued north, skirting Canton, North Carolina. Avoiding populated areas was taking much more time than Sam would have liked, but the goal was to get home without having the truck stolen and with everyone in one piece. So Sam pressed on, taking back roads and reaching the outskirts of Leicester, North Carolina, two hours and forty-five minutes after leaving Franklin. The houses began getting closer together, indicating they were getting close to town. They were just coming out of an S-curve when Becky spotted a roadblock.

"Not again," Moondust said.

It seemed even adrenaline junkies like Moondust had their limits.

A man in his late sixties appeared wearing blue jeans, overalls, and a bandanna over his head. He waved and gestured for them to pull up. He smiled and pointed toward an opening between the tractor and the large road graders blocking the lanes.

"Is this a trick?" Moondust asked. She was catching on quickly. Gone was the friendly, trusting hippie type he'd met back in Gainesville, Georgia.

Sam looked in the rearview mirror. "I'm not sure. Becky, you've got the right side of the road."

"Got it," Becky said, resting the barrel of her rifle on the window opening.

Tumbleweed was standing, leaning against the back glass. Sam heard the thump of Tumbleweed's shotgun as he plopped it onto the roof of the truck for a supported firing position and was glad his travel companions were such quick learners. Sam eased forward, keeping his eyes on the older gentleman and the left side of the roadway.

"What do you see, Becky?" Sam asked as they came within twenty feet of the 70s Caterpillar road grader. The tractor had been placed in the opposite lane ten feet farther north, creating a staggered checkpoint instead of a solid barrier to slow traffic without stopping it completely. From the horse poop piles, Sam imagined it was to allow farmers to ride into town.

"Nice truck," the gentleman said as he pumped his arm like a traffic cop guiding Sam through the checkpoint.

"Thanks," Sam said. "How are things in town?"

"Fair to middling. The gospel singing just started about an hour ago. If you hurry, you can still make it. Betty Sanders brought blackberry cobbler."

"She did, did she? Sounds good," Sam responded.

"I've been asking her for some ever since she had to shut down the Salty Goat. Momma and me used to go there after church every Sunday, and I'd get me a big helping of her berry cobbler with a huge scoop of her cinnamon ice cream."

The talk of cobbler had Sam's mouth salivating. Cinnamon ice cream? It would be winter before they'd be able to eat ice cream again.

Sam waved back as he cleared the grader and tractor. "Thanks for the info," Sam shouted.

"Is this for real?" Moondust asked. "Can they really be having a church revival meeting and serving dessert?"

"Life might not have changed all that much in small rural towns like this one. Folks adjust and then come together to help one another," Becky said. She was quiet for a moment. "That's how I imagine my hometown right now."

The Power Wagon bounced along the bridge over the French Broad River and passed by the Alexander, North Carolina Post Office. A few people came out of their homes and stopped in the driveways to stare at the old truck as it passed through town. Five minutes later, Sam steered the truck onto the on-ramp of Interstate 26. If the lanes had been cleared of vehicles, that would mean he'd be home in a little over an hour, but anything could happen in fifty miles.

Becky leaned back and stared out the Power Wagon's split windshield. "I'm looking forward to seeing my momma."

Moondust shifted in the seat, placed one hand on the dash, and twisted to look into the bed of the truck. "It's going to be a long, long hike to New Hampshire before I see my mother." She nodded toward Tumbleweed. "He's from Arizona. I can't imagine how he feels. What's the chance he'll ever make it home?"

Neither Sam nor Becky answered her question. They all knew the likelihood was next to zero. No one spoke a word for the next twenty miles.

"Sam's Gap," Moondust said as they drove over the Appalachian Trail where it crossed under the highway.

"There's the Tennessee state line," Becky said.

A knot formed in Sam's throat at the sight of the sign and the word, "Tennessee," painted on it. He was almost home. All he had to do was backtrack fifteen miles, drop off Becky at her home along Shelton Laurel Creek near White Rock, and then hop back onto Interstate 26 and push the old beast as fast as she'd go for the thirty or so miles to Unicoi.

Becky sat upright and put her hand over her mouth as the truck came out of a hairpin turn approaching the gravel road leading to Becky's childhood cabin.

Sam slowed the truck to a stop. Both sides of the road were lined with blackened trees sticking up from scorched earth. All that was left of Becky's childhood home were ashes. The whole forest looked as if it had been on fire. No one said a word, each staring out the split window at the heart-wrenching sight.

"Was that...?" Moondust broke the silence.

"My Papaw Shelton built that cabin in 1912," Becky said, easing open the passenger-side door and climbing out of the truck.

"I'm so sorry, Becky," Tumbleweed said, hopping down from the bed of the truck.

Sam couldn't find the words to comfort her as he fought back his own fears of what he would find when he reached home.

Becky walked up the hill and began sifting through her family's burned belongings.

"They got out," Moondust said. "Your momma is probably with another family member."

Becky nodded, wiped her ash-covered hands on her cargo pants, and turned back toward the truck as tears streamed down her cheeks.

"Just tell me which way, and we'll go find her," Sam said.

~

At the end of the gravel road, they turned south and followed Shelton Laurel Creek a quarter mile.

"There. That dirt road on the left," Becky said.

Sam made the turn, but as soon as he did, he stopped in the middle of the roadway. All that was left of the manufactured home was the steel frame and burned appliances.

"It was a forest fire," Moondust said.

They sat there in the truck for several minutes as Becky gathered herself. Sam put the truck into reverse and backed onto the blacktop. As he started to accelerate, Tumbleweed banged on the roof of the truck. Sam looked back, and he was kneeling in the bed with his shotgun pointed at something behind them.

Becky twisted and looked out her window. "Stop! Stop the truck, Sam!"

Sam had barely put the truck into park when Becky's door flung open, and she jumped out. As he climbed out, Sam spotted the couple standing in the roadway a hundred feet behind them.

Becky ran to them and threw her arms around the woman. She looked much too young to have been Becky's mother, but she was definitely family. Sam gave them a moment and then began to approach. He was within five feet when Becky dropped to her knees and began to wail. "I'm sorry, Beck. I'm sorry," the young man said. "We tried to get 'em out. It was just too hot."

"Momma! Momma!" Becky cried softly.

Sam stopped for a moment, allowing Becky's family to console her. He was almost numb inside as flashes of his losing his own parents washed over him, bringing a fresh round of grief for the loss. Sam walked over and placed a hand on Becky's shuddering shoulder. "I'm sorry, Becky."

She stiffened and then quickly shot to her feet. "I'm okay, Sam. You don't have to hang around. I know you need to get home to your family." She burst into tears at the word, and Sam reached out and pulled her into an embrace.

"I would never leave you like this. I couldn't."

"They're all gone. My momma, my brother, and his wife and kids."

Sam said nothing, allowing her time to process the pain.

"I have no one now. Not really. I have uncles, aunts, and cousins, but I can't expect them to take me in." She spun in a circle. "I have to find an abandoned cabin or trailer house or something."

The man pointed across the creek. "There's great-granddad's old homestead," the man said.

Becky nodded. "This is my cousin, Robbie, and his girlfriend."

Sam gave the couple a polite nod. "Becky, you can come home with me. You don't have to stay here unless you want to."

Becky was quiet for a moment. She glanced across the creek and back toward her family's burned mobile home. Her gaze turned toward the truck where Moondust and Tumbleweed stood. "I wouldn't want to be a burden to—"

"Don't. You could never be a burden. You know you'd be an asset. I've already told you that. We need you, Becky."

Becky turned to her cousin. "I think I'm going to stay with my friend here until I figure things out."

They hugged, and Sam wrapped his arm around Becky's shoulder and led her back to the truck. Moondust was already in the cab, and Tumbleweed held the door open for Becky and helped her climb up into the truck. Becky sobbed softly as Sam pulled the Power Wagon back onto the interstate and drove north toward Unicoi.

They saw virtually no cars. The few semis they passed on the road had been broken into and the contents spilled all over the ground. With each passing mile, the knot in Sam's stomach grew larger to the point he could feel it in his throat by the time they passed over Unaka Springs Road that led to the Nolichucky River and the A.T. trailhead south of Erwin, Tennessee. He was so close to home, and his heart was pounding in anticipation—and fear.

Just before the Unicoi County Hospital came into view, someone ran toward the truck from a side road. Monty West, the Unicoi County surveyor, was waving his arms, trying to stop Sam who pulled up next to Monty. "Don't drive into Erwin, Sam. I'd turn around and get the hell out of here if I were you."

THIRTY-EIGHT

Lauren

Unicoi City Hall
Unicoi, Tennessee
Day 23

"He straight up denied it," Benny said. "Ralph said he'd never seen the man before in his life. He swore on his dying grandson's life. Can you believe that? The guilty always do that."

"Disgusting. I knew he'd deny it. So the spy had no legitimate reason to be at Ralph's or he would have said so. We have to deduce from that denial that Ralph is hiding something. After my conversation with Bradshaw just a few moments ago, I think I know what that something is."

After Lauren relayed what Bradshaw had told her, Benny stood and paced the floor of her office. "What do you think? Should we bring this to the entire board? Should we have a trial and lay out all the evidence against him?" Lauren asked.

"I'd wait until Bradshaw gathers all his statements and for Vince and Dave to return from Watauga Lake. We'll need the extra security. This might start a civil war, Lauren. It could get extremely ugly. You know that, right?"

"What are we supposed to do, let him steal from the town and collude with the Corbins on who knows what evil plot he has planned for the town?"

"I agree. We can't ignore it. I'm just saying we need to be prepared for the fallout."

"Do what you need to do. I'm going to finish up here and run home to check on my dad."

"How's he doing?"

Lauren shook her head. She couldn't bring herself to say the words out loud.

"I'm sorry, Lauren."

"Thanks, Benny. Go help Bradshaw make his case against Ralph so we can put that issue to bed and move on to the next: what to do about State Senator Phelps' proposal."

After Benny left, Lauren found it impossible to concentrate. She'd added a list of numbers six times and finally thrown the old manual calculator across the room.

"Alan Mayberry is here, Mayor," her assistant, Natasha, said.

Lauren sighed loudly.

Alan appeared. "If I'm disturbing you, I can come back later."

"No. I'm just…" Lauren closed the notebook on her desk and steepled her fingers with her elbows on her desk. "What bad news do you have for me?"

Alan slid into the chair and began by telling her how the kidnapper had watched the compound for days to learn the routines and discover a way in. "His orders were to slip in and get the children without being detected. He would have if Charlie hadn't stopped him."

"And Charlie is okay? He didn't get hurt?" Lauren asked.

Benny rushed into the room; behind him were his confidential informant, Verónica "Ronnie" Morales, and Nick's former girlfriend, Cindy Plummer.

"We have to get you out of here and to the compound," Benny said.

Lauren rose from her chair. "Why? What's happened?"

Benny stepped back and allowed Ronnie and Cindy to enter Lauren's office. Alan stood and moved toward the window.

"Ma'am, I've been inside Nigel Corbin's group since he got out of jail. I've been sending Benny information about their activities," Ronnie said. She looked back at Benny. "He has this former special forces type guy on his team that came up with a plan to attack the town."

Lauren's heart lurched. "When?"

"Soon is all I know. Mario came back from Unicoi all upset because someone here killed his brother."

He had to be talking about the man that Lauren had killed. Was that what he'd meant when he said she'd unleashed the hounds of hell?

"The head of security took him into Corbin's office and I could hear yelling inside. The guy told Corbin they were ready to act but were waiting for Russo's kids to arrive in Erwin," Ronnie said.

"Mayor, after I left the compound, I went to stay with my ex-boyfriend, Clay Cross, at his parent's house. I overheard Ralph and Ray Peters talking about how Ralph had evidence that you were stealing. Ray was furious. Ralph was talking about rounding up folks to come arrest you and take control of the town," Cindy said.

Raised voices echoed through the streets outside the municipal building. It sounded like half the town was in the parking lot. Lauren ran to the window. Her hand dropped to her revolver at the sight of at least two hundred angry residents armed with baseball bats and clubs.

"Mayor, we need to get you out of here," Mayberry said, rushing over and grabbing Lauren's arm.

"Take her out the back and get her up to the compound. Then come back and help me handle this," Benny said, checking the number of rounds in his weapon's magazine before running outside to stop the crowd from storming the building.

"Bring her out, Benny. You bring that thief out and have her face us," Ray Peters yelled.

Others shouted their agreement and then began chanting, "Lock her up! Lock her up!"

THIRTY-NINE

Lauren
_____

Unicoi City Hall
Unicoi, Tennessee
Day 23

"I'm not going to the compound, Alan. I can't leave my parents and I'm not going to abandon the town in the middle of a crisis," Lauren said.

Mayberry pointed to the concrete block building to the back of city hall. "Let me at least get you over to the police station. We can secure that building better than this one."

"I'm going to get my sister. We'll come back and help you guard her," Ronnie said.

"No, Ronnie. It's too dangerous, but you can go tell everyone you see to stay indoors until this is resolved. I don't want innocent people hurt," Lauren said.

"I'll do that, but I'm sure Marie will want to come and back up her boyfriend."

"We have to go, Lauren." Alan was practically dragging her down the corridor.

They ran to the back door, and Alan peered around the door jamb. "Shit. There's a bunch of them standing around watching the back.

"Here, I'm on it," Ronnie said. "Join me, Cindy?"

"Why not?" Cindy said, tugging up her strapless shirt.

The two young women stepped outside and ran toward the crowd of ten or so people. "She got away. Did you see her run past? I think she slipped out the window and ran south," Ronnie said.

"Yeah, I saw her. She went that way and ran into the woods," Cindy pointed to the tree line across the street that ran behind city hall.

"Where?" a taller man asked. "Show us."

As soon as Ronnie and Cindy led the crowd away, Alan pushed open the door, and he and Lauren ran toward the police station and entered through a side door of the concrete block building. Alan locked the heavy steel door and led Lauren through the station past the desk sergeant, Belinda Salter.

"Get her into the arms room," Belinda said, rushing to unlock the door.

Along one wall was a row of weapons lockers. The opposite wall contained shelves stacked with cardboard boxes. "I'm not getting locked inside there," Lauren said.

"It's the most secure place unless you want to be locked into the jail cell in the back," Belinda said.

"Hell no!" I'll stay right here. If they breach the door, I'll fight right alongside you," Lauren said.

The mob outside grew louder as the chants of "lock her up" also increased in volume. Some shouted for Lauren to be hanged, while others wanted her placed in the same stocks they used for thieves.

"I can't believe Ralph did this," Lauren said as she checked the rounds in her revolver.

"Here," Alan said, handing Lauren an AR-15 and four spare

magazines from a weapons locker. "You know how to use this?"

"Oh, yeah. She's an excellent shot. I trained with her out at their shooting range," Belinda said.

Belinda had been dating a member of the survival group at the time and had applied to be a part of the group. When the EMP happened, she'd chosen to help defend the town instead of moving to the compound, a decision Lauren was grateful for at the moment. It seemed they needed all the loyal citizens they could find to save the town now. Lauren had anticipated having to fight enemies outside of the town, but she'd not considered having to protect herself from the citizens she'd served for the last three years.

"Save the mayor! Save the mayor!" someone outside yelled.

"Someone's on your side," Belinda said.

Lauren took a step toward the window to see who was supporting her, but Alan stepped up and grabbed her arm. "You have to stay away from the windows."

Belinda ignored him and moved to the glass door. "You will not believe who's out there rallying for you," she said.

The chants in support of her grew louder. "They're making a line in front of city hall," Belinda said.

Lauren strained to see around Alan's broad shoulders. "Who? Who is it?"

"The girls from the motel. The ones that Pastor Billings took in after Billy Mahon was killed.

"Go home. This is not how we settle things in Unicoi," someone else outside yelled.

"Is that Pastor Billings?" Lauren asked. She desperately wanted to see for herself, but Alan stood his ground as an unmovable force.

"It sure is," Belinda said.

"What in the world?" Lauren was shocked. He and those poor young girls Mahon had used and abused were out there now, putting their lives in danger for her and the town.

"The security force just pulled up," Belinda said.

A second later, the back door opened, and Lauren spun around, ready to shoot to defend herself.

"It's me," Wilson said. He ran down the short hall and rounded the corner, flying past Lauren and Alan and into the arms room. Chief sent me to get the tear gas and rubber bullets. I never thought we'd have to use these in Unicoi."

"We have riot gear?" Lauren had never imagined they'd have to repel a crowd in tiny Unicoi, either.

"Yes, ma'am. It was donated when another agency upgraded. It's all old, but it's better than nothing." He grabbed several large cans of pepper spray.

"Is that really necessary?" Lauren could not accept it had come to this.

"We could use live rounds." Wilson wasn't smiling.

"I'd like this settled with minimal violence to the protesters," Lauren said.

"Those aren't protesters, ma'am. Some of them want you dead. Others want you in stocks."

Lauren was at a loss for words.

"Trey King and his sons are among the protesters. They're armed," Wilson said.

Alan shook his head. "Stay here with the mayor. I'll deliver the crowd control weapons and then deal with that King bunch."

"Alan?" Lauren stepped in front of him. I don't want to start a civil war."

"I'm sorry to tell you this, mayor, but someone already did."

"Let me in!" someone outside yelled. The voice sounded like Angela's.

No way!

There was no way her parent's nurse would turn against her. If she'd wanted to hurt Lauren, she could have easily done so on hundreds of occasions.

"Lauren! It's Angela. You have to come quick."

"Angela?" Lauren pushed past Wilson and ran to the door. Her parents' nurse stood outside with her hands pressed against the glass. Lauren looked past her to the flames coming from the shops across the street from city hall. "Belinda, unlock it."

Belinda fumbled with the keys for a moment before getting the door open and yanked Angela inside just as a brick slammed into the concrete building.

"Is that glass going to hold?" Angela asked.

"They can't get through those bars on the windows."

"What's wrong, Angela?" Lauren asked, taking her hand.

"A bunch of them are outside your parents' house. Lindsay is holding them off, but she's low on shells."

"Bullets." Lauren couldn't help correcting her. "Shells are for shotguns."

"I have to get back. Your father...." Angela spun around and hit the door handle. She was halfway out the door.

"What about my father?"

"I have to get back," she said, racing across the parking lot and disappearing behind city hall.

"I have to go. I have to protect my parents."

"Well, shit!" Belinda said. "Wilson, they're going to need the rest of those weapons and ammo. You gotta make sure no unauthorized persons get into that arms room."

Wilson spun, ran back to the armory, and slammed the door shut. "No one's getting in here without authorization."

Lauren clutched the AR to her chest as she and Belinda raced out the back door of the police station, crossed the street behind the hardware store, and ran into the woods behind city hall, arriving at her parents' neighbor's home several minutes later.

A group of twenty or so people was hunkered down behind an SUV near her parents' driveway. Belinda dropped down into the drainage ditch and moved toward Buddy French's newer model lifted F450 truck. She placed the barrel of her rifle on its massive bumper and peered through her rifle scope.

"Are they armed? Do you see weapons?" Lauren asked, moving in next to her.

"Ray and Brian Peters are carrying rifles, but I can't see whether anyone else is armed."

"Where's Lindsay?"

"Over there behind the pad-mounted transformer in Buddy's front yard. I think Buddy is with her."

"That's a surprise." Lauren half expected him to have joined the crowd wanting her head. Had she misjudged him?

Ray poked his head up and popped off several rounds in Lindsay's direction. Lindsay returned fire from her position and then dropped back out of sight. Belinda and Lauren both fired, striking Ray in the side. He fell forward. Brian checked his brother and then spun toward them, firing wildly without aiming. The rounds slammed into Buddy's brand new truck, shattering the windshield and breaking the huge side mirrors. When Brian stopped to reload, Belinda fired, striking Brian in the head. Several of the rioters ran from the SUV and took cover behind Mrs. Utley's silver sedan parked in her driveway. Lindsay fired several rounds into it, causing the people hiding behind it to flee in all directions.

As Belinda moved to secure Ray and Brian's weapons, Lauren ran over to Lindsay and Buddy. "We have to get to my house. I have to get to my parents," she said.

"Go! Belinda and I will handle the rest of them," Buddy said.

Lauren stared at him for a second.

"See, they're running away. We'll make sure they don't come back. Go! Go to your dad," Buddy said.

"What the hell is going on, Lauren? Buddy came running up the street yelling that a group of folks were heading this way aiming to hurt you and your parents," Lindsay said as she and Lauren ran toward the front door of her parents' home.

"Ralph," was all Lauren could manage to say.

Lauren shouldered the door open and ran to her father's side. "Daddy!" His oxygen mask was off, and his face was blue.

FORTY

Sam
___

Interstate 23, Exit 34
Unicoi, Tennessee
Day 23

Sam raced north along the interstate, intending to take the Walmart exit, but just after passing Elks Lodge, he discovered a roadblock constructed of shipping containers and tractor-trailers lined up to form a steel wall blocking all four lanes of the interstate. The fortress extended across the field toward town as far as he could see.

"Looks like someone's been busy," Sam said. "We'll have to go on foot, everyone. Becky, are you up for this?"

"Let's roll," Becky said, wiping a tear from her swollen eyes, throwing open the passenger door, and jumping out.

"Becky, hop back in. I'm going to get right up next to one of those Conexes with the truck and we can use it to get on top of the wall." Becky did what he asked and Sam maneuvered the truck so the passenger side was parked sideways right up against one of the Conexes sitting on the highway.

"Alright, I'll go over first. When I'm over and it's clear, I'll holler at y'all to come on over," Sam said.

In the distance, on the other side of the barrier, they heard sporadic gunfire. His heart sank as he realized what was happening.

Sam, Moondust, and Becky exited the cab through the driver's door, and Sam got himself into the truck bed. As he was attempting to get himself and his bum leg on top of the cab, Tumbleweed said, "Sam, let me go first. I can help break your fall when you go to drop down on the other side,"

"How 'bout if you help me balance here and give me a shove so I can get on top of the truck, and then onto the Conex? I'll crawl over and check things out, then call you up and you can drop down and help me to the ground over there. If this wall is being guarded by the city, I may know the guards. They don't know you, though, and you might catch a bullet.

"Sounds fair to me," Tumbleweed said, swallowing hard.

Tumbleweed gave him a shove and Sam rolled onto the top of the shipping container flopping over onto his back, right next to a dead body.

It was Neil Foster. Sam and Neil had played high school football together. Neil's milky eyes stared blankly up into the sky. The metal Conex acted like a frying pan in the hot sun, cooking Neil's body in his own blood pooled underneath him. Some of the blood was still liquid, indicating how recently Foster had been shot.

Not the welcome home Sam was hoping to receive.

The sound of more distant gunfire echoed off the shipping container wall. Sam's instinct was to run toward the sound, but with his leg, he knew he wasn't running anywhere. He needed the assistance of his travel companions if he was going to make it to his wife and son.

"Guys, come on up, but be aware there's a body up here," Sam said. "Just try not to look at it."

Tumbleweed sprang from the top of the truck onto the Conex,

took in the whole gruesome scene, then gingerly turned and reached down to help the ladies up.

"The gunfire sounds like it's coming from downtown. We need to get moving," Sam said, standing next to Tumbleweed, between the body and the ladies. Fear and dread curled around Sam's heart at the thought of his wife and son being caught up in the distant firefight.

"I'll drop down and help everyone down," Tumbleweed said, rolling over the edge of the Conex and dropping to the ground inside the wall.

Sam guided the ladies around the body and lowered each of them down as Tumbleweed reached up to help them to the ground, then Sam rolled over the edge himself.

"I didn't look—did you?" Moondust asked Becky.

"Nope."

"Follow me," Sam said, heading off into the woods. The hikers followed him single file into the trees, heading toward the sound of more gunfire.

The sporadic gunfire increased in volume the closer Sam and his companions got to town. Through the tree line, Sam made out the outline of the back of the elementary school. Two men were running along its concrete facade. They stopped at the far corner where they began engaging with their rifles.

That's Benny and Alan!

"You guys wait here in the wood line—I'm going to make contact with them," Sam said, pointing to the men.

"Chief Jameson, this is Simpson, over," radioed Tyler Simpson

"Simpson, Jameson, over."

"Chief, there's eight of 'em. We won't be able to hold 'em off once they smash through the front door. It's only me and one guard inside here."

"Benny! Alan!" Sam shouted, hobbling up to them.

Benny and Alan both turned, mouths agape, staring at Sam in shock. He was afraid they might not recognize him unshaven and with his apocalyptic weight loss.

"Sam, it's damn good to see you, man!" Benny said.

"How can I help?" Sam asked, pointing in the direction of the shooters.

Without skipping a beat, Alan said, "I'll run up to the front and distract them on this side of the building."

"We'll flank 'em. Follow me, Sam," said Benny, and took off back along the concrete facade toward the far corner of the elementary school."

Sam looked toward the wood line and signaled for his three companions to follow as he limped after Benny. When Becky and the hikers got closer, he waved them on and pointed toward Benny. Moondust, Becky, and Tumbleweed looked at each other in mock-comic astonishment, shrugging their shoulders, then jogged ahead of Sam to follow the uniformed man with the rifle.

Chief Benny Jameson rounded the other back corner of the school and headed toward the front. He crouched and scurried along behind a concrete pony wall that extended the side wall past the front corner of the school. Then he stopped, rested his rifle barrel on top of the wall, and glassed the school's front yard with his rifle scope, evaluating the situation in front of him. Moondust, Tumbleweed, and Becky followed suit behind Benny. Becky and Tumbleweed stopped and rested the business ends of their weapons atop the wall.

"Who the hell are...?" Benny asked, turning his head, expecting to find Sam. Instead, a slender woman in shorts and running shoes wearing a purple backpack crouched next to him. Moondust held a knife in one hand and a can of bear spray in the other. Her big messy bun was flopped to one side of her head, too much for her hair tie to handle. Benny glanced past her to the other two civilians with long guns crouched next to her. Sam had rounded the corner behind them and, with his bum leg, was only just catching up now. Benny looked at him over the top of the three hikers and Sam gave him a thumbs up. "They're with me."

Extended automatic rifle fire from the far side of the school got their attention. From the sound of it, Alan had emptied an entire thirty-round magazine as a signal. Benny pointed at the wall and said, "We have eight bad guys dressed in red shirts and black body armor. They're trying to take control of our food storage facility." He reached down, drew his service pistol, and handed it, butt first, to Moondust. "Let's not let that happen, shall we?" he said. Moondust smiled and nodded. Sam, crouched beside Becky, laid his rifle barrel on top of the wall, and they all turned and opened fire on Corbin's Z-Nation crew.

In just a few minutes. Benny, Becky, the hikers, and Sam had dispatched all eight of the Z-Nation crew. The elementary school's front yard was littered with gangbangers' bodies.

"Benny, where are my wife and son?" Sam asked.

"Charlie's at the compound. We left Lauren at the police station when we heard gunfire over here—right after we used all of our rubber bullets, bean bags, and pepper spray to disperse an angry mob there. Wilson and Belinda are at the police station with her," Benny said.

Sam felt lightheaded. He bent over and placed his hands on his knees. His wife and son were alive. Charlie had made it off the plane and Lauren had managed to get them home from Knoxville. Three weeks of unbearable stress of not knowing whether they were alive had just been lifted from his shoulders. "I have to get to her."

Becky put a hand on Sam's shoulder, and Sam placed a hand on hers as he straightened upright to embrace her in a hug. Becky smiled. "They made it home."

"We need more folks to secure the school—we've only got Simpson and one other guard here right now," Benny said. "This is our distribution center for the food we grow and gather from the farms up near your in-laws' place, Sam."

"Becky," Sam said, also looking at Moondust and Tumbleweed. "Will you three stay here and help guard the school?"

The three looked at each other and nodded.

"Roger that, Sam," Tumbleweed said.

"The truck's over here," Benny said.

Sam rode shotgun while Benny drove. Alan stood in the bed with his rifle lying on top of the cab as they raced through town toward the police station. People were running back and forth across the street in front of them.

"Chief, huh? Congrats. Should I ask what happened to Avery?" Sam asked.

"Killed by Billy Mahon. What happened to your leg?"

"Got shot," Sam said.

Benny had to hit the brakes to keep from running over a man. They passed the fire department and post office, which were both ablaze, just before screeching to a stop at the police department.

"What the hell is happening here?" Sam asked, hopping out of the truck and then turning and hobbling toward the entrance to the police station. Benny beat him there and went inside. By the time Sam got to the door, Benny was bursting back out.

"There's no one here," Benny yelled to Alan, who was still standing in the truck bed pulling security. "Radio Belinda and find out where they are."

Before Alan could respond, Lindsay's voice crackled through the radio.

"Alan, this is Lindsay. I'm here at Lauren's house—there's a mob outside looking for Lauren."

Benny started the truck and pulled around the police station, intending to head to Lauren and Sam's place, but very nearly ran straight into the Wagoneer as it came barreling around the building from the other direction. Vince was behind the wheel of the Wagoneer staring wildly through the windshield at his brother—not fifteen feet in front of him and staring back.

"Lindsay, this is Vince. Me, Dave, and Nick are back from the lake. We're following the chief and Mayberry. We'll be there as fast as we can!"

A bullet hit the truck and Alan slapped the top of the cab. "Step on it, Chief," he yelled.

Benny cranked the wheel, drove around the Wagoneer, and stomped the gas. Vince, Dave, and Nick followed as they all raced north toward the Taylors' subdivision. Benny took the next turn a little too fast and nearly ran off the roadway. He pushed the truck to its limits, racing to get there in time.

Up ahead, the Johnson & Carter Farms packinghouse sat on a hill above the roadway on the right. As the two vehicles approached the plant, the truck was hit by a barrage of bullets. Sam turned to see Alan's body tumble out of the truck bed and across the road into the ditch on the left.

"Alan!" Benny yelled as he slammed on the brakes and pointed the truck toward the far side of a tractor-trailer parked parallel with the road in the packinghouse's overflow lot on the left, across the road from the packinghouse. The truck skidded to a stop with the tractor-trailer for cover between them and the shooters at the packinghouse.

Sam heard the Wagoneer accelerate, then saw, through the space under the tractor-trailer, both of the Wagoneer's front tires suddenly blow out and it lurch to the right, causing the vehicle to immediately roll onto the driver's side and then flip in a spiraling pirouette, end-to-end, past the tractor-trailer until it stopped upside down in the middle of the road blocking both lanes. Nick was thrown from the vehicle, high into the air, landing on the side of the hill on the right side of the road. Sam peered under the tractor-trailer at the over-turned Wagoneer. There was no movement from the crippled vehicle.

"Sam, there are men crossing the road coming toward us," Benny said. "Engage!"

Sam flattened himself on the ground and rolled left under the trailer until he spotted the men. There were half a dozen or more of them wearing body armor like the Z-Nation guys back at the elementary school. Sam glassed them with the red dot mounted to the top of his AR, exhaled slowly, and squeezed the trigger.

Bang!

One down.

Benny let loose with automatic weapon fire from around the front bumper of the truck. The men scattered into the ditch at the bottom of the packinghouse hill. Sam zeroed in on the next man, exhaled, and...

Bang!

Two down.

"Brrrrrt!" Benny took out two more.

Another man popped his head out of the ditch and Sam squeezed his trigger again.

Bang!

That's three.

Gravel flew into the air in front of Sam, hitting him in the face, followed by the report of several shots originating from some-where on the other side of the road. Several more shots rang out from across the road, hitting the tractor-trailer and the pickup, and throwing more gravel in Sam's direction.

In the distance, through the sound of the gunfire, Sam heard the deep rumble of what he thought was a Harley Davidson V-twin, downshifting, and then cutting out.

More rifle fire from across the road. Sam took careful aim again and took out another man who had stuck his head up from the ditch.

Four.

One shot—one kill. How many more can there be?

Several men ran down the hill and took cover in the ditch to his left near the overturned Wagoneer.

"Shit!"

He no longer had any cover whatsoever. Sam took aim again and squeezed the trigger, but nothing happened.

"Shit!"

He rolled back toward the tractor-trailer, still out in the open in front of the new men in the ditch across the road, then scrambled back awkwardly behind the truck's rear wheels, using his good leg to push himself, and dropped his magazine.

Empty.

"Shit!"

He was out of ammo for his AR. He dropped the rifle, drew his 1911 from his cross-draw holster, and aimed it at the new threat across the road. He looked toward the Wagoneer—still no movement at all from the old Jeep.

Two men broke cover from the ditch, ran, and took cover behind the Jeep's rear bumper. One peered inside the rear hatch and ducked back down. He shook his head at the other man, and the two ran across the road to the rear of the trailer. Sam took a shot at them as they crossed and hit one of them, who fell to the asphalt holding his side screaming. The other kept going and took cover behind the driver's side rear wheels of the trailer.

"Brrrrrt." Benny's automatic sounded again from the pickup.

The men from the ditch began concentrating their fire on Benny's position. Shot after shot flew in his direction.

Sam fired his 1911 at another man across the road.

Bang!

He couldn't tell whether he'd hit the man, or not.

Another high-powered rifle round took out a man in the ditch, followed by yet another high-powered round hitting another man.

Suddenly, silence descended on their war zone, then Sam heard the sound of gravel under the boots of the man who had taken cover at the end of the tractor-trailer.

More shots from across the road. More gravel pelted Sam.

A high-powered rifle report followed by a man's scream from the packing plant ditch filled the air.

Silence again.

Ten seconds went by. Twenty. Thirty seconds—still silence.

Sam dropped down and rolled back toward the pickup, looking underneath in Benny's direction. Benny lay on his back, his rifle beyond his reach, unmoving.

The silence increased, suddenly drowned out by Sam's heartbeat pounding in his ears, rushing to a crescendo.

Boots on gravel snapped Sam's attention toward the rear of the semitrailer. The man who had taken cover there was running toward Sam, firing his rifle at him. Sam rolled and squeezed off two rounds—missing both times. The slide on his 1911 locked to the rear, and the man kept coming, firing wildly. More gravel sprayed him in the face. Sam closed his eyes, reaching out a hand to shield himself.

Another high-powered rifle shot.

Silence.

A man crumpled to the gravel right in front of Sam, his rifle skidding a few feet away.

Silence. The silence seemed to go on forever.

"Sam!" someone yelled. "Sam!"

Who the hell is that?

Sam looked around. He didn't see movement in any direction.

"Sam!"

"Holy shit!"

"Matt!" Sam yelled.

He couldn't believe it. Could this really be his army buddy, Matt Cruz? Had he somehow made it all the way from the CDC in Atlanta, Georgia?

"Yeah, I don't see any movement. Where are you?"

Sam stood and hobbled around the back of the pickup toward the sound of Matt's voice. Benny lay on the ground in front of the passenger front tire. Sam bent to feel for a pulse. Benny was alive, but he appeared to have been hit in the head by a bullet.

"Benny!" Sam said. "Benny!"

Benny stirred, lifting his hand to his head.

"Sam, you all right?" Matt asked, walking up.

"Yeah, you okay?"

"Yeah," Matt said.

"Matt Cruz, this is Police Chief Benny Jameson." Benny opened his eyes and looked around. "Benny, this is my buddy. We served together—he's going to take care of you. Matt, make sure Benny's not hit anywhere else if you would. I've got to check on my brother in the Wagoneer."

Vince and Dave were both unconscious, still strapped in the Jeep and hanging upside down.

"Matt, if Benny's okay, I could use a hand here."

"How is he?" Sam asked as Matt ran around to the passenger side of the Wagoneer.

"He has a concussion, but nothing broken."

Vince and Dave began to stir as Sam and Matt worked to unlatch their seatbelts without letting them fall. There was no major trauma to their bodies that Sam could see.

"Matt, we had a man thrown from the truck. He's back down the road in the ditch on the right. Did you see him when you were coming up here?"

"Sam, that man's dead."

Nick had been left alone on the hillside by Nigel Corbin's men, who evidently thought he was dead. With Vince and Dave safely extracted from the Wagoneer, Sam went to check on him. As Sam approached, Nick sat up, wincing.

"I think my left shoulder's broken."

"Move your legs. Do you hurt anywhere else?"

"Nah, I just got a few scratches."

Sam turned back toward Matt and yelled, "My wife's in trouble, I've got to go. Can you do your best to take care of my friends until I return with someone who can provide medical assistance?"

"You got it, brother. Take my bike. It's back there past the last curve at the end of a driveway," Matt said, tossing him the keys.

Sam limped back toward Matt's motorcycle, past Mayberry, who was lying dead in the ditch, a tangle of broken bones and torn flesh. As he hobbled closer to the bike, he realized he had a problem. The motorcycle had to be kick started. Thinking out of the box, Sam mounted the bike from the right side—the wrong side—throwing his bum leg over the seat. Leaving the vintage Harley leaning on its stand, Sam worked the kick peddle, then balanced himself as he lifted his body above the bike. With one kick, the Harley roared to life, and Sam struggled to keep the heavy machine from falling over. He gasped at the searing pain in his left leg.

Accelerating through the packinghouse battleground, Sam rumbled past his friends with his hand in the air, counting five other hands going up in response.

FORTY-ONE

Lauren

Taylor Residence
Unicoi Tennessee
Day 23

Edna was in her rocking chair, staring out the back window singing an old church hymn. Lauren released her father's limp hand and crumpled to the floor beside his bed. The music moved through her, settling her soul and encompassing her like a cocoon. Lauren lay on the floor, spent, with nothing left, her heart aching from a wound so deep she could hardly breathe. A hand touched her. She didn't respond. She couldn't move. Her mind was blank and unaware of anything going on around her.

He's gone. He can't be gone. Oh, Daddy. I'm so sorry I wasn't here.

As she rocked back and forth, a hand slid under her arm.

"Lauren."

It was Sam's voice. Through the haze of tears, she looked at him.

Was this a dream? Could this be real?

Her husband lifted her from the floor.

"Sam?"

"I'm here, my love. I'm home."

Her heart wouldn't allow her to hope. If this was a dream, it would be the end of her. She couldn't bear to have Sam back only to lose him again to a vision.

"You're not real."

"I'm real, love. I'm real. I'm home. Everything is going to be all right."

Lauren looked into Sam's eyes. She clasped his face between her hands, her eyes wide, tears streaming down her cheeks. "My Sam! Is it you?" She touched his beard and ran her fingers across his brow. "Oh, Sam! You made it. You came home to me."

"Nothing on earth would have stopped me, my love. Nothing."

"Daddy. My dad. He's gone, Sam. The town… it's…" Lauren sobbed into his shoulder.

"I'm sorry I wasn't here for you. I'm so, so sorry. I'm here now. I will never, ever leave you again."

Lauren squeezed him tighter. Her gaze fell onto her father's lifeless body. Sam was home, but everything wasn't going to be all right. How could it be?

Edna continued rocking and singing, not acknowledging the death of her husband or Sam's arrival.

Sam gently led Lauren to a chair next to Bill's bed. He removed Bill's oxygen mask from his face and placed it on the table next to the bed, then smoothed a strand of her father's hair back and closed the elderly man's eyes. He took Lauren's hand in his, and the two stared at the strongest man Lauren had ever known.

The passage of time was fleeting as Lauren sat silently with her father. Memories flooded her mind: images of fishing trips, Sunday stops at the ice cream parlor, the road trip—just the two of them when she'd been choosing which college to attend. Lauren couldn't imagine life without her dad.

Sam squeezed her hand. "I need to go speak to Lindsay. I have to check on Vince and the others and then see about Charlie. I won't be long."

Lauren stood and threw her hands around his neck. "Thank God you're home. Thank God. I needed you. I can't—"

"You're not alone anymore, Lauren. I'm here now. Everything is going to be all right."

He held her tight and kissed her cheek.

"I want to take my dad home to our farm, Sam. Let's go home. Let's go to the farm. I want to sit on our porch and watch the sunset."

"Then that's what we'll do. I've got to radio the compound and dispatch some medical help."

Lauren thought to ask who the medical help was for, but she couldn't bear to know.

Late that afternoon, Lauren and Sam led Edna out the front door where one of the compound's old trucks was parked in the driveway. The bodies of the rioters had been removed, but blood still stained the driveway and street in front of the home. Lauren was surprised to see Sam's old army buddy, Matt Cruz, but assumed he and Sam had traveled from Atlanta together. She attempted a smile.

Sam helped Edna into the passenger seat and Lauren sat next to her as Matt, Vince, and Dave carried her father's quilt-wrapped body from the house and placed it in the bed of the truck.

"I'll ride back here with him," Lindsay said, patting Lauren's shoulder. Angela stepped around the front of the vehicle. "I'll ride back there with him, too."

"We'll be right behind you," Vince said, stepping back next to Nick, Dave, and Matt.

Buddy French stood on the sidewalk in front of his house. Lauren knew she should thank him for protecting her parents from the rioters, but she didn't have the strength to form the words. She raised her hand and waved. It was the best she could do.

"Dad!" Charlie ran toward them. "Dad!" His tone was desperate, and he yelled, "You're home!"

Sam climbed out of the truck, and Charlie ran over to him, throwing his arms around his father's neck. The touching scene sent Lauren into uncontrollable tears. She covered her face and leaned forward, her head resting on the dash. She felt her mother's hand on her back, patting her. "It's okay, Lauren Michelle. It's okay. You let those tears out. It's okay to cry. You don't always have to be so tough."

Lauren turned and hugged her mother, sobbing into her mother's shoulder like she had when she was a little girl. Edna stroked her hair and sang softly in her ear.

"Amazing grace, how sweet the sound..."

"You're home, Dad. I knew you'd make it. I knew you would," Charlie said.

"You okay, Charlie Brown?" Sam pulled his son into an embrace.

"I'm good now," Charlie said. "What took you so long?"

"That's a long story, son. Let's get Lauren and Edna inside, and I'll tell you all about it on our way up to the cemetery."

Lindsay and Angela hopped down from the truck bed and opened Lauren's door. "Come on, Lauren. Let's get your mother inside." Angela helped Edna up the walkway to Lauren's front porch and steadied her as she lowered herself into a rocking chair.

Lauren glanced around. "What happened with Benny and the town, Lindsay?"

"Benny's fine. We can talk about all that after we get you settled."

Lauren followed her up the steps and sat in her favorite chair. She looked out at the mountain peaks in the distance as Matt, Dave, and Vince carried her father's body toward the hill.

FORTY-TWO

Sam

Taylor Residence
Unicoi, Tennessee
Day 26

It was moving day for the Wallace family. Sam picked up a box of
clothes and handed it to Charlie. "You can take this one."

Lauren had been in her parents' room for over an hour, getting
her mother's things ready to move out to their farm. Sam eased
Bill and Edna's door open. He half expected to see Bill sitting in
his wheelchair next to Edna as he always did. "Lauren, it's time."
He pushed the door open the rest of the way and stepped into the
room. "We have to go."

Lauren glanced up at him. The pain on her face nearly ripped
his heart from his chest. This was the day she'd always dreaded.
She'd fought so hard to keep her parents in their home. She wanted
her mother to be able to live out her last days and die in her own
bed as her father had. She'd promised Bill that very thing when
they'd moved in there with them—but that was before. It just
wasn't possible to keep that promise now, not with the condition of

the town as it was. They weren't safe there even now. Not after the riots and attack by Nigel Corbin's men. Many of the people who'd taken part in the riots still lived in the town despite the damage to the buildings. Those who remained were doing their best to secure the borders against future attacks, but Sam wasn't taking chances with his family's safety.

"Sam. We gotta go, bud," Vince called from the living room.

"Lauren," Sam said, moving toward her. "I'll help you."

Sam took Lauren's arm and lifted her from her chair. "Charlie and Vince will grab your mother's chair," Sam said.

"She's going to love it at the farm," Angela said, holding Edna's suitcase in her hand.

"She'll love all the lambs and baby animals. She'll get to sit in the rocker on the front porch with Maggie's little girl and pet baby bunnies," Lindsay said as Sam led Lauren to the truck.

"Hold up. I have one last thing I want to get," Lauren said, running back inside.

"Stay here, Charlie," Sam said, following after Lauren.

After a search of the house, Sam found Lauren in the attic. "What are you doing up here?" he asked.

She continued ripping open a large box. "Help me."

Sam grabbed the box, and she pulled out a wooden baby cradle.

"I think Maggie's boy is too big for this, Lauren."

Lauren looked up. "It's not for him."

"Who's it for, then?" Sam asked.

Lauren smiled. "Sam Junior."

"What?" Sam wasn't sure he'd heard her right.

She nodded.

"You?"

Her smile grew wider. "Yep!"

"Are you sure?"

"As Mom would say, the rabbit died."

"What does that mean?"

"It's an old saying. It means the pregnancy test was positive. Mrs. Miller says she won't be able to detect a heartbeat until around eighteen to twenty weeks gestation, so I guess we won't know for sure until then. Maggie said I might be showing weeks before that though."

Sam was still in shock. He'd wanted more children, but he thought Lauren didn't. With their careers and taking care of Bill and Edna, it seemed like that wasn't in the cards, but he was wrong.

"I'm the most blessed man on earth." He took her in his arms and kissed her softly on the lips. "Sam Junior. I like the sound of that."

~

Driving past Unicoi's burned-out homes and businesses that had been there all his life was hard. So much had changed. People they'd grown up with were dead or had moved away to be with family. Those who remained would rebuild what they could. Benny, Richardson, Tyler Simpson, Bradshaw, Sid, Belinda, Mr. Lawless, and others who'd been there for Lauren and the town through the worst days of its history were attempting to pick up the pieces and start new lives on its outskirts. They would all work together to build a community that was strong and resilient. One they would be able to defend against an attack like the one that had caused the destruction.

~

Sam pulled the truck up to the steel gate that spanned the entrance to the Wallace compound. Dave greeted them and pushed open the heavy steel gate, allowing Sam to drive through. "How's your neck today, Dave?" Angela asked as Sam drove past.

"Better, thanks to Mrs. Miller's brownies." Dave chuckled.

"Better not let Vince hear you say that," Lindsay said.

Charlie laughed. "He ate two brownies after dinner last night."

Inside the perimeter, Sam looked up toward the hill to the west and covered his eyes from the glaring sun. Without binoculars or a scope, he couldn't make out who was on duty at that guard post, but he knew someone was, and they could see the truck very well. So could the person on duty on the hill to the east. From their perches high up on the hills, they could see the whole Wallace compound, as well as the road beyond.

Sam pulled the vehicle to a stop in front of the farmhouse. Edna was sitting in the rocker on the porch. Next to her were Moondust, Tumbleweed, and Becky.

"Welcome home, Lauren. I have a little girl who is very anxious to see you again," Maggie said. She held Charlotte in the air. "Hi, Ms. Lauren. You wanna come play with my bubbles? Uncle Vince got them for me."

Lauren smiled at the little girl. "I'd love to, Charlotte."

Sam left Lauren on the front porch with her mother and Charlotte to visit the compound's operation center with Vince. He needed to get the rundown on where they stood foodwise, as well as with weapons and ammo. If they were going to fend off an attack like the one in Unicoi, they needed to be prepared.

"How many people do we have on guard rotation?" Sam asked.

"We have thirty-two trained guards plus another fifteen that have some weapons training, mostly through hunting, but they have yet to be taught about securing a perimeter. Mel Brower has been in the process of training everyone over the age of ten to be proficient with a rifle and pistol," Vince said.

"Well, I can start helping her train folks today. Do you have a list?"

He handed Sam a handwritten list with thirty names on it.

"None of these folks have weapons training?"

"Nope," Vince said. "We didn't have time, big brother. It was all we could do to keep the perimeter guarded with the guys we had. We never prepared for training dozens of refugees."

"I'm not busting your balls, Vince. I understand. It's just—"

"You want to take more time and get settled in?" Vince asked.

"We need to go to Erwin and deal with Nigel once and for all—before he amasses another army and comes at us again here."

"I doubt they'll come at us this soon after we took out so many of their men."

"No. We can't let our guard down. If the attack on Unicoi taught us anything at all, it was that every person in the community needs to know how to defend themselves. There would have been no way for fifty people to attack a town of three thousand and kill so many if everyone had been trained and armed to defend the town."

"We didn't have enough guns for three thousand people, Sam."

"A baseball bat in the hands of someone properly trained to use it in self-defense could have done a lot of damage."

"True," Vince said. He looked at his shoes.

"I know you all did the best you could. I'm not saying I could have done any better under the circumstances. But now, we need to work together and make the community here at the compound as safe as we can—for all our families." As he said the word families, a huge smile formed. He still couldn't wrap his head around the fact that he and Lauren were going to have a baby.

"Lauren told you?" Vince asked, a sheepish grin forming on his face.

"She did."

Sam had barely had time to process this new information. It changed things for him in ways that he didn't yet fully understand. When he and Vince first spoke of creating a "prepper compound" for like-minded people to survive an apocalypse, Sam had envisioned a community much like a small town where people would bring their wives and children.

"We not only owe it to the people taking refuge inside the wire here, but to all those to come to secure a place where they can live safely. We've done the work to provide food, water, and shelter. Now we have to train everyone to defend it."

"That's what we'll do then. We'll concentrate our efforts on raising an army that will cause the likes of the Corbins and Russos to quake in their boots and make them think twice about trying to destroy our community."

The door banged open, and Sam heard someone running toward the communications room.

"Vince!" It was Dave's voice.

"Someone's at the gate," he said, nearly breathless.

"Corbin's group?" Sam asked, grabbing his rifle and moving toward the door.

"No, State Senator Phelps. He wants to talk to Lauren. He said it was urgent."

Thank you for reading Brink of Chaos, book two in the Survive the Collapse series. **The story continues in book three, Brink of Panic. Order your copy today at Amazon.com!**

If you enjoyed this book, I'd like to hear from you and hope that you could take a moment and post an honest review on Amazon. Your support and feedback will help this author improve for future projects. Without the support of readers like yourself, self-publishing would not be possible. **Don't forget to sign up for my spam-free newsletter at www.tlpayne.com to be the first to know of new releases, giveaways, and special offers.**

Brink of Chaos has gone through several layers of editing. If you found a typographical, grammatical, or other error which impacted your enjoyment of the book, I offer my apologies and ask that you let me know so I can fix it for future readers. To do so, click here and fill out the form or email me at contact@tl-payne.com. In appreciation, I would like to offer you a free ebook copy of my next book prior to it's release.

Have you read my Days of Want series? Order your copy of Turbulent, book one in the series!

Also by T. L. Payne

Survive the Collapse Series

Brink of Darkness

Brink of Chaos

Brink of Panic

Brink of Collapse

Brink of Destruction: A FREE Novelette

The Days of Want Series

Turbulent

Hunted

Turmoil

Uprising

Upheaval

Mayhem

Defiance

Fall of Houston Series

A Days of Want Companion Series

No Way Out

No Other Choice

No Turning Back

No Surrender

No Man's Land

The Gateway to Chaos Series

Seeking Safety

Seeking Refuge

Seeking Justice

Seeking Hope

Acknowledgments

I'd like to thank everyone who helped me with Brink of Chaos.

Beta Readers Samuel Bradshaw, Sam Stokes, Lee Reed, Carolyn Rahnema, Sue Jackson, and for their tremendously valuable feedback and suggestions.

About the Author

T. L. Payne is the author of several bestselling post-apocalyptic series. T. L. lives and writes in the Osage Hills region of Oklahoma and enjoys many outdoor activities including kayaking, rock-hounding, metal detecting, and fishing the many lakes and rivers of the area.

Don't forget to sign up for T. L.'s VIP Readers Club at www. tlpayne.com to be the first to know of new releases, giveaways, and special offers.

T. L. loves to hear from readers. You may email T. L. at contact@tlpayne.com or join the Facebook reader group at https://www.facebook.com/groups/tlpaynereadergroup

Join TL on Social Media

Facebook Author Page
Instagram
Website: tlpayne.com
Email: contact@tlpayne.com

facebook.com/tlpayneauthor
instagram.com/tl.payne.author

Made in the USA
Middletown, DE
29 July 2023

35917586R00177